POST ROE
Alternatives
Fighting Back

Edited by
Debora Godfrey, Phyllis Irene
Radford, Lou J Berger, Tom Easton,
K.G. Anderson. Marleen S. Barr,
Elé Killian, Rebecca McFarland
Kyle, Manny Frishberg, and
Bob Brown

Also from B Cubed Press

Alternative Truths
More Alternative Truths: Tales from the Resistance
After the Orange: Ruin and Recovery
Alternative Truths: End Game
Alternative Theologies
Poetry for the Thoughtful Young
Stories for the Thoughtful Young
When Trump Changed, by Marleen S. Barr
Firedancer, by S.A. Bolich
Alternative Apocalypse
OZ Is Burning
Destinies: Issues to Shape Our Future, by Tom Easton
Alternative Deathiness
Alternative War
Spawn of War and Deathiness
The Protest Diaries
Alternative Holidays

POST ROE ALTERNATIVES
Fighting Back

Edited by

Debora Godfrey, Phyllis Irene Radford,
Lou J Berger, Tom Easton, K.G. Anderson.
Elé Killian, Rebecca McFarland Kyle,
Marleen S. Barr, Manny Frishberg, and
Bob Brown

Cover Design
Bob Brown

Published by

B Cubed Press
Kiona, WA

Copyright

DEDICATION

This book is dedicated to the people of Kansas.
You stood up when it mattered and told the
autocratic Theocrats exactly what you thought about
them trying to take away your liberties.

POST ROE Alternatives

Foreword

Hillary Clinton once shocked the world when she stated that "Women's Rights are Human Rights."

These words are as true today as they were when she spoke to them to the Chinese government and are even *more* true when directed at the theocratic and political hacks that form the conservative majority of the Supreme Court.

In their pointless goal to appease the religious right minority and the politicians they vote for, the Court successfully diminished the rights of all women in this country.

By denying women's bodily autonomy, they have reduced the rights of *all* citizens, regardless of gender.

When Kansas, in all its conservative red glory, rebuked this assault on Human Rights, many of us rejoiced. The overwhelming rejection of the SCOTUS decision exposed a deliberate effort to end reproductive rights, to force unwanted and often unsafe pregnancies on children, rape victims, and unwilling mothers, as a dehumanizing objective of a religious few. An effort by a minority to dominate the many.

And we *are* many.

We believe that the sanctity of our bodies is our own domain, and *not* the playground of those who would punish us in the name of their own religious fervor. This is *not* a fight just about gender, but of separation of Church and State.

This is a struggle to maintain bodily autonomy for *everyone*.

We are all victims, today and tomorrow, of the overturn of Roe v. Wade.

Failing to fight back, on behalf of the women affected, means no one will fight back for us, when we lose even more rights, tomorrow.

So, fight back! Women's Rights are, indeed, Human Rights.

CONTENTS

Kansas Rules

J. Yolen

Who would have guessed,
flat as it is,
that Kansas has a sharp spine,
acknowledging women
can make their own body choices,
the Supremes tried to dance
on the corpse of freedom,
the spikes of their fascist boots
leaving marks in the flat soil
that will be erased by the prairie winds,
trampled into nothing by lines of voters,
and turned under in time
by America's plowshares.

The Practical Solutions Club

D.L. Godfrey

Good afternoon, sir, Officer, sir.

You received a complaint about the Practical Solutions Club? I'm Barbie Richards, one of the founders.

Yes, feel free to come in and look around. This is a private club, we started it for ladies, something to do in the afternoon, but now we have activities for kids and families, just answering demand.

What do we do? Ladies' stuff, mostly. You know.

Like what? Well, we play bingo on Thursday afternoons, and Mahjong twice a week because my mother inherited a set from her grandmother, and I like to play.

Guns? Well, yes, we do offer classes on gun safety. Afternoons, Monday through Friday, and on Sunday, because, after all, everyone needs to feel safe.

Handguns, mostly, suitable for small hands, because our junior division starts with 10-year-olds. Never too young to learn to defend yourself, right, Officer?

Oh, yes. This is one of the paper targets we use for practice. Is there some sort of statute that says that the bull's-eye has to center on the heart? No, no, sir, it's not designed to look like any politician in particular, not that I'm aware of, anyway. And no, none of the ladies have any problem with the bull's-eye location—seems to improve their aim.

Yes, we do have weekly shooting competitions on Fridays, both a senior and a junior division. You'd be surprised how well some of those 10-year-olds can shoot. Get that bull's-eye every time. We encourage everyone to keep their weapon stored safely at their home, ready in case an occasion comes up where they might need to protect themselves.

Yes, Charlotte Rose is in the club, one of our best 12-year-olds. True, that business about her shooting her Uncle Ralph was unfortunate, particularly him being the mayor's brother-in-law and all, but I never did hear a good explanation as to why he was in her bedroom at 2 o'clock in the morning, either. She just shot her normal target area. Let's hope reconstructive surgery can do wonders for him.

No, we don't have any classes on Saturday. That's the day our shooting clubs go compete. Sometimes we have meets here, sometimes in neighboring states. We load everyone up on our bus, guns and all, mothers, fathers, children. And we go shoot.

Yeah, Rita Mae told me there had been some sort of misunderstanding this morning, said Officer Reedy tried to pull the bus over.

No, she had no trouble with him checking out her license to drive, but she said that he got creepy with the young girls on the bus. She said they were getting nervous, feeling unsafe, and that she was afraid he was going to make them late for the tournament.

You know that Jerome White is a lawyer, and he was on the bus, right? Well, he said that Officer Reedy had no right to detain the whole bus for an unfounded suspicion that some girl might be pregnant and seeking an abortion out of state, and that Officer Reedy would need a court order to stop the bus.

Okay, maybe they could have waited while he radioed in, but they were going to be late for the meet. Couldn't disappoint the kids, could they?

Yes, we have meets every week, mostly we travel to them. Some people are regulars, there are always a few along for the first time. If they find they don't like it, they don't have to go out again. For some people, once is enough. They can still shoot at the club, even if they never go to another meet.

Why are we doing this? Well, we're training survivors, Officer. We're all just trying to survive in the world we've got. The ability to shoot straight eliminates a lot of arguments, and we're just answering demand.

Did that address your concerns, Officer? Feel free to come anytime. You've got daughters, don't you? Do let them know we'll be here for them if they ever feel the need to join the club.

How It Feels

M. Belanger

This dizzy, breathless slide
down a bank, all mud and water,
with no handholds in sight.
Choking on such
hopelessness and rage

I need to know
we're not alone in this,
that our suffocating trepidation
will have some end
beyond the obvious.

Will there come a turning point
where ordinary people
can choose to stop?
Will we even get that option?
Who diverts the flood?

If you were alive
in Germany
when it all went wrong
can you tell me:
did it feel like this?

Did it feel exactly like this?

With the Wheeze of a Glass Sentence

A.T. Castro

Cecily's pregnancy manifested with a hole through her palm.

There were in her world any number of reasons why a woman's hand might possess a hole substantial enough to pass daylight. There was the toxic worm and there was the wasting disease and there was plain old-fashioned crucifixion. But those were wounds. Her palm had just turned transparent and insubstantial, part of a condition that sometimes happened to women, known in the common vernacular as "turning to glass."

It wasn't literally glass, of course. It was air, a hole in her work-calloused palm through which she could poke the index finger of her other hand to demonstrate just how permeable it had become.

It meant that she was pregnant.

~~~

Cecily's palm was the first part of her body to make the transformation, though it could have just as easily been her breasts or her hip or her face. She had known women who had begun their metamorphoses into "glass" from all these places, and others; had heard her blessed mother's stories of the smoky texture that had overtaken her jaw, making the sight of her gaping mouth and visible throat so disgusting that her grandfather, a less than empathetic man, had banished her to a back room so that her condition wouldn't ruin anybody's appetite.

Cecily could peer through the hole in her hand the way she might peer through a knothole in some wooden fence. It was fun, and it was terrifying, to gaze upon the three rooms her husband Job had provided and pretend that she was gazing through some gaping wound in the very nature of things, from the world where she had been simply Cecily, to the world where she would be a mother bringing precious new life into being. She supposed she was happy that she would soon give her husband a child, and to feel the looming promise of that child, a new personality yet to manifest.

But, in the hours before he came home, she felt an odd and discomfiting joy that was more connected to her coming months of invisibility than it was to that distant future, still months away, of daily wiping shit from her baby's bottom. *What is it with me, that I cherish the joys of disappearance even more? Why do I find that so promising?*

This was a common reaction, she knew; certainly, her sister Anyi had confided about having a similar mixed joy the day her feet disappeared. Anyi had said, "I don't mind disappearing. I just mind that I must come *back*." She had said it where people could hear her and, so, she had been flogged, her last physical experience before she had disappeared completely, for months.

There were sentiments that should not be voiced.

Cecily was not a perfect wife, and Job was not a perfect husband. He was often surly, and frequently unfaithful, and had once or twice passed on a disease from some tavern slut he'd dallied with on a night when he was too drunk to come home. He was still, mostly, a good man, and she knew that fatherhood would give him more of a reason to not stray so much.

This was, at least, the advice of their church leaders and of the council of women, and so, she had been trying in all the ways available to women, to maximize their time in bed together, ultimately resulting in conception. He was, to the best of her knowledge, wholly oblivious to these measures, which had ranged from pharmaceuticals to an extra avidity she would show during certain days of the month. This had been her secret project for almost a year, and it had shown no results.

Until today.

She did not reveal her surprise to Job until after dinner. She could not. The Man's Hour was, by tradition, the time from any husband's arrival home from whatever work he did to put bread and bacon on the table, to the last bite of whatever meal his wife had provided him. It was not a law, written in books, like so many of the rules that dictated the lives of women. You would not go to prison for it. You would not be hauled to the public square to have the sins of your disobedience branded on your forehead. It was possible, she knew, to theoretically live a fulfilling life with a warm and open man who *wanted* to engage from the moment he arrived, tired and sweaty from his daily labors. A man who liked the company of his woman enough to laugh with her and to be her friend.

Job was a traditionalist. He believed that a woman's silent time was part of the marriage sacrament. He did not want to hear from Cecily until he put his fork down at the end of the evening meal, and he sometimes did not want to hear from her even then, instead admonishing her to a silence that would last through the rest of the night. There were, Cecily knew, men who demanded silence of their women throughout the entirety of their marriage, men who would not tolerate an uttered word, ever, forcing their wives into eternally mute lives.

She could not imagine being one of those women. She had words burning within her, words that demanded release, and life as one of those women would have been a living death. Job, whose demands for extended silence were infrequent, was a much better man, one who, for the most part, seemed to greet the return of her voice with a relief that came from the loneliness he must have felt while she was silent. Tonight, he seemed to be in an expansive mood when he put down his fork, forming a crossbeam with his knife, at a right angle in the glistening remnants of the night's stew.

"So," he said. "Tell me about your day."

She removed the single, pink glove she had worn to hide her marvelous vacancy.

~~~

His reaction was everything she had hoped for.

~~~

Oh, the celebration! The joy in his eyes and in his laughter! She had always known that Job loved her, even though he went weeks or months without saying so; even though his eyes sometimes grew unfocused when she spoke. She had known because of his tenderness in bed, because of the relative rarity of his corporal punishments, and because he sometimes forgot that he was supposed to be the stone voice of authority and let her advise him in matters that should have been his decision alone.

Tonight, he was not too manly to erupt in tears. He said things like, *our son,* just assuming it would be a boy, and *you'll make such a great mother. H*e sat at the table's lone chair and rested his great tanned brow against her midsection, whispering nonsensical words to the baby that he could not yet see, but that would soon be the only part of Cecily he *could* see. He gazed up at her and said the one thing that made her break: *I'll miss you when you're glass,* and it was so clearly true that she bent down and kissed him on the top of his head, just as if she might have were she a mother and he the blessed child she had been put on this Earth to comfort.

Not for the first time, Cecily thought that the members of her own powerless gender were the only adults in all the world because men, despite all their authority, were forbidden to show weakness and, therefore, held no positions other than absolute strength or abject fragility.

Men, unlike women, were permitted to break, which they did often, and this was something women knew and spent their lives obligated to fix. Then he shuddered and announced that they would go to bed, that they would make love, because they both knew that this was an activity that would soon be impossible, and she followed him into the curtained alcove of their home where he mounted her from behind and made animal noises, praising God for the gifts He had given.

Midway through the act, certain other parts of Cecily numbed as they, too, became glass, and she stopped feeling anything at all.

~~~

Cecily went to see one of her female friends the next day, to ask what she should expect. She knew what the answers would be, of course, from her mother and from other women who had gone through the same process. Maia, who had been through it eight times in the last decade and had therefore spent about half of her married life as glass, listened to her and said, "What do you want me to tell you? That it's a blessing? Sure, it's a blessing. You get children out of it."

"And, while you're glass?"

Maia hesitated. "While you're glass, you find out who you are, and who your husband is."

"What do you mean?"

"I mean that you are not *there*. Some men take too much license in that. They think that just because you're not there, you can't see them. It's different for a family with many children. The first time, Zyke used my absence as a form of freedom. He became a child. After I had children, there were other eyes in the house and he could not misbehave with them watching. I don't know what Job will be like. Neither do you, and you'll learn. By God, you will learn."

~~~

The earliest they could get a master of medicine to see her was two days later and, by then, the transparency had spread halfway up her right arm, with an odd second path taking off the top of her head at an angle that made her look lopsided from multiple angles. The master was a typical savant: gray-haired, wizened, marked with the forehead-brands of his sort, with eyes like flaming coals.

He examined her and said, "It's moving fast. You'll be all glass before long."

Cecily gave him a joyous smile but didn't say the obvious part: that she was terrified.

All girls grew up knowing that the process of making babies included months of virtual nonexistence, but who among them really wanted to be intangible? Who wanted to be a ghost in her own home, unseen and unheard, beings who might as well not exist and only did because they carried creatures who would be taking all their substance for many months on end?

Her mother had said, "It is the way of things. You are not as important as the child to come. God arranged such things to protect the unborn from our imperfections and our whims." She had talked about months of standing, unseen and unheard, not eating or sleeping or engaging with the world and unable to do anything at all until it was over. "It almost killed me," her mother said, and there was more than a tinge of accusation there, the traditional charge that all mothers have against those they have birthed—that sacrifices have been made and that offspring should regard these sacrifices not with mere appreciation but with deep guilt.

Cecily had long ago sworn that she would never wield such guilt as a weapon against any children she might be blessed by God to bear, but with nonexistence now looming large before her, she knew that this was a base lie and that she would take what was coming and hone it, like the blade of a knife, to flay her children with for any insufficient fealty.

Job bragged that he would keep the house just as clean as Cecily had and would take advantage of her virtual absence to also make all the foods that she had never agreed to, even allowing that he would enjoy the silence for a change, ha ha ha.

"But, I'll also miss you," he said in a hurry. "I don't know what I'm going to do without you."

Cecily smiled the way she was supposed to and said, "I'll be right there, all the time," but her voice, already weakened by her delicate condition, sounded as faint as a distant whisper, spoken through a wall, and it occurred to her that she wanted another meal while she could still eat, something that might keep her during all the months to come.

She asked the master if this would be all right, and he gave her a printed list of things she should not have this close to her transformation. They included a few of the things that she would have made for herself if there had still been time, not that there was, because her free hand had also started to fade during the examination and there was no possibility of her being able to prepare anything at all.

The master advised Job to treat her to anything she wanted because it would likely be her last meal, and Job scowled a bit at this, showing the annoyance he always showed at moments of unnecessary expense. The prospect of becoming a father, however, had softened him enough to agree, though by the time they accepted the master's last recommendations and reached the parts of the city where it was possible to buy prepared meals, it was swiftly becoming moot, her pregnant state coming up on her more swiftly than either one of them could have foretold.

~~~

Most expectant mothers took weeks to disappear completely; in some cases, as long as a couple of months. But, for a few unlucky ones, such as Cecily, it only took days, and they experienced the phantasmic state for almost the full gestation.

She had once heard tell of a woman who had remained visible, yet as transparent as glass, from her breasts up, until the moment the baby dropped. But for those close to disincorporation, it was too risky to spend any time in public, and so she and Job took the food home in bags because the alternative was to risk Cecily becoming glass in public and be lost, at that location, for the duration of her pregnancy.

Because she no longer had arms, Job fed her, lovingly, one morsel at a time, and for a little bit she felt a surge of adoration for him, gratitude for a husband who was, at times scattered, something approaching a good man. But the food itself had no flavor, going down. She could feel her system accepting it but not the weight of its presence in her belly, and so she knew that this part of her was already gone, and would not be coming back until her baby was born.

~~~

Every home has an unused place, somewhere that the furnishings exist only to require dusting.

Job and Cecily had long talked about theirs, an alcove beside their most comfortable chair. None of the light of their home reached this corner. It was forever dark when the rest of the house was bright, and never a home when the rest of the house was welcoming. It was always shadowed, and at night when the house was a dim place where the furnishings were only recognizable shapes, that corner was black indeed, an alcove for imagined monsters to hide, for murderous invaders to lurk with their strangle-cords while they plotted the evil things that they, as predators, would do.

No arrangement of lanterns or candles had ever succeeded in fully bringing light to that forgotten corner, and so Cecily had been surprised to note, as the sensations of her everyday unimpregnated existence fled her, that Job did not have any problem designating that corner as her place for the months to come. *Was it not appropriate*, she asked herself, thoughts swirling with gray. *A haunted corner for me, who is about to become a ghost?* It seemed like the kind of thought that should have upset her, though it did not.

She went to stand in that corner and, for a while, as Job watched her disappear, it was like she had retreated to this place too early. For a long time, she could still feel her own weight, even if enough of her had disappeared so that it had become a weight far less substantial than the one she knew.

Then, her legs went away, and even that weight went. She tried to flash a brave smile but there were no lips to spread, no teeth to reflect what light somehow made it to this place. She tried to say something, but her voice was like something shouted at such a great distance that even these urgent sounds did not resolve into words.

It took hours, hours that were exactly what Cecily's mother had once promised her: a little like drowning. *This is what it is like*, she thought, *to be dead*, and this made perfect sense, because it was an unborn baby's job to take everything of its mother that made her real, everything of her substance that made her a creature who could feel and accept touch. Just before the last of herself went away, she felt a little flutter in her belly, though it was surely too soon for the baby to be moving. This was just the last agitation of the butterflies, reflecting her fear as she entered that part of her life that everybody called a woman's first real taste of death.

~~~

The first thing Job did when she was gone—she was there, from her own point of view, but she was gone to the rest of the world—was a comical, common reaction of men upon the disincorporation of their women.

He drew close and he stared, as wide-eyed and as flummoxed as she had ever seen him, at the empty space she now occupied. Every man knew that this happened, and many men had seen it with their mothers and their siblings, but no man ever got used to it. No man ever treated it with equanimity, because it was the most baffling trick women had out of, oh God, so many. It was a comic premise and, to Cecily, for whom all the rest of the world now felt as emotionally distant as a little circle of daylight at the end of a tube, it did not escape being comic.

If she could have laughed, she might have. If she could have called his reaction cute, she would have. There was an element of secret amusement in her reaction to the sight of her man reaching out with an extended index finger to probe the empty space where she had been. When his hand passed through her at collarbone altitude, that amusement was like a taste of delicious spring water. His awe, his thunderstruck amusement, made her fall in love with him all over again, cutting past all the nonsense that went with being a wife in a world of men.

I'm here, she told him, though of course she made no sound and he did not hear.

He glanced down at her belly, at the approximate location of their baby and, of course, there was nothing yet to see. The baby was not large enough. But there were things to know from the way he looked, entire volumes to be read in the wonder in his eyes, and still other things to be inferred from the movement of his lips, when he faced the approximate location of her eyes and spoke words she could not hear. She did not need to hear them to know the import of what he was saying, the assurances that he loved her and that he would wait for her and that he looked forward to watching their child grow. It was all a million miles away and it warmed her, even though she knew that his fealty to this promise would last no time at all.

~~~

Other women had said that the time would crawl. What happened was that it did not move at all. She was an insect, stuck in amber, who felt no hunger, no thirst, no need to sleep, no stirrings of her body and certainly no sense of a living child growing within the space where she had been; all she felt was a stasis, and in that stasis she thought inconsequential thoughts that had nothing to do with the needs of a body that no longer existed and of a life that was, for the moment, interrupted by intangibility.

Sometimes it was day and sometimes it was night. Sometimes she thought of the life to come and sometimes she thought of the life she missed. Sometimes Job was with her, saying things that she could not hear, and sometimes he was elsewhere, either at his labors as a working man or for any number of the other important items of business that a man could get up to. She did notice that, while he stayed with her for hours at a time near the beginning, his eyes earnest and compassionate and filled with the love she knew he had for her, after a while the pointlessness of this exercise must have begun to weigh on him in any number of small ways. His gaze faltered while he thought of other things. She did not resent him for this. God had, in his wisdom, prevented disincorporated pregnant women from fully experiencing time the way that women of flesh and blood did. During pregnancy, it was up to the men to feel the tedium.

~~~

Someday soon, she thought, *I will be a mother.* It was a startling thought, because she still thought of herself as a child, really. In a world very close to this one, she was still a little thing in a shapeless sack of a dress, exhausting the adult world with her endless energy and with her endless questions about *why*.

She had loved asking *why* and had never stopped demanding to know why the sky was blue and why it sometimes rained and why birds could fly and people could not and why some animals had fur and others had scales, and why fish were perfectly happy darting back and forth under water when the same lifestyle would have killed dogs and cats and little girls. Never once, in all those questions, when the most frequent replies were *I don't know,* or *nobody knows,* or, most commonly, *you'll ruin your brain with all these questions*, did she stop wanting to *know*.

When her mother had gotten pregnant again, with the child who would become her younger brother, the one who hadn't lived, she had asked another set of questions, *where did Mommy go? Why do women disappear when they have babies growing inside them? If Mommy's like a ghost standing over there, like you say, can she see me? Does she still love me? Can I hug someone who can't be felt? Can she be hugging me back even if I can't feel her?*

And the answers had always been things like, *It's what God wants, it's the way the world is,* and *little girls shouldn't ask questions because it's just a way of not accepting what they've been given.*

When it was time to eat, in the room where her pregnant mother and her doomed baby brother were unseen, she had not sat at the table where she was supposed to but, instead, in the bare spot against the wall, opposite the place where her mother had last been seen, and she'd asked *does it bother her that we're eating in front of her, when she can't have anything? Is she hungry? Is she upset that we didn't save dinner for her?*

Her grandmother, who had lived through it herself, had said *she can't have anything because she has no solid teeth to chew with, or any solid throat to deliver it to her stomach, and for that matter no stomach, but as for being hungry, God would not do anything so stupid and sloppy and inconsiderate. She is not hungry. She is not* there. *For a few months, she does not exist. She is the idea of herself, remembering something her body has forgotten. And no, it does not bother her that she must watch us eat. Because the sight of you is a reminder of what she will have again, and what she will teach you about what being a woman means, even as I had to teach her. You are a joy to her, the way she was a joy to me.*

These were answers that still satisfied Cecily in the

place where she was, now. But they only led to more questions, things that her asking reflex insisted that she demand of the universe as she endured the long gray hours before Job's return. *Why can't I exist at the same time as my baby? Why must I disappear? Isn't there another way for nature to do this thing?* She pictured one especially bizarre possibility, living and physically present women carrying their unborn children, in their arms she supposed, for the long months it took them to grow, and she amused herself with thoughts of the back strain, of the exhaustion, of the frustration with a burden that they could not put down. Surely, she thought, that made no sense. But how did *this* make sense? Who would arrange a universe this way, basing the future of humanity on making the development of a new child a purgatory of waiting? *Why*, she wanted to know. *Why, why, why?*

And it was while thinking such things that she felt the first stirrings of a sensation that had no place being felt at all, because women only actively suffered in pregnancy if something had gone terribly wrong inside them. By all the rules that were supposed to work, they were supposed to feel nothing.

Experience, of any kind, was a bad sign. And, so, she was startled when, for a fraction of a second—or at least what *felt* like a fraction of a second because she was a pregnant woman and any real sense of time had gone where all irrelevancies went, during this particular life passage—she had felt or imagined she felt a faraway rumble, like distant clouds promising an eruption of storms. It was a passing thing, and it was so ephemeral that she was left wondering whether it was imaginary; something she felt because her mind was already tired of feeling nothing and was busily concocting phantoms for her.

In that fraction of a second it arrived, hinted at itself, and then vanished, as fleeting as a dream. She did not take a deep breath, because breathing was currently beyond her, but she hesitated for an interval that was the equivalent of that and wondered what had happened. It had not been pain, not precisely. It had not been nausea, or stomach upset, two things that were horrifying to imagine afflicting somebody who was pregnant. It had not been anything like those things. It had just been a murmur, the hint of *something* and, though she performed what little self-inventory she could, trying to claim hold of the phenomenon, it was already gone.

Imagination, then.

Or something terribly wrong.

~~~

Within what seemed a few weeks, from the way the light played upon their home's walls, he stopped coming home at the regular times.

In less time than she had dared to believe, his attitude toward her invisible space reflected that he did not feel much comforted; he, rather, looked sullen, resentful, and tempted, in a way, to blame her for the virtual unfaithfulness she had demonstrated by leaving him and this world in favor of one where she could not be touched or felt.

It occurred to her that what he really was, was drunk, and on one of the nights when he came home especially late, she performed as careful a visual analysis as she could, and noted his visible clumsiness, the unsteadiness of his walk, the redness of his cheeks,

24

the glassiness of his eyes.

Sometimes, he talked for a long time and there was just enough sadness in his eyes that she felt for him and indulged herself in guilt for abandoning him. Sometimes, he seemed to yell, to curse, to fulminate, and she wanted to hate him and to tell herself that she had always hated him: a perception that she realized was not entirely untrue. Hatred was part of the tapestry of emotions she felt for this man she had married, and not a small part; for she hated his small-mindedness, his self-importance, and his husbandly prerogative of being able to declare when she could speak and when she could not. And, now, for this: for interpreting her most difficult time as if *he* were the one who was suffering because of her disappearance.

How *dare* he?

She wanted to rage and, of course, she could not, so she did nothing.

It was part of the plan of God that she do nothing.

All of this was normal, or so other women had told her. *A man is a wailing baby,* they said, *and while you are glass you are his mirror.* And this, too, was proof of the wisdom of God for, in her invisibility, she was like a window set with curtains instead of shutters. A thing that did not shatter in the wind but was merely blown about and could survive such tempests intact. *Glass,* they called her, a word that seemed less appropriate all the time, because glass shattered, and she would not.

But the rumblings continued and grew worse.

~~~

Multiple times, deep in her season of glass, he brought home prostitutes. On the first occasion, he was blind, staggering drunk, supported as much by the woman as he was by his own legs. The first one led him into the room, dumped him to the floor as soon as she reached a place to put him, and straddled him where he fell. Milking him of what little capacity for performance remained in him, while he lay there and did nothing. She ushered him into a messy sleep too deep to remain aware of the woman's presence, his mouth agape in a snore that Cecily could not hear but knew well. The woman lit a pipe and filled the room with smoke while she puffed away, looking irritated and alone.

Then she turned and faced the empty spot where Cecily stood and, whether he had told her that his wife was glass or whether it was some instinct of her sort that enlightened her to the presence of an intangible spectator, her face brightened with a clear look of recognition.

She stood and approached, her nakedness unapologetic, her painted smile both an insolent challenge and a secret confidence, speaking volumes to the unseen woman she knew nothing about, whose only known quality was that she was glass. Her gaze flickered downward, to the place where the baby was growing; and then she looked back up, attempting eye contact but missing by inches, looking at what would have been Cecily's mouth. *No*, she mouthed. And *not yet*. And then she gathered her clothes and hurried out.

Cecily never saw that one again, but on the half-dozen instances over the next three months when Job brought other women home—and it was far from certain that they were the only times he paid for solace because he was gone for long periods and it was very possible that he met others at the houses where they worked, or in the dark alcoves where their sort allowed themselves

26

to be taken against alley walls—the ones who returned with him were the same two. An exotic one from the north, whose face was an unfamiliar shape and whose long, sleek hair was a shade of black wholly uncommon in this country; the other a very small one with fiery hair and the demeanor of a child, which might have been the chief attribute of her success in her industry, despite an apparent age that showed itself only when she drew close and regarded the invisible Cecily from across a span of inches.

The dark-haired one made Job drink something from a bottle of black glass, then held him until he passed out, lit her pipe and crossed the room to blow black smoke into Cecily's spot; the childlike one with the fiery hair actually delivered the service Job must have paid for, held him until he fell asleep and then came to where Cecily stood to say things that Cecily could only presume to be confidences. It was on her third visit that she knelt below Cecily's static field of vision and then rose again with hands held a couple of inches apart. She seemed joyous as she mouthed, *I can see your baby.*

~~~

The rumbles came once or twice a day, now, as far as she could tell, and she never knew what to think about them because they corresponded to no experience that she had ever been warned about. She knew only that they had been getting more powerful, and more unpleasant, and that she would categorize them as things that hurt. She wished she could tell the sweet little harlot, whom she liked better than the nasty northern one who blew smoke, that something was wrong and that she needed help. But she was glass, unable to offer confidences. *I wonder if I'm dying,* she thought. And then she thought, with a sudden savage fury, powerful enough to pierce the enforced placidity of the pregnant, *that would serve Job right!*

~~~

One day, Anyi and Maia arrived with the master of medicine.

It was the first time Cecily had seen her sister or her friend since the onset of her season of glass. It was rare that she saw Anyi, at all. The two had been close in childhood, and would have still been close in adulthood, if not for the happenstance that Job hated Anyi's voice for its volume and for its nasal brassiness, things that he maintained made her less than a proper woman. He had forbidden Anyi's entry into their home and limited how often Cecily could visit her. There was a wall between the sisters because of that, but here Anyi was, bringing the master of medicine with her, looking like she'd had to drag him.

Cecily had no idea how her sister knew to lead the learned man straight to the specific spot where she stood, unless the whispering network of women had somehow spread the news of the specific place where she had been positioned to spend her season of nonexistence; unless word had gotten out, past whatever barriers Job had erected to keep it in.

This did not make Cecily grateful. Instead, she felt violated. But there was no objection she could raise, and so she waited as the master of medicine knelt before her, donned spectacles from his vest pocket, and peered at the space in her midsection. He was one of those men who made even most joyous expressions look dour, with a thick mustache that obscured his lips and made them impossible to read. Cecily could tell that he was saying something because the mustache trembled with his breath, but that was not enough of a clue for her to reconstruct words, let alone meaning. Anyi was, alas, more transparent. Her hand shot to her mouth, and her eyes glittered with unshed tears. She asked the master of medicine a question under the cloak of her hand, and he said something over his shoulder that made Anyi turn and stride away.

He produced a slate, wrote on it with a dusty chalk, and showed it to her.

There is trouble.

She did not find out that day, or the day after, what he meant.

~~~

The rumbling hurt, now. It was not agony. It was nothing she could fail to live with in an everyday life where she was not made of glass. But it was unpleasant, the sensation of cracks spreading across the substance of her, creating fault lines that became outright fissures wherever they met, and dropping little shards of herself to the floor. The sensation was so much that of shattering crystal that she realized something that no one had ever mentioned to her, not her mother or her grandmother or Anyi or any of the many friends or relatives who had become mothers and lit this path for her: that to become glass, even a metaphorical kind of glass, was to become fragile and indeed, able to break.

She thought that, if she could look down at her feet, she would see a fine little halo of the little pieces of herself that had already broken off, that were, by their very presence, testimony that more would continue to break off until there was nothing left of her, at all. The

29

pain alone was not enough to make her scream, but she did scream, even though she would not be heard, and even though it had never been her lot to be heard.

~~~

Anyi returned with the master of medicine, who once again knelt before Cecily but, this time, carried a device that consisted of two mirrors attached to opposite ends of a vertical tube. The device allowed him to show Cecily her baby. It looked like it had grown quite a bit, to about the size of a clenched fist, and it held its little knuckles to its chin as if musing over some deep philosophical point upon which it would soon make some wise and learned pronouncement.

It was not the first time she had seen an unborn child growing inside a woman of glass, and she was used to them not being tranquil, to the stirrings of their little limbs, to the random facial expressions that sometimes processed as wonder, and sometimes processed as rage, and finally to the sense with every random movement that this was just not a potential human being but that very miracle in totality, only smaller.

But what she saw through the mirror held up before her eyes was something else, something that she had never seen before: a pattern of jagged red lines, radiating from that unborn child in all directions. The scarlet colors throbbed in sync with the rumbling inside her, each flare a vivid and ludicrous cartoon of Cecily's pain. He took the contraption with the mirrors away, handed it to Anyi and produced a slate board upon which he had written, *I know it hurts.*

The maddening nature of this form of communication is that it only permitted one sentence at a time. But, over the next few minutes, he was able to build on what he had already said, with a series of similarly brief dispatches.

The baby is hurting you.

The baby is dangerous.

We can take the baby...

He wrote more.

...and save you...

...before there is too much damage.

We know it hurts.

Job should have seen these lines.

Job should have called me to help.

Job needs to decide.

There was not much more: the declaration that they had been looking for her husband for days and had been unable to find him. Cecily could not understand why they were bothering her with such details. If she'd had a voice, she could have told them about the harlots she had seen him with, about the drunken and heedless state into which he had fallen.

~~~

More days passed. Job came home a few more times, always gray-skinned and always looking like he had been many nights without sleep. Sometimes he bothered to look at her. Most of the time he did not.

If he was aware of a decision he had to make, he did not show it.

Meanwhile, Cecily's pain was like an eclipse of the moon. It was an occluding presence that hid the world from her. It chipped away at her and it became so vast that, had she been corporeal, she would have screamed, fallen to the floor, broken things, gone mad. She began to think of the baby in her womb of glass like a toxic presence, a cancer. She knew that this was not true, that she should hate herself for thinking such a thing. If he lived to be born, he would want everything that every child wants, including sweet things to eat and the warm touch of the midday sun upon his face, and that he would find the silliest things funny and his laughter over the things that all the adults in his life had long since forgotten to laugh at would be a reminder to them that such splendid jokes existed, and make them laugh just as hard.

But she also knew that this being she loved was killing her, and that he was killing her slowly and yet in far less time than she could bear to believe, and that her life and his life were incompatible in this world that God had created. She lived in a fury of self-recrimination and of the lust for life and she made endless silent speeches in this darkness, declaring to a world incapable of hearing her that she wanted to live, too, that she also wanted the taste of sweet things and the feel of the sun on her face and that these were things she was entitled to, because she was not done with life's blessings and wanted to clutch them with both hands.

She thought all of this in the time of this red eclipse and at times she screamed it to all the presences who appeared before her loveless, lightless alcove, to observe the progress of her illness and of the baby's development: Anyi, the master of medicine, the childlike whore Job brought home during the worst of her suffering, several supportive relatives, and multiple faces Cecily did not know: all peering at the emptiness where Cecily stood and, shaking their heads sadly before turning away, in clear concurrence with the verdict.

At one point, Cecily saw Anyi gesturing toward her and screaming at Job, the way one would scream at a slow child who didn't get it, and she saw Job turn the color of scarlet and she thought, *no, that is the look he has before he hits, and he will hit you if you continue to confront him, even though you belong to another.* The world returned to one of its frequent intervals of darkness before that happened, and she next saw Job sitting in the dark, hands dangling impotently between his knees as he stared at a place on the floor. A trick of the available light turned his eyes into black holes that might as well have been bottomless, that might have harbored entire worlds, including one where this was not happening, where they were a man and a woman waiting in breathless joy for the arrival of a baby.

She thought, *Save me.*

Somebody please save *me.*

~~~

She was unprepared for just how desperately she wanted to live.

She wanted to walk waist-deep in cool water. She wanted the breeze to whip her hair against her cheeks, to be annoyed and yet pleased by it as she took the offending locks and tucked them behind her ear. To just do that, during those few seconds on a day when the air wanted to move, and when it felt cool being pulled into her nostrils and filling her chest. She wanted the tart irritation that went with biting a hot pepper, feeling it land, acidic but insistent, on her tongue. She wanted to glance up at the sky and watch the clouds that looked like fish, like turtles, like an old, hooded woman whose toothlessness made her chin and the tip of her nose almost touch.

She wanted to hold babies, if not necessarily *her* baby, then at least somebody else's baby, the child of a friend, of a sister, of someone who counted on her to watch over the child for a moment. She wanted the feeling of hot, wet sand between her toes. She even wanted to make love to a man again: and, she found, she did not necessarily mean Job, though the images that formed in her mind were of him, on those occasions in the past, when he'd taken direction and shown willingness to work a little harder to please her.

For what seemed like hours, she waxed nostalgic about the sensual pleasures to be found in a nice satisfying shit, the feel of it emerging from those places inside her, and relieving the pressure inside with a suddenness that made her status as a physical being feel balanced again. Even that, she thought, is a joy.

I want the world. I miss the world. I want my Mommy. I want to cry tears so nasty and so ugly that my eyes burn as they come out like fire. I want the sudden pain of a needle pricking my finger and of the blood forming a bright red drop that sits in that fissure of skin, like a ruby, capturing the light; and I want to place that finger between my lips and I want to suck that finger clean, tasting the coppery freshness of it, being attached to myself in the way I used to take for granted. These are all things I should have, and wanting them is not selfish. Give them to me. Give them to me, now. I want to live. I want to live. I want to live. I want I want I want to I want to live want want want want want.

And then the pain, too, became glass: first transparent, and then invisible.

~~~

The master of medicine held a mirror up to her face.

She was astonished to be able to see herself.

This, by itself, was almost enough to make her weep.

"No!" he said, sharply. "Look!"

She complied and saw that things had happened to her face in her time of glass. It had become wan and shadowed. Her cheekbones protruded like those of a starving woman. Dark semi-circles underlined her eyes, which appeared yellow and aged. And, though she could see herself, what she saw was a face still glass, features through which she could see the texture of the wall behind her, clearly visible through the eyes of someone starving.

She asked, "Has the baby been born?"

Her voice was like a ripple, like a ripple in a dying person's last gasp.

The master of medicine said, "No. It will be. But you and he are very close to death. It never should have gone this far, but it has, and we can still save one of you."

She peered past his bearded presence to those in the room beyond: her sister, her mother, Maia, several other faces she knew and loved, many who were craning their necks to be seen by the flickering woman of glass. Behind them all was Job, still with hooded eyes, and it somehow surprised her not at all that beside him stood the childlike whore, decent enough to weep but yet holding his hand, as if he were a young boy and needed a mother's guidance to make his way across a road where carriages were racing.

Cecily knew that, if these were her last minutes on Earth, he would not mourn her for long. She was like the precious family cat who cuddled in bed and purred when treated with kindness but who, after a brief flurry of tears, could be replaced by another, just as cute.

She told the master of medicine that she needed to live.

She told him that she did not care what Job said, that her own decision was that she wanted to live.

But whatever had given her a voice had turned to glass again, and the image in the mirror was now a shadow too insubstantial for anyone to discern her facial features, and what voice she'd had, for just a moment, disappeared again, replaced by a wheeze that could have meant anything at all.

Cecily saw the flurry of activity around her husband. She saw Anyi and several of her friends screaming at him. She saw him shaking his head and understood that it was a mistake for her to think that this decision was easy for him. He was a weak man, and not a very good one, and not one to whom hard decisions came easily. What choice he made now was being made out of default, one answer chosen because all the others were too unthinkable. Cecily could not see his face at the moment he made it. But she expected precisely what happened; saw her sister cry out, saw her mother scream, saw the master of medicine press him for confirmation. Then she closed her eyes, and discovered a grand advantage of being glass; that if you shut your eyes to the sight that is your only window to the world of life, you need not witness what you would rather die than see.

She did not feel the moment when her son was removed from her.

~~~

One day, the boy was five.

His name was Naoh. They had intended to call him Noah, as Cecily had always wanted, but there had been a misspelling during the ceremony that matched him to his name and no one had ever seen fit to issue a correction. There is an oddly specific difference between a natural name and an unnatural one, between the one with a substantial weight of legend and tradition and history behind it and the one that is just a strange combination of sounds, a *Na* followed by an *Oh* that no one is in the habit of saying, and that requires constant correction when teaching it to strangers. It made Naoh seem odd. Not that he wasn't odd, with his facial disfigurements and with a mind that took slowly to lessons. No one would ever say that his life was not worth living.

He enjoyed all the things his mother had loved, including the sunlight and the feel of the wind in his hair, not to mention the occasional visits from his Aunt Anyi, who had three children of her own and could not justify bringing this child into a family where the others would have to do without in order to make room for him. His blessings did not quite make up for his problems, or for the loveless existence of a state ward cared for by people who, while not unkind, saw him as a daily problem to be wrangled. They added up to something more than zero on the tally of whether a given life is worth living, or not. Just not much more than that.

No one, in the family or the community, knew where Job had fled only a few months after Naoh's birth. For them, it was like he had become glass himself. We do know where he ended up, and understand that he passed out in a ditch and drowned in shallow water.

A day came where Job was too drunk to put up a fight against two robbers who beat him and left him in a ditch, hours before a sudden rainstorm filled that ditch with six inches of water. His corpse wasn't found until the smell could be discerned from the road. No one claimed it. No one identified it. No one particularly missed him. No speeches were made. Men like Job come and go all the time. When they die, the atmosphere rushes in to fill the empty spaces, and if this is cold-hearted to understand, it is yet better than what happens to women who are allowed to die while glass.

The house where Job and Cecily had lived sat abandoned for a few months, but by the end it was outlasting the attraction empty places have always had for the people who need places to fill. By the start of winter, it was the home of a struggling family of five, recently moved to town after a personal disaster in another city.

There was a father named Zedediah, a mother named Sarah, and three daughters named Rachel, Irina, and Seska, all of whom were at the cusp between childhood and marriageable age. Seska was, at the time they moved in, four months away from seduction by a man who would impregnate her and disappear, thinking himself a victor, to meet a fate as terrible as Job's.

It was another series of life problems, by another gathering of lives, none of which would mean anything at all to us if not for the happenstance that the family believed in taking care of its own and that they stood by Seska as her ears and her eyes and her hands all turned to glass on the same day, announcing to one and all what she'd been up to; and that they were very kind to her as she disappeared by degrees, and when they had to tell her that they'd see her again when her baby was born and she was no longer glass. That child, Arryn, would live a long, and healthy, and largely happy life, and this is nice to know, even though he also doesn't concern us much.

What does, alas, is that at the moment Seska turned to glass and found herself facing the season of silence and isolation that went with her months of pregnancy, finding it an adventure, she gazed out across her loving family's main room at the only tableau the lot or her gender permitted here, and saw for the first time something that no member of her family had noticed during the long months they had been staying there: another glass woman, still standing where she'd been left, in the spot that she would now remain forever, because of the decision that had been made for her.

Seska saw that this other woman was not quite alive but also not quite dead, that she was aware and that she was a permanently helpless witness to everything that would ever happen in her presence.

Seska could say nothing to this other, nameless woman, who in turn could say nothing to her. It was not like they had conversations. But much was communicated between the two sets of immobile eyes and by the time Seska gave birth to her fully healthy child and returned to a tangible solidity, the silly and shallow girl she'd been had become a quite different person.

She was less prone to smiles, more prone to anger. She had turned humorless. Her vulnerability to the attention of men, once healthy, was reduced to less than nothing. Her disgust for them so humorless than she lashed out at any who showed interest. She was a solid, if stern and unforgiving, mother and if anybody ever noticed that she sometimes glanced at the empty alcove

39

across the room where she had stood in silence for all those months, they never said anything. Nor did she. For what would have been the point?

All that is necessary to know about her is this: For the twenty-seven remaining years of her life, she never invited pregnancy again.

Bounty Blues

C. Carmichael

There's a bounty on your head,
there's a mob beside your bed,
and they don't care who it is or how.
This madness rides on wild,
when a child must have a child,
and your rapist wants his baby now.
From the courtesy of Texas.
and the shallows on the court,
jackbooted robes of power
are whom we should abort.

A Better World

J. Wright

I *want* to live in a nation where there is no abortion.

That's right.

What's that?

Oh. You're already mad, aren't you?

I didn't even make it a full paragraph into this and I've already pissed you off because I said I wanted to live in a nation, a world, where there was no abortion.

Sure, you're mad and why wouldn't you be? But, before you stop reading, hear me out. Just give me a minute to explain. Please.

What did you *think* I meant by that?

I didn't say "I want to live in a world where abortion is *illegal.*"

I didn't say "I want to live in a world where women are forced to endure pregnancy against their will."

And I sure didn't say, "Hey, I wish we could somehow magically brainwash women (and men too, I suppose) into wanting every pregnancy."

But that's the thing, isn't it? This ... well, I guess we really can't call it a "debate" given that it's being imposed on us against our will, but this subject, this fight, this fundamental right, whatever we choose to call it, it's so charged with emotion, so loaded with baggage, we don't even hear the words anymore.

There aren't any neutral parties in this war.

We're all in this fight and you're either with us, or you're against us.

Pretty big talk, I guess, from a straight, white male with all that implies.

Given the battlespace, I admit a case could certainly be made that I implied all those things in the previous paragraphs. And so, when I say, hey, I'd love to live in a world where there's no abortion, I can't really blame you for taking it at face value, making certain assumptions about me, and not looking any further.

But, again, please, give me a minute to explain.

America, we're not supposed to make laws based on one group's ideology, political or religious. The Constitution specifically prohibits imposing your beliefs and ideology on any other person—and it expressly forbids the government from doing so.

And, yet, that's exactly what's happening.

Yes, it is.

Because, ultimately, *every* justification for outlawing abortion comes down to this: morality as defined by a narrow slice of theocracy.

And that idea of morality is always, always, every time, based on one concept: Human life is sacred.

Not just special, or valuable, or unique, but *sacred.*

Sacred: a gift bestowed by someone's god.

Sacred doesn't have any meaning *without* a deity involved.

And thus, neither does the *moral* imperative behind it.

This idea of some right to life, that (some, but we'll get to that) human life itself is sacred, must always, ultimately, be based on belief in some higher power.

And that, right there, is the ironic part, isn't it?

Sacred. A *right* to life. I mean, you do see the staggering irony of that belief, don't you?

Imagine that world.

No. Really, imagine that world, that nation, where every life actually *is* sacred. Where every human life no matter how great or how small is sincerely regarded as a gift from some divine agency.

Where every person, be they a 6-week-old fetus or a geriatric case, really *does* matter, where *all* of us, even the least of us, are truly important to each other and to some god.

Imagine *that* world.

I know I'm now repeating myself, but it's important.

Imagine if there really *was* a right to life, if human life itself really *was* sacred, if there really *was* a god up there who actually cared and commanded you to do his bidding: to protect human life.

Oh yes, let us imagine if it really was about *morality*.

See, if we *really* believed life was sacred—be that some special quality endowed by a god—then it would be our moral duty as citizens of that religion and/or that nation to ensure *every* human has *every* opportunity for the best life possible.

That's right, our moral duty. To our god. To our nation. To the world. To *life*.

That's what holy men tell us.

That's what those politicians who claim the moral high ground tell us, is it not?

So, before human life is even conceived, it would be our moral duty to optimize the conditions for its growth.

If indeed life is sacred.

Optimize conditions for its growth? What does that

mean? Well, that means a healthy environment: to include clean air, safe water, nutritious and balanced diet, shelter, and so on. Moreover, we would expect that environment to endure for the duration of the life in question, to *improve* even. Because what good is it to value human *life*, if there's no world for it to *live* in? If the warm seas rise, if the air is foul and the water toxic, if the oceans are choked with plastic, what chance does that life have for a better future?

No, if we truly value *human* life, if we truly believe it to be sacred, as these alleged Christian Conservatives tell us we must, then before it even begins we as a people and *as a nation* must bend every effort to ensure not only its survival, but that it *thrives* to reach its full potential.

Anything less is immoral.

If life *is* truly sacred.

We would have to be that nation of safety, and stability, and opportunity, *now and into the future.*

And that's just for starters.

Those who bring that life into the world, the parent(s), they must have opportunity to provide the best start.

If life is indeed *sacred*, then surely we can agree to that bare minimum? Morally?

For that life to have the best start possible, the parents need comprehensive and responsive healthcare, a decent standard of living and economic opportunity, good jobs with a living wage, education, community, support, etc.

But it's more than that.

If life is born to parents who are not full and equal members of society for whatever reason, race, color, sex,

46

orientation, identity, beliefs, who are *de facto* denied the same rights and opportunities as other, more privileged members of that nation, then we fail right out of the gate.

For, if you truly believe that all human life is sacred, if you really believe that, then *morally* you must work to ensure that all human life is given equal opportunity to thrive. If we truly—*truly*—believe in the sacredness of life, then we, as a people, must every single day work to build a civilization where all are valued, where all members have access and opportunity, without regard to their differences. We must work to truly be that shining city on the hill for all, not just a privileged few, not just those who can afford it.

And that's just the groundwork.

When that life comes, when that baby is born, what then?

If that life *is* truly sacred as you say it must be, what then?

No, *no*, don't look away.

What then?

It's often said that for the pro-life crowd "life begins at conception and ends at birth." Whether or not you agree with that, in America, that's the *de facto* truth. We must change that and, so, if you truly believe that new human life is sacred, do we not then have a moral obligation both as a nation and as a people to provide for that life? To provide the best possible environment, the possible best future, *no matter the expense?*

America tells me life is sacred but then tells me that to provide the best possible future for it costs too much, because we are a nation of capitalists and that, too, must change. Because *if* human life is indeed sacred, then you can't tell me profits *now* matter more than peace, equality, justice, healthcare, education, and a better environment for that life in the future.

Heh heh.

I've lost you, haven't I?

That's always where it happens: money.

Life is sacred, unless it cuts into profit.

You tell me *all* life is sacred, but you don't really mean that. You don't. You don't mean *all* life, or even all *human* life. You don't really believe it. No. Those shouting loudest about the sacredness of life are the very same people who, daily, divide humanity into the valued and the worthless, who put profit over human life.

Every. Single. Day.

That's where morality always breaks down, right there.

Because building the world where there is no need for abortion is *hard.*

You see, if you honestly believe human life to be sacred, then it's not enough to demand every conception be carried to term and every baby be born. No. That's the easy part.

If you *truly* value human life, then you must build a world where that life is *truly* valued, encouraged, and celebrated for itself. If you *truly* believe no pregnancy should be terminated, no matter what, no matter the circumstances of conception, no matter for birth defects, no matter the risk to the mother's life or health, then you must work every single day to fully eliminate those conditions.

You must build a society where women are not impregnated against *their* will, be it by force or deception or failure of technology.

Thus, we must first hold *men* accountable. No exceptions. No excuses.

If life is sacred, then those who create it must be *responsible* for it until it can function on its own.

(NOTE, let me very clear here: I said men should be held *responsible* for their actions, not that men should have any right to force their presence into the mother's life if they are not wanted. Those laws that give rapists and abusers parental rights and force women to interact with them are travesties of justice *and* morality.)

If you allow no exemptions for impregnation by force, then you must work diligently and aggressively to ensure rape does not happen (I know. I see you, barely holding in a scream of unbelieving rage. I know. I know exactly what I just said, and exactly how it sounds. I said it on purpose, with malice aforethought. Give me another minute. Stay with me to the end. Please.) You must *change* society, you must *change* how we think, you must *change* the entrenched power structure. You must *change men*.

What it comes to is this: if women are allowed no exceptions, then men cannot be allowed any, either.

If you allow no exemptions for intention, you must ensure to the greatest possible extent the right of women *not* to get pregnant, even by accident, even by force. That means full and unlimited access to birth control for every woman by *her* choice. If you allow no exemptions for technology, then you must actively work to reduce the likelihood of failure. Birth control must be safe, 100% reliable, affordable, convenient, ubiquitous, continuously improved, and the woman's decision—and that decision must include her legal control over men.

That is: if the woman must bear the burden of pregnancy without recourse to its termination, then she *and only she* must have authority over its prevention. So, the woman must be given full *legal* authority over whether a man wears protection or not.

That's right.

Remember, this was about *morality.*

Thus, if you put the *entire* legal burden for life on one person, then *that* person must then have *entire* legal authority. You can't hold people morally accountable if you don't give them full legal authority over the decision. So, women must be legally empowered to determine when and where and what type of birth control *a man* uses.

If society holds a woman personally, morally, and legally accountable for pregnancy—and that's what these new laws do—then PREGNANCY MUST BE *SOLELY* THE CHOICE OF THE MOTHER AND THAT CHOICE MUST BE RESPECTED AND PROTECTED BY LAW.

No exceptions. No excuses.

Bet you didn't see that coming, did you fellas?

No pun intended.

If you allow no exemption for defect, then you must put every possible effort into preventing that defect, curing that disease, repairing that damage. In fact, as a society you must put *more* effort into that research than you do into ending life, than you do into weapons and war. It must be one of society's highest priorities.

Ah, but it doesn't end there.

A society which believes its moral imperative is to protect human life, well, *that* society must have a *radically* different foreign policy than we do today, one that promotes this better future for *all* humanity, not just babies born to our nation.

Ironic, no? If we truly believe human life is sacred, that every pregnancy is indeed a divine gift, then we actually have to live up to those commandments of that deity used to justify this alleged morality.

We would actually have to feed the hungry, clothe the poor, and care for the sick.

We would have to *truly* do unto others as we would have them do unto us.

But *that* civilization, the one which truly values human life, which welcomes life in the delivery room *and* at the border, we're not really talking about that, are we?

Because this has never been about the sanctity of life or any right to it.

That alleged morality is bullshit, nothing more than a convenient fiction.

No, this is about power.

It's about bending others to your will.

It's about imposing your religion and your political ideology on others by force.

This isn't about *morality*.

And it's for damn certain not about some god or his alleged will. Q.E.D.

It's about power and that's *all* it's about.

Yes, I do want to live in a nation where life *is* considered sacred.

I want to live in a nation where *every* life matters.

I want to live in a world where all of us are important to each other and where every life can reach its potential, one where there is no rape, no accidents, no failures of birth control, no unwanted pregnancies, where every child is cared for and valued and likely to grow up in a better future. A world where we put more energy and creativity and effort into giving human life the best chance at a decent future instead of one where we devote more than half of our national budget to its destruction.

Yes, I would love to live in that world.

The one where there is no abortion, *not* because it is illegal, but because it is *unnecessary*.

If you want to talk about building *that* world, I'll listen.

But until then, until we live in a world where we actually do hold life sacred and act as if it is, then, *morally*, abortion must be safe, legal, available, and solely the choice of the mother.

Abortion isn't a constitutional right.

Abortion isn't a state's right.

Abortion is a *human* right.

No Country for Young Women

S. Bryant

"Does the crowd seem off to you tonight?" Henry gestured at the room behind him. It was a good crowd for a Tuesday night. He could hear the pool balls clacking and loud laughter. The clientele seemed to be having a good time, but he couldn't shake the feeling that something wasn't right. No crackling lightning like a fight about to erupt or anything like that—just a feeling that something was missing. Dale, the bartender, wiped at the wet rings on the bar with a towel, then tossed it up on his shoulder, and squinted at the room, considering. "Not many babes here tonight," he said, after looking the room over, as he slid a glass of bourbon—the good stuff, of course—to his boss. "Kind of a sausage fest."

Henry took a sip and then turned around on the stool, sloshing the alcohol around in his glass. It was difficult to count people when they were moving around, but Henry gave it a go, starting with the groups playing pool. One table with four young men. Another with four older guys. The third table had two women, there with their husbands, regulars he recognized.

Shifting his attention to the booths, he counted only two women there, too, and they'd come together. Henry didn't really understand dykes, but he'd take their money on a Tuesday night same as anybody. Usually there'd be a crowd of girls from the college, just barely old enough to drink and looking for a cowboy to take home, or at least a couple of middle-aged ladies nursing wine glasses and people-watching while they bitched about their husbands. But not tonight.

Finally, he leaned out so he could see the row of barstools. Eight stools, and eight male rear ends. Not a rounded feminine curve down the entire row. Weird.

Finishing his drink, he left the glass on the bar and headed up the stairs to his office. He picked up the newspaper and flipped to the calendar and events part, wondering if there was an event attracting all the female clientele tonight, but he didn't see anything. Downstairs, he heard the drums kick up and a roar of approval from the crowd. Good, the band was ready.

Turning around, he checked the calendar on the wall to see who was playing: *No Rest*. Henry liked them. Solid young country sound. Their singer had a set of pipes, waist length blonde curls, and a flirtatious way about her that the crowd loved. She might go on to be somebody someday. Maybe he'd go watch for a bit before he headed home for the night.

Applause sounded, and Henry figured that was his cue, so he headed downstairs. He paused at the top landing to listen and was surprised to hear Randy instead of Sue on vocals. He recognized the song and knew it was one she usually sang, so he sped his steps to see what was going on. When he rounded the corner and could see the stage, he frowned.

No Sue.

He scanned the faces of the crowd and saw some of

his own disappointment mirrored there. Leaning into a quiet corner, he listened until the song ended. The crowd still applauded, but it was nothing like the reception that song had gotten when Sue sang.

"Thank you," Randy spoke into the microphone. "Welcome to the show. We're No Rest." He went on to introduce the rest of the band members, without any mention of Sue or her absence from the stage.

Henry sought out Dale again. "Did Randy say anything about why Sue's not here tonight?"

"She split."

"Split?"

"Yeah. He said she packed up her shit and left a week or so ago."

"Where'd she go?"

Dale shrugged. "East, I think."

"Isn't she from Houston?"

Another shrug.

Henry took another look at the crowd. Everything seemed okay. "I'm going to head out. Text me if you need anything."

Dale nodded. "See you tomorrow."

~~~

Henry didn't sleep well, but he was still awake at six, however unwillingly. He couldn't remember any dreams, but a cloudy discomfort lingered between his ears and his throat felt raw, like he'd been days without water. Rolling up to a seated position, he groaned and rubbed his hands over his head. His hair was greasy and his jaw was stubbly, so he decided he'd better shower before stumbling to the coffee shop for a bit of liquid motivation.

He turned on the radio, expecting the usual

Saturday morning talk show with Gwen Rogers, whose show featured interviews with local celebrities and often gave him a lead on events or guests for the bar. But instead of Gwen's deep and delicious voice, a young man with a nasal tone rattled on about the new ridiculousness out of the state legislature, an attempt to lump birth control in with abortion.

Grunting his disgust, he spun the dial until he found some nice wordless jazz and padded to the shower. Confirmed bachelor that he was, stuff like that had nothing to do with him and he didn't want to hear it.

A few minutes later, he had washed the worst of the night off his flesh and considered himself publicly presentable. So, he picked up his phone, wallet, and keys and walked out the door. A nice indie coffee shop was only a few blocks away and Henry decided to walk it, hoping the still chilly morning air would do some of the work of waking him up.

He got there by seven-thirty. The coffee shop was still relatively empty this early on a Saturday, so he walked straight up to the counter. The blue-haired boy behind the counter was reading a magazine. Henry cleared his throat to get his attention.

The boy slid off the stool and sidled to the counter. "What can I get you?" he asked. Henry gave his order and turned to look at the room while the machine steamed and whirred his concoction into life behind him. When the boy handed it to him, Henry took a sip. Not warm enough.

"Can you warm this up a little? It's not really hot enough," he said.

The boy ducked his head and took the cup back,

dumping the whole thing back into a metal pitcher and sticking the heating wand back inside. The two watched the milk and coffee steam for a long moment, and then the boy passed it back again.

"Thanks, man," Henry said, dropping a couple of dollars into the tip cup. "Where's Luisa this morning? She sick or something?"

"Naw, she quit a couple of days ago. Said it was time to try somewhere else."

Henry frowned. That was too bad. He'd liked the girl. She made good coffee and served it with a pleasant smile. She read a lot, too, and he liked hearing about the books she chose. He'd even read a few of them himself on her recommendation. A little heavy and serious for him—he tended to like old-fashioned escapism—but still interesting.

"Bummer," he offered.

"Yeah. It was weird. All of them quit on the same day."

"All of them?"

"Yeah, all the girls." The boy tossed the spoon and metal pitcher into the sink. "Oh well, more shifts for me, I guess."

Henry lifted his cup in salute and went back outside.

Back out on the street, Henry sat for a moment at one of the rickety tables, watching cars drive by and thinking. After a few minutes, he realized he'd been keeping a tally of all the people he saw: twenty-four men, six women. Was that more or less than usual? He had no idea. Shifting in his seat so he could watch the pedestrian traffic without being too obvious about it, he continued to sip his mediocre coffee.

He'd been sitting there for fifteen minutes when he spotted a familiar face. "Cass!" he called out, waving.

Cass had been walking with her head down, moving slowly, hands shoved into the front pockets of her jeans, but she lifted her head at the sound of her name, smiled, and headed his direction. At his invitation, she dropped her brightly colored bag in the chair opposite and went inside to get her own cuppa.

He'd known Cass nearly as long as he could remember. She grew up down the street from him, and they'd always been friends. Unlike him, the incorrigible bachelor, she'd been an incurable romantic. At his last count, she'd been married five times, and he'd lost track of how many times she'd been in love. Each and every time, she thought she'd found "the one," and Henry was amazed at her ability to keep brushing herself off and giving love another chance when she'd been smacked down so many times.

When they'd been in high school, she'd gotten in trouble. She hadn't been able to talk to her mama about it, so he'd been the one to drive her to get an abortion when her then-boyfriend refused to take responsibility for his part in their unplanned "blessing." She had only been sixteen years old, her whole life ahead of her. She'd never have made it through nursing school if she'd had to provide for a kid at the same time.

He wasn't sure what had him thinking about that day. Maybe the story on the radio. But he could still feel the acid atmosphere of that dark waiting room all those years ago. He shivered, remembering all the eyes on him where he sat in the molded plastic chair trying not to shift around too much while he waited to take Cass back home.

Everyone assumed he'd gotten that pretty little blonde in trouble and was making her "take care of it" rather than stepping up. He'd felt almost as guilty as if that had been the truth, even though he was damned careful when it came to birth control, even back then.

Luckily, he'd been able to avoid such situations since. He hadn't had that many relationships, maybe five or six over the past twenty years, and he knew he wasn't fit to be anybody's father, so he'd had a vasectomy when he was in his thirties. No little Henrys or Henriettas would come into the world because of him.

Cass came back with her drink and flopped into the chair, her face puffy and her eyes red from crying. He hadn't noticed when he invited her to sit with him, between the bright sun and her white-blonde bangs hanging low over her brow.

Bracing himself for another tale of love gone wrong, he asked, "You, okay, Cass?"

Reaching across the table, she squeezed his fingers and he noticed that hers, like his own, had become spotted and on the way to gnarled-looking. When did they get old? Seemed like just yesterday that she was drinking beer with him under the bleachers and making fun of the height of the hair on the homecoming queen.

"Maggie's left," she said.

Henry blinked. "Maggie?"

Cass nodded, biting her lower lip, then looked away from him. "Packed her bags yesterday and took the bus."

"How old is she now?"

"Twenty."

Henry whistled. That seemed awfully young to him. Young to be setting out on your own. Of course, in his mind, Maggie was still the gap-toothed six-year-old who could twist something in his heart by calling him "Uncle Henry." Maggie was gone?

"Where'd she go?"

Cass sighed. "Portland."

"Maine?"

"Oregon."

Henry considered that. "Why? I mean, last I heard, she wanted to be a nurse. Texas has plenty of need for nurses right here. They just put in that new hospital."

"I told her all of that, but she said she couldn't stay here anymore. Not even for me."

"Did you all have a fight or something?"

"No. And nobody broke her heart neither. She's always been smarter than me about men." Cass wrapped both hands around the paper cup, her hands heartbreakingly small. "It's these new laws. She says it's no place for a young woman, anymore. Not if there's any chance you could get pregnant."

Henry colored, his ears glowing hot. He tried to cover his embarrassment with a sip of coffee, but his cup had been empty for a few minutes now. "I see," he said, not really sure that he did.

Cass squinted at him, highlighting the lines around her pale-blue eyes. "You heard about it, didn't you?

"I heard something on the radio this morning. I guess I didn't realize it was such a big deal."

Cass snorted. "Of course you didn't."

Henry was hurt. "What's that supposed to mean?"

"Ah, Hank." Cass's voice softened, but there was still some acid in it. "You mean well. You've always meant well, but you don't get it."

He fought down a spike of anger. What was that supposed to mean? Hadn't he been a good friend to her all their lives? What didn't he get?

Biting down his retort, he said, "Maybe you should explain it to me." This was Cass, after all. He owed it to her to listen.

"The thing is, that all of you think that this 'woman stuff' has nothing to do with you. You'll sing the praises of us Texas girls up one side and down the other, but you don't want to hear about the messy bits—the blood and guts part of it."

"I figured that's not my business."

A sound somewhere between a growl and a groan escaped Cass's throat. "That's the problem right there. You don't bother to learn about it and understand it, because you think it's got nothing to do with you, and then assholes whose cowboy hats are bigger than their brains get away with passing bullshit laws that make our daughters think that Texas is a hellhole instead of their home!"

Cass's voice cracked at the end, and Henry sat there in silent shock. He'd never heard such language out of Cass in all the years of their friendship. He scrambled mentally, trying to think of something to say, but his brain was a wasteland of white static, caught between stations and nothing tuned in. He wanted to defend himself—he hadn't passed those laws. He was just a guy who owned a bar—he just wanted people to have a good time.

"I don't know what to say, Cass," he finally managed.

Cass smiled with one side of her mouth, showing her crooked front teeth with the gap she'd never had fixed. Pushing her cup away, she gathered her hair into fistfuls and tugged it around her face, like pigtails, pulling them like she'd always done when she was frustrated. She sat in silence for a while, and Henry started counting passersby again, giving her time to find her peace.

Finally, she sighed. "I'm sorry, Hank." Cass dropped her head into her hands, speaking to the table instead of looking him in the eyes. "This isn't your fault, or at least not just your fault. You might think this has nothing to do with you, but what affects one of us affects us all. You know what they say: if you're not part of the solution, then you're part of the problem."

Henry didn't know what to do, so he sat in silence, hands wrapped around his empty coffee cup. After a while, Cass reached out and patted his arm. He looked into her eyes, maybe the pair of eyes most familiar to him in all this world, outside his own. A question burned there, and he wasn't sure he understood what he was being asked, let alone how to answer.

"I don't know what to say, Cass," he said again.

She nodded. "Well, I hope you figure it out soon." She stood up, swinging her bag over her shoulder, the tangled ends of her hair catching under the strap. "Because if you don't, if we all don't figure this out together? It'll be too late. They'll all be gone, and then where will we be?"

Henry sat there long after Cass had gone. A string of customers came and went around him and when he finally stood and cleared away the two paper cups, his hips were stiff. He'd been sitting too long. Maybe it was time to move.

The Devil You Know

J. Mierisch

"Please," begged Mary, the dark-haired young woman in the hospital gown. "There is no time for this!"

Nurse Burkhart, squat and blonde and heavily made-up, arched an eyebrow at her patient. "Sorry Honey, the rules require a transvaginal ultrasound to ensure you're not past the six-week cutoff for a legal abortion."

"Yeah," muttered Mary. "Thanks a lot Governor Hensler. But I've already waited three weeks for this appointment. I have to get this thing out of me! It's the spawn of Satan!"

The nurse smirked. "Sure it is sweetheart."

"You don't understand," Mary said. "I thought he was just a hot guy from Tinder. He bought me one drink. The next thing I knew, I was waking up in his bed, and he was flying around the room chanting that he'd planted the seed that would bring about the end of the world!"

"Really," said Nurse Burkhart, "there's no need to make up stories just because you're unhappy with your life choices."

The black-and-white ultrasound image was grainy, but it looked a lot like an embryo with miniature horns, budding wings, and tiny hooves. A forked tongue flickered from its mouth.

"See?" shouted Mary.

"The law makes no exception for physical abnormalities." Nurse Burkhart squinted at the monitor and then smiled. "The baby measures six weeks and one day. You're past the cutoff."

"Come on! You're really going to make me give birth? To that?"

Burkhart rolled her eyes. "Should have thought of that before you opened your legs, sugar."

~~~

Nurse Burkhart did a double take at the patient's chart. She hadn't recognized Mary when the orderly wheeled her into the maternity ward.

In the months since the ultrasound, the young woman had aged decades, her face sallow, her skin a sickly gray. Her protruding belly twitched and the gown fell open, exposing an abdomen marred by purple bruises.

Armand, the medical technician, peered at Mary's chart. "She measured six weeks on April 14?" he muttered to Nurse Burkhart. "That's only four months ago. How is she this big already?"

Nurse Burkhart shrugged, fingering the gold cross around her neck. "God works in mysterious ways."

"It's coming," Mary croaked. "I tried to warn you." Her abdomen contracted, and she screamed, a primal shriek of misery that split the sterile air.

"Are we going to have melodrama again?" sighed Nurse Burkhart. "You think you're the only woman who ever went through labor pains?"

"I'm telling you," gasped Mary, "it's the spawn of Satan. It is going to destroy me, then you, then all of humanity."

Nurse Burkhart tsk-tsked and shook her head. "A baby is a gift from God, no matter how you personally feel about it," she said.

"A gift? From *God?*" Mary laughed hysterically as the nurse bent over to examine her.

Armand, his brows furrowed in concern, approached holding an IV kit and a vial of narcotics.

"Too late for painkillers," declared Nurse Burkhart, setting the speculum aside. "She's ten centimeters. Time to push."

"What?!" shrieked Mary. "No! I need drugs. It's ripping me apart from the inside!"

"Should have thought of that before you went and got yourself pregnant," said the nurse.

Mary wailed as a fierce contraction gripped her innards.

The baby slithered out so fast that Nurse Burkhart barely caught it.

"Please kill it," sobbed Mary.

"Killing babies is evil, young lady," Nurse Burkhart declared. "Given your emotional state, I highly recommend adoption." But when she got a good look at what she held, she dropped it onto the scale like a hot potato and quickly crossed herself.

The creature, slimy with mucus and amniotic fluid, blinked yellow eyes in a fat, red face. With a loud snap, it unfolded scaly wings, spattering the room with blood. It leaped into the air and soared around the room, giggling gleefully, shattering a light fixture in an explosion of sparks.

Nurse Burkhart backed against the wall behind a cabinet. "This damage will be your financial responsibility!" she yelled at Mary.

The demon's clawed hands overturned a bookcase, seized a medical textbook, and hurled it at Nurse Burkhart, smacking her in the face.

Armand's screams brought others running in from the hallway. The demon grinned and licked its lips. It cackled as it dove for one person after another, shredding blue scrubs with shark-like teeth.

"Run," cried Mary. "Save yourselves!" Her straining body fell limp as she passed out in a pool of her own blood. The demon flapped its wings, screeched, and burst through the hospital window.

~~~

"Governor Hensler," said the reporter from ABC7 News. "City Hospital has just reported that the patient who gave birth to the creature has died. Can you comment?"

Reporters whispered and pointed at the sky above the press conference. What appeared to be a cloud of massive birds approached rapidly from downtown.

The long-faced man brushed lint off the shoulder of his blue suit. "Death is a sad, but real, part of life," he said. "Events that may seem tragic are merely God's will."

"God's will?" said the reporter. "It was God's will that the spawn of Satan be unleashed upon the earth?"

The crowd's murmurs swelled to panicked shouts as a flying creature broke off from the group and buzzed directly over their heads.

"God knows all," said the governor. "Who are we to question Him?"

The flying demons swarmed overhead, dropping flaming brimstone onto the assembled members of the media. Reporters and camera operators screamed and ran for their news vans.

"The hospital also stated," the reporter shouted, shielding his head with his clipboard, "that the patient was denied an abortion four months ago, after you signed Bill 780 into law."

"I urge you to consider the real evil here," said Governor Hensler, ducking a dive-bombing demon.

"Real evil?" demanded the reporter. "What could be more evil than hell-beasts summoning their minions to destroy us all?" An imp landed on his shoulder and began gnawing on his ear.

"Pre-marital sex!" hollered the Governor, just before a demon bit off his head.

Leeli's Choice

K.G. Anderson

Late afternoon light filtered through the towering pecan trees in our back yard and lit the cavernous room Jenn insists on referring to as my study. I sat at the desk, a monstrous dark wood thing her interior designer had picked out, and stared at my laptop. But my attention wasn't on the case file open on my screen. My attention was on the voices in the kitchen. My daughter's voice, soft and hesitant, and my wife's voice, as strident and peremptory as one of her campaign speeches.

I'd offered to go with her, but Leeli wanted to tell her mother herself. Now I could hear Leeli's voice tentatively offering the plan, then halting.

There was no answer from Jenn.

"Mom?" Leeli asked, her voice trembling.

More silence. Then the clack, clack, clack of high heels as Jenn crossed the tile floor. The splash of iced tea poured from a pitcher. The rattle of ice cubes stirred impatiently in a glass. The clank of a dirty spoon tossed into the stainless-steel sink.

Then, finally, Jenn's voice. "You'll have the baby," she said. "End of discussion."

"But Mom, I don't want to have a kid senior year. I can just drive up to Maryland and get an abortion.

That's what people do now."

"*People*?" My wife's laugh was mirthless. "*People?* Well, that may be what 'people' do, but you aren't 'people.' You're the daughter of a candidate for governor of this state. A candidate who wrote this state's anti-abortion legislation. Do you realize that if you were to get an abortion—which you will not do—just the fact that you and I even *talked* about it could put both of us in prison?"

"Mom!" Leeli tried again. "Mom, get real. I am not going to have a kid. You don't even know this guy, he's not—"

"I don't care who he is." Here I could imagine Jenn giving that tight politician's smile she uses on TV when she doesn't like the interviewer's questions. "This boy and his parents are going to make nice for the cameras and you two are going to have a nice little wedding. Look, you can always get divorced after the kid is born. Divorce is legal in this state. Murdering babies is not."

Rage flooded through me. I stood up from the desk, the desk chair scraping the floor. The shotgun wedding scenario? Jenn knew it only too well—because she'd acted it out with me 18 years earlier. In a week's time I'd gone from packing a backpack for a year of post-law-school travel around the world, to standing at the altar with a woman I'd met at a friend's graduation party and had sex with once. And not very good sex, at that. One date with Jenn, one broken condom, and I'd been chained to her for life. Her father, a local judge, saw to that.

When Leeli came to me about her unexpected pregnancy I knew immediately that I wanted to spare her the same fate I'd suffered. I told her I'd take her up

70

to Maryland for an abortion. My law partner's girlfriend had gone up there last summer. They knew an excellent clinic. I would have explained all this to Jenn, but Leeli was afraid that would trigger another one of our epic fights.

"But Mom," Leeli wailed as I strode down the hall, "I'm only six or seven weeks pregnant. It's not a baby."

Oh no, I thought. *Wrong argument.*

Jenn launched into her campaign speech about baby killers. "You are carrying a life, a human being, and a little one who can hear—"

"Shut up," I said.

They both spun around. Leeli, perched on a stool at the granite counter. Jenn, hands on hips in the middle of the kitchen.

"Leeli made a mistake," I resorted to the calm, even tones I use when presenting a case in court. "She went to a party, had a few beers, and let a friend of Nate Jackson's drive her home. They ended up in the back seat of his car."

I took a few steps into the kitchen and put a hand on Leeli's shoulder. At my touch, she burst into tears, turning and burying her head in my shirt just the way she had when she was five and had fallen off the swing set. "I'm taking Leeli up to Maryland. I've made arrangements. The hell with your campaign, Jenn. This is our daughter. This is her *life.*"

"It's the baby's life *I'm* concerned about, Derek," Jenn shot back.

"Spare me," I said. "It's your campaign you're worried about. Babies? They're just planks in your party's platform."

Jenn's eyes blazed. Her lips curled back.

Leeli was shivering. Jenn was about to unleash a threat. For a second I thought she might report me to the police for planning an abortion and then publicly cast herself as the family martyr. But that tactic was too incredible, even for my publicity-crazed wife.

"Look," Jenn took a deep breath and spoke slowly. Her glass was now empty of tea, but she swirled it, rattling the ice cubes. "I'll make you two a deal. Leeli and this boy get married privately. Just so there's something on paper. She'll have the baby, and then there's a divorce. We'll pay all the expenses and help Leeli raise the kid. Problem solved."

"Mom, the guy—" Leeli hesitated. She looked up at me.

I gave her shoulder a squeeze and nodded, "Go ahead."

"The baby's father..." Leeli said, and stopped.

I looked hard at Jenn and finished the sentence. "The baby's father is Black."

Jenn's iced tea glass hit the floor and shattered. Ice cubes and sharp shards flew across the tile. She slammed her manicured hands flat on the counter, and lowered her head. "Fuck. Fuck."

"So, how does that work with your plans?" I asked. "Is your party ready for a White governor with a Black grandchild?"

Jenn shook her freshly dyed auburn curls and raised her head. Her eyes gleamed with hate and anger. "OK. Fine. Go to up Maryland, you two. Just make goddamn sure that no one hears anything about it."

I felt my daughter's shoulders relax. The worst was over. We'd get to Maryland.

An ugly smile crept over Jenn's finely sculpted features. "When you two come back," she said. "You'll do anything I ask. Because if you don't, well, I'd just have to obey the law and turn both of you in." She whirled and clattered out of the kitchen, leaving the broken glass on the floor. "Unbelievable," she muttered as she crossed through the dining room.

It was unbelievable, all right.

Leeli, still sobbing, slid off the stool, took a broom from the closet, and began sweeping up the glass. I brought over the dustpan and held it as she swept.

"I'll finish the arrangements," I whispered. "I have a special cell phone and Uncle Pete is handling all the email. Don't tell any of your friends." I let the broken glass slide off the dustpan and rattle into the trash.

"I won't," Leeli whispered back. "Shit. I wish I hadn't said anything to Mom."

I didn't answer, just gave her a hug before she headed upstairs to her room.

I went back to my study. The sun had set, and a chill breeze from the garden poured in through the open French doors. I closed them, sank into the desk chair, and reached for my laptop. I opened a password-protected file labeled Future. I read, once again, my carefully prepared petition for divorce from Jenn. Now, I knew it would be many, many years before I dared file it. If ever.

~~~

Early the next morning Leeli and I started for Maryland, where we'd stay with my brother Pete and his wife, Lorraine. With any luck, the clinic would give Leeli the abortion pill—two pills, actually—and she'd spend the next few days recuperating in Pete's guest room.

"Been there, done that," Lorraine, had said over the phone. "I'll take the best care of her."

Lorraine, a nurse, explained that it might take a few days to make sure the pills had worked completely. "So you can't take the chance of driving back home, and then her needing to get more medicine or go to a hospital," she said. "People down your way are being sentenced to prison just for having miscarriages. If those folks think Leeli's had an abortion—well, never mind. She'll stay right here with us until we're absolutely sure that everything's fine."

We drove north along scenic back roads—I didn't tell Leeli I was trying to avoid leaving any evidence of our trip on highway security cameras—and when we got lunch at a drive-through burger place, I paid cash. There could be no traces of this trip. I was so wrapped up in figuring out security issues that we were halfway to Maryland before I registered Leeli's silence. She's always been a quiet girl, but a cheerful one. Now, as we drove, she looked haunted. She'd barely nibbled at her hamburger.

"Dad?" she said.

"Sweetie?"

More silence.

"Dad, what if I changed my mind?"

I opened my mouth to tell her not to be ridiculous, but fortunately stopped myself. "Well," I said, "You could do that. Tell me what you're thinking."

She shrugged, her shoulders bony and narrow in her white cotton t-shirt. She stared out the window at the lush green farmland as she spoke. "I... I think I want to keep the baby and raise them by myself. Or, at least, have the baby and then a family could adopt them."

"Wait. Did your mother—"

She shook her head vigorously, then looked over at me. "No. Dad, this was my idea. I just... feel this way. I'm... sorry."

I felt ridiculous speeding along a winding country road to an appointment it now appeared we would not be keeping, staring at the road when I should be looking at my little girl. I spotted a fruit and vegetable stand up ahead, pulled into their gravel parking lot, and turned off the engine. There we were, surrounded by wheatfield. We rolled down the windows. The hot, humid air poured in, but along with it the sweet smells of the fields.

I was reluctant to look at Leeli, but when I turned to her, she gave me her wonderful, shy smile.

"Is this OK, Dad? I know that you've gone to so much trouble..."

"It's OK." Actually, it was very OK. I'd had nightmares imagining Leeli at the clinic. Now I realized I could easily imagine her pregnant, having the baby, and giving it up to a good home. Or, even keeping it. She'd be a good mother, though I couldn't imagine how she'd turned out that way, growing up with Jenn.

And, I realized with a jolt, with her new decision I'd regained my own dream. The one of finally getting free of Jenn. Of taking that backpacking trip around the world that I'd delayed for nearly 20 years.

I thought for a moment of telling Leeli about the circumstances of her own birth. But that was for some time much, much later. Or maybe never. This kid had plenty to handle already with the pregnancy, her mother's blinding political ambitions, and possibly the responsibilities of impending motherhood.

"So, you're OK with this, Dad?" Leeli asked. She picked up her milkshake and took a healthy sip, apparently confident of my reply.

I smiled. "Sweetie, this is completely your choice. All I want is for you to be able to make a choice."

She nodded.

So I texted Pete on the burner phone, telling him our plans had changed, to please cancel Leeli's appointment, and I'd explain later. I'd call him tonight and ask him to donate a substantial sum to the abortion clinic.

Then I started the car, turned around, and we headed back home. Leeli and I were silent as we drove, both of us imagining the future. A future that we'd chosen.

Signs of Blood

J. Yolen

The sign of blood
is not a mark of Cain.
We young women bleed
every single month,
a purge eggs that cannot live,
unfertile or maimed or simply
not meant to be babies.

I stood in the garden once.
the blood that waterfalled
down my legs was not the color
of hair, or skin, or love.

The doctor explained it to me.
But the loss followed like a shadow
into my 80s.

I will always wonder who that child
might have been, sandwiched between
my first and second children.
A poet, poseur, mathematician, or matron?

We do not bleed away eggs, zygotes,
imps or impulses easily.
But we know better than most men,
that not every egg is meant to be held
in a mother's arms.
Or a father's.

Wanted Woman

R. Dawson

Mother Jones's Tavern was fairly busy for a Wednesday. Clearly there were still a few progressive folkies left in Texas—at least here in Austin, the "blueberry in the tomato soup" as the joke had it. Rosa Kinneard had already got more in tips than Eddie and Jim were paying her for the gig, and Eddie and Jim paid *well*. And the audience showed respect, listening quietly while she performed.

How much longer would she be able to keep performing like this? Already half the bars in Texas were back to being the smoky hells of her youth. She could survive there with her asthma puffer, if she was lucky, but no way could she sing a set in that poisonous murk. And Kentucky, with its big tobacco industry, had brought in a law in 2031 declaring no-smoking zones illegal. The State Supreme Court had ruled that the Smoker's Rights Act violated the first amendment, but Washington had agreed to hear an appeal, and other red states were already drafting copycat laws. She sighed. Joni Mitchell had it right: you don't know what you've got till it's gone.

The set was almost over. Could she do her signature piece? She'd already tested the water with "The Four Marys," and "Gypsies, Tramps, and Thieves," two songs about unwanted pregnancies, watching the audience closely through each one. Nothing set her alarms off. *Time to commit.* She took a deep breath.

"Okay, folks! For my last song this evening, I'm going to sing 'Wanted Woman.'" She waited for the applause to die down. "The tune's by Bob Dylan, though Johnny Cash made it famous. And I wrote my own words." She played the tune through once on guitar, then began to sing.

> *I'm a wanted gal in Gilead, come listen to my tale:*
> *Wanted gal for sending sisters* mifepristone *in the mail.*
> *Wanted gal in Oklahoma, wanted gal in Texas too,*
> *When your urine test says "pregnant," honey, I'll be there for you.*

A scattering of audience members applauded again, just for long enough to show they were on the same team. Nobody cursed, or got up and left. A good start.

> *Wanted woman in Biloxi, wanted woman in Mobile,*
> *For those drives to California with me behind the wheel,*
> *Wanted woman in Wyoming, in Dakota, North and South,*
> *If you see me driving by you, tie your shoe and shut your mouth.*

She stopped singing and let her guitar take the next sixteen bars, fingers on autopilot, while she scanned the room again. No veins popping on foreheads, nobody shifting their ass to get easier access to a holster, not even anybody recording her on a phone. Any evening when the atmosphere turned nasty, she'd deliberately break a guitar string: she'd practised doing that until she could make it sound natural to anybody but another guitarist. Whichever string broke, she'd pretend it was the G string and get the good old boys laughing with a corny stripper joke. Then when she'd changed the snapped string and retuned, why, she'd just sing something completely different, as if that was what she'd planned all along. "Amazing Grace", if that was what it took to calm them down. But tonight it looked as if she'd judged her audience right.

I was fifteen and in trouble thirty-seven years ago,
When the waters rose around me, couldn't wade but I could row.
Now the rowboat's lying broken at the bottom of the creek,
But I help a sister cross it almost every single week.

One of the waiters, the tall one, Francis, was looking at her, almost twitching, trying to catch her eye. She looked toward him: for a moment his eyes dipped toward a young woman sitting at a table just ahead of him. *Really* young—how the hell had she got past Makaela at the door? Especially the way she was dressed? Eddie and Jim weren't stupid enough to risk the tavern's license by allowing underaged hookers to work the place. Why wasn't Francis just telling the kid to scram?

Wanted woman in Miami, Chattanooga, Lafayette,

*In Columbus and Savannah, but they haven't caught
me yet.*
*Wanted woman down in Dallas, wanted woman in
Walhall',*
*And till every child's a wanted child, I'll be a wanted
gal.*
Take it away, guitar...

She must have ID, then. *Real* ID, it would take a lot
to fool Makaela. But what sort of grown woman tries to
look like jailbait for a night out? Maybe she's got a
boyfriend who's kinky that way, but smart enough to
keep it strictly to cosplay? No, that dog wouldn't hunt:
the other three seats at her table were empty.

Rosa's brain flicked through possibilities. Only one
explanation made sense: a plain clothes police officer,
dressed for a pedo sting. But why here? No john in his
right mind would come here looking to find a hooker:
Eddie and Jim made damned sure it wasn't that sort of
bar. Adult sex workers were welcome—strictly outside
their working hours. It stayed on the right side of the
law, and it saved the other customers from harassment.

For a panicky moment she thought she'd lost her
place in the song. No, it was okay: her clever fingers
were still enjoying their solo, giving her time to think.
Officer Jailbait was here for a sting, but it wasn't a john
she was after. Suddenly Rosa understood, and her
stomach lurched. *That outfit would be the plain clothes
section's idea of what a "bad girl" looked like.*

She wasn't pretending to be a hooker, she was
pretending to be knocked up. It would never occur to
them that a pregnant teenager might look like the police
chief's daughter—let alone *be* the police chief's daughter

(but, honey, could I tell you a tale or two!) So, if that was right, Officer Jailbait was there to entrap an abortion-runner. And that was problematic... because to the best of Rosa's knowledge, there was only one abortion-runner in Mother Jones's that night, and that particular person had to start singing again in just about two bars. Too late to break a string: she'd already sung most of the song. She'd have to brazen it out. She hadn't done anything illegal yet.

Well, the Pope says I'm a sinner, but I'm just the gal you want
When you're overdue to visit with that California aunt,
Wanted woman in Kentucky, wanted gal in Salt Lake City,
Wanted woman in Atlanta, ain't it just a fucking pity?

More applause... where was Jailbait's backup? Nobody in the room looked the part—and Rosa had been able to spot cops at a hundred paces ever since the old days when she'd made a small fortune selling organic homegrown marijuana. Was she getting rusty in her retirement career? One more verse–should she sing the polite version? No, fuck that shit, there were no kids in the room. Not even Jailbait. Might as well go out in style.

I've got Justice "Handmaid" Barrett's face tattooed upon my ass,
Justice Kavanaugh can kiss it—any time that I've got gas!
Wanted woman in Topeka, and in Tuscaloosa, AL,

And till every child's a wanted child, I'll be a wanted gal.

Laughter, hoots, and applause filled the room. She stood up, took several bows, gestured that she didn't have the energy for an encore, and left the stage.

With shaking hands, she staggered into the tiny private change room that was one of the perks of playing Mother Jones's, and locked the door behind her. She slipped off her shoes, and flopped into the shabby armchair, avoiding the familiar broken spring; then she closed her eyes and waited. It was about five minutes before the knock came.

"Ms. Kinneard?" The voice through the door sounded young and scared.

"Yes?" Rosa did not get up, did not even open her eyes.

"I need to talk to you. Please open the door. It's important."

"Just a moment." She stood up, and opened the door. "Come in."

Jailbait stepped in, hesitantly. From close up, Rosa could see the lying makeup, the deliberately naive eyeshadow and unsophisticated blusher that would have taken ten years off her age under a streetlight. The woman closed the door behind her. "Hi, Ms. Kinneard: my name's Emma. Emma Murphy. I came back here to, uh, ask you about that last song you sang."

"What about it?"

"Is it, like, real?"

Play dumb. "It's a real song, yes. Real words set to real music."

"Because... I'd like to meet somebody like that."

There was a quaver in her voice. She sounded utterly sincere.

For a terrible moment, Rosa wondered if she'd misjudged the woman: logic is only as good as the data you give it. But she'd stayed mostly out of jail for thirty years by trusting her gut, and this was no time to start second-guessing. Time to pull the plug. "I'm sure you'd love to. It'd look good on your record, maybe even get you a promotion. Only I don't know anybody like that." She reached into her backpack, brought out a slim pink-and-fuchsia cardboard box. "There's a toilet next door. Why don't you go there and try this test kit? Just for the sake of staying in character?"

"I don't know what you mean." But the sound of sincerity had gone. She did not reach out to take the kit.

"Honey? That song I sang? It's a *song*. People have been singing about lawbreakers as long as people have been breaking laws. Do you guys still have an open file on Johnny Cash for shooting a man in Reno? Because I can give him an alibi."

"Huh?"

"He was in my bed at the time."

"He was..." She snorted "Okay. You got me good with that one." She smiled wryly. "I don't suppose June Cash would have appreciated that much."

Rosa grinned. "Then it had better stay our little secret, hadn't it?"

Jailbait touched a fingertip to her lips—*silence!* Then from somewhere in that improbably skimpy costume she produced a black Sharpie. (What else did she have hidden?) She bent over the strong aluminum microphone case, lined with thick foam and supposedly safe even against the assaults of airline baggage handlers, that protected Rosa's favorite mike between gigs. On the top she scrawled SOUNDPROOF?

Rosa nodded.

The police officer straightened up, slid a hand into her top and pulled out a wire, wincing as the tape pulled away from her skin. She put the gadget into the travel case and closed the lid. Then, as Rosa stared, she took off her top and Daisy Duke shorts, put them on top of the case, and turned, slowly. Her belly was flat—if she *was* pregnant, it was early days yet. And... those panties could not conceal a gun. "Satisfied?" she asked in a calm voice.

"Satisfied about what?

"I need to talk to you—without the wire. And I need you to *know* it's without the wire." She smiled ruefully. "Besides, I feel more decent in bare skin than that tacky teenage-tart costume."

"You're police," said Rosa. "Even in your skivvies, you're police. Fuzz, we used to say. The heat. And for some unknown reason you suspect me of something. So, just because of that, and because the Supreme Court hasn't yet managed to annul the Fifth Amendment, I'm not saying another god-damned word, not even if you do a fucking pole dance. You put some clothes on, show me your badge and a warrant, and I'll phone my lawyer, and then maybe we can talk—if she says it's okay."

"No, you don't understand." She bit her lip. "You're quite right, I'm not pregnant. But my kid sister *is*. Her boyfriend's ghosted her, and she's afraid to tell our parents. That's why I volunteered for this undercover assignment—as a way to talk to you."

Rosa had trusted her gut for thirty years. She thought for a long time. "Put your clothes on—or this robe, if you prefer—and we'll talk. Has she seen a doctor?"

~~~

An hour later, Rosa strode out of Mother Jones's, guitar case in one hand and microphone case in the other. In a week or so, the police officer's sister would get a package in the mail with some organic radish seeds, pesticide-free and suitable for sprouting, from a cooperative in Oregon. They sold good seeds, but their hippie workers were sometimes careless: every so often, a few pills found their way into a package. She hummed to herself: "*And till every child's a wanted child, I'll be a wanted gal.*"

It felt *good* to be wanted.

We Tell You This

A. Alexander

We who have been forced into this sad world
by politics and posturing and grim
pursuit of agendas to be unfurled,
and ideas important only to HIM

never asking an opinion from HER -
we speak to you, who claim to be "pro-life"
and yet treat us worse than the lowest cur
dooming us to hunger and endless strife

leaving us—low, beaten, unclothed, unfed—
most especially if our skin is brown—
we cry out to you. Something must be said
before there's so much blood that we all drown.

We tell you this, with pity, and with scorn.
We needed to be loved, not merely born.

On Maintaining a Domestic Supply of Infants

P. Hammond

We are in a population crisis. For much of our history, we have enjoyed a healthy, growing population, which has, in turn, made us successful and prosperous. Since 2011, however, birth rates have been falling by at least 400,000 annually. It was clear, as early as 2035, that the unthinkable—zero population growth—was just around the corner.

Shrinking populations produce stagnant economies: something had to be done. And it was. The resulting legislation has turned the tide to some degree but, as recent Sundered States senators have noted, the Christian is still producing fewer offspring, globally, than the Muslim or the Hindu. If the States are to thrive, then a domestic supply of infants must be maintained by any means necessary. It is with this very serious consideration in mind that this document has been produced.

The topics covered in this short pamphlet are those which will, we hope, prove of great assistance to all those who are planning to keep one or more brood cows.

Within, you will find a lexicon offering helpful descriptions of the different divisions of brood cows. For clarity, charts are provided which summarize the various yields and quantity of offspring to be expected, plus the optimal conditions in which to produce viable and healthy issue.

An appendix deals with so-called free-range cows, which can be hired on a birth-by-birth basis via one of the State-approved brothels. While perfectly comparable to standard brood cows, these can be a less expensive option for the beginner breeder who is looking to gain experience in the field.

How Many Is Too Many?

For those wondering whether to invest in a brood farm and, if so, how many brood cows it is practical or desirable to keep, we offer the following words of wisdom from Over Pastor Aversion Peterson:

"One can compare a woman to a fruit tree. The sap of the tree provides the vigor needed to promote the development of the fruit. When a tree gives but little fruit, that sap turns to waste. Better then, to abandon the barren and unprofitable tree and gain what financial reward you can from its wood, rather than continue to waste God-given resources. Quality will always win over quantity, just as, in the end, Christianity will prevail over the infidel."

Brood Banks or Live Pens?

When the first breeding programs were established, huge manpower costs were involved in keeping brood cows permanently contained. Since then, a number of different approaches have been trialed and, of those, three have come to dominate modern husbandry.

1. Induced comas have been found to be effective in the short term. Such brood banks are able to function with the minimum of staff and security. The difficulties of keeping cows healthy during successive pregnancies, while insensible, remains an issue.

2. Targeted leucotomies, more popularly known as lobotomies, have been found to reduce aggression in newly acquired brood cows. But breeder beware! The procedure also creates apathy and a lack of initiative, which may result in high infant mortality should you decide to allow cows to breast-feed their offspring.

3. Your State keeps a register of brood lines which allows you to select cows for desirable traits, such as passivity. The advantages of what has become known as the live pen approach are twofold. (a.) A reduction in the need for sedative hypnotic drugs such as propofol, pentobarbital, and thiopental. (b.) Cows can be entrusted with basic infant care tasks. This significantly reduces overheads and is believed to be less stressful for the cow.

Is Inbreeding an Issue?

While it has been a practice for decades to mate cows with members of their own family, in order to breed in (or out) desirable qualities, the dangers of inbreeding should be noted. Good genetics, after all, is one of the key determinants of economic growth.

Line breeding, where cows are artificially inseminated with the sperm of their grandchildren or cousins, will avoid many of the genetic problems associated with inbreeding, while ensuring the offspring retain the desirable qualities of its parent.

Is There an Ideal Age to Begin Breeding?

There has been much debate as to the timeframe in which you can expect a brood cow to produce viable offspring. As outlined in Pamphlet 3247 ("When and How: A Guide To Successful Breeding") the well cared for cow may produce as many as forty to forty-five offspring over the course of their life. Recent studies have suggested that these figures should not be taken as an absolute baseline. To avoid physical fatigue, no more than one birth annually is now recommended. The conscientious farm manager may increase his yields by breeding as soon as puberty starts, although rising medical costs, and the possibility of stillbirths, or permanent damage to the brood cow, need to be weighed against any product gains. This pamphlet recommends first insemination no earlier than 14 years of age. See Chart 1.1 for an overview of age versus yield data.

Does Better Feed Produce Better Offspring?

Since 2050, it has been observed that, where brood cows are fed a high-end roughage, plus concentrate, product quality is improved. This is true even for brood cows who have been raised on low-quality roughage: their offspring will be superior if they are fed an enhanced diet during pregnancy.

Since the focus of many breeders within the Sundered States is on producing strong bodies for hard labor, it is suggested that vitamin-rich concentrate is added to all feed for at least the first trimester. See Chart 1.2 for a comparison of roughage quality versus miscarriages and birth defects.

Choosing Your Cow

Ultimately, every breeder must choose their stock to suit the needs of the local economy but, for the beginner, this pamphlet recommends one of three classic brood line divisions, which combine productivity with manageability.

1. *The Curved Line.* The archetypal Sundered State brood cow, the Curved Line combines endurance with traditional feminine aesthetics. Initial costs may be higher, but the Curved Line has the potential to produce an appealing and high value product.

2. *The Demijohn.* This strong, stocky, wide-hipped cow is rightly known as 'the baby maker.' Consistently outperforming other divisions of brood cow, this is a solid choice for the breeder looking for a product that sells consistently, regardless of fashion or market demands.

3. *The Hay Bale.* This small but durable cow requires less fodder and space, making it ideal for a starter farm on a small budget.

See Chart 1.3 for an outline of average maintenance costs per live birth.

Maximizing Profits

One of the most prominent breeders of the last decade, Mr. Aspic Spalding, Jr., has written extensively on the importance of keeping the profit margin in mind when raising infants intended for laboring, mining, and other non-dexterous work. With his thanks, we summarize his recommendations below:

1. As to the accommodation: an indoor space, 20 feet by 20 feet is sufficient for six cows.

2. You will need a self-contained concrete courtyard, where the cows can take the air and be washed and deloused. Do not use electric containment fences in areas where running water is accessible, as cows have been known to electrocute themselves.

3. A cow is seldom inclined to exercise their locomotive powers more than necessary to secure food, so the courtyard need not be large. A covered area, where the cow may take shade during the summer is, however, recommended. Only the foolish breeder allows cattle to come to harm for want of a few dollars' worth of tarpaulin.

4. An outdoor latrine should be provided near the sleeping area. Care should be taken to train your cows to use the latrine on command, no more than three times a day, to reduce manpower costs.

5. Sleeping cots should be raised off the ground to avoid the spread of disease. Clean bedding should be supplied every fortnight for the same reason.

6. When the birth due date is near, farrowing crates will prevent the cow from moving and injuring herself or the infant after birth.
7. Clothing is not necessary, but should you feel the urge to anthropomorphize your breeders, then meal sacks are adequate, durable, and cheap.

Final Notes

Throughout this pamphlet, the term brood cow has been used rather than the more emotive word 'woman', which has modern day connotations never intended by our Founding Fathers.

Bedside Manner

A. MayClair

Pumpkin, just stop fiddling with your IVs.

No, I won't read you a story. The surgeon will be coming for you soon enough. He's one of my most trusted colleagues. I'm only here to keep an eye on you. In the meantime, I must finish documenting these charts. I've explained how important my work is.

Patient 02892

> *27-year-old female. Current chemotherapy regime includes medications which are also known abortifacients. Ordered stop of all chemotherapy. Prognosis: patient is likely to become deceased before parturition. Referring to palliative care.*

Patient 04738

> *12-year-old female. During monthly women's health check visit, patient made mention of prohibited pharmaceutical contraception. Form 37 completed and filed with monitoring agency for any legal follow up.*

Patient 00900

> *44-year-old female. Verified fetal death due to natural causes one week prior. Treating symptoms*

of sepsis. Prognosis is poor. Scheduling husband for palliative care support.

What now?

Your mother? You know full well why your mother isn't here. She decided that she was above the law. How dare she, escaping to Canada for a tubal ligation, without my permission!

Yes, she was caught at the border. I told you, I refuse to post bail. She's a criminal, and we are a law-abiding family, aren't we. Aren't we?! Just nod. Now hush, I need to finish these."

Patient 003689

13-year-old female. Patient attempted suicide by ingestion of illegally acquired insulin, prescribed for her grandfather. Form 54-b, Bodily Infraction, completed and filed with monitoring agency. Due to mental health evaluation, implementing procedure 27, induced medical coma to ensure continuation of pregnancy until due date. Sole visitation is genetic father, advised legal team at father's request due to desire to sue patient in event of murder charges rendered by the district attorney. Offspring legally declared property of the genetic father.

Patient 002022

26-year-old female. Patient attempted self-induced abortion. Verified existence of fetal heartbeat. Form 2-3a, 3b, and 3c completed and filed with agency. Implementing procedure 7, holding in protective custody until expected parturition date.

Immediate move to women's primary lockup. Arm restraints when prone and restraint jacket at all times until post parturition. Supervision during all toilet visits. Due to mental incapacity, offspring to be remanded to legal custody of social services for enrollment at the Orphan League.

Patient 03001

19-year-old female. Patient moved to women's enclave 17 awaiting parturition. Maintain close supervision, flight risk. Fetal material property of client 671 to be packaged for stem cell and organs upon parturition. See related chart for transport of liver, kidney, stomach lining, eyes, skin, heart. Stem cells to be housed in government cryogenic facility 12.

Patient 03710

14-year-old female. Enforced pregnancy as part of hormonal treatment included within the updated mental reorientation program. Maintenance of hormone therapy subsequent to parturition in order to counteract any further sexual misidentification tendencies.

Don't you start crying. Brave girls don't cry. You're saving my mother's life, Pumpkin.

I don't care if it hurts when she pinches you. Stop complaining, it's just love touch. I can't imagine who you've been talking to.

That's all nonsense, puerile leftist propaganda. You exist for the good of *all* society. They'll take what they need this time, and then you won't ever have to worry

101

about all this ever again.

Boyfriends? Who would want you, especially with all the scars?

Patient 01500

> *30-year-old male. Routine stem cell matching found suitable recipient, see related chart. Patient shot at southern border attempting to flee the country post notification. Liver damaged, no longer useful as transplant. Form 1528 completed and filed with monitoring agency. Holding patient in medical facility until charges including murder, destruction of private property, and others are filed.*

Patient 789, VIP

> *71-year-old male. Various organs failing due to long term alcoholism and lingering Covid complications. After initial visitation, referred to scheduling department for review of addition to prime recipient list.*

Well, well, looks like we may get a new wing in the hospital soon enough. That last one was a VIP. You know, a very important person, someone with wealth and power. Someone not like you.

I won't tell you again. Stop that sniveling. Crying is so unattractive. Don't look at me that way. I'm your father, Pumpkin. God commanded that you love and honor your father. You are a good, God-fearing girl, aren't you?"

Enough! Stop overreacting. You'll get over it. Just lay back and shut your eyes. This won't hurt a bit.

Consequences

P.E. Thompson

It started at the Walpole Mississippi Gentlemen's Club, known locally as just The Club. Actually, it was known to its non-gentlemen patrons as the whorehouse, but let Miss Jenny hear you use that term, or any derivation, about either the house or the "girls" and you'd be spending the next six months limited to the internet for your indulgences.

The sign went up on the red door with the fancy glass. inside the wrap-around screen porch that allowed patrons the pleasure of evening breezes free of both prying eyes and mosquitos.

Jasper Maddox, the Mayor of Walpole, was heaving his form up the wood steps when he saw Old Tom attaching the sign. Two bright brass screw-in hooks held the sign, hung from a short length of equally bright chain such as you might find hanging from an overhead fan.

"What you doing there Tom?"

"What's it look like?" said Tom. He checked his work with a small level. Miss Jenny didn't tolerate half-assed work. That suited Tom just fine. He worked hard and kept the place looking good. His shack was on the river about a hundred yards back of the club where he still had his shop, and Miss Jenny paid him in cash. He'd asked once about services for services, and the glare Miss Jenny had given him had made him drop his eyes in shame.

"My people aren't trade goods," she'd said.

Tom understood and never broached the subject again.

Jasper stepped closer and peered at the sign.

Tom frowned, as if to say that if Jasper couldn't read the sign from the steps, he likely shouldn't be driving the faded red Cadillac out in the dirt parking lot.

Jasper let the screen go shut behind him and settled into one of the padded wicker chairs. "What's this nonsense?"

Tom shrugged. "Don't ask me. I'm just the help." He turned back to the door and, satisfied with his work, reached a liver-spotted hand down and picked up his worn canvas tool bag.

He was turning to leave when the door opened, and Miss Jenny herself stepped onto the porch. She didn't spare Jasper a glance but reached out a tumbler of sweet tea to Tom.

She gave the sign a brief inspection. "Nice lettering job, Tom." She brushed her fingers lightly over the gilt lettering. "You might as well sit a spell. It's gonna be quiet around here for a bit."

Tom accepted the tea and sat down. He looked approving at the crushed mint leaf nestled among the ice cubes. Clearly, Miss Jenny might not do services for services, but she was a pleasure to work for.

"That sure looks good, Miss Jenny," said Jasper. "Don't suppose I could ask for one myself."

Miss Jenny pointed her chin towards the sign. "You can read, can't you?" she said sweetly.

"Well, yeah," said Jasper. "It just don't make no sense. "'Closed due to State Permit Requirements,'" he read the gold lettered sign slowly. "Come on, Miss Jenny." He gave what passed for a smile. "You ain't exactly operating under no state permit as it is."

Miss Jenny smiled a sad smile. "You read the papers, Jasper?"

He nodded.

"You know what a trigger law is?"

"That means I got a right to my gun?" he said hesitantly.

"No, that means that when some law happens in Washington, DC, other laws in the Great State of Mississippi go into effect automatically."

He nodded. Awareness dawning on his jowly face.

"Then you know it means the State of Mississippi has now laid claim to my body. It isn't mine anymore."

"Aw now Miss Jenny, you ain't serious." He tried to smile, but he couldn't. "A man has needs." He looked longingly again at Tom's sweet tea and then at the sign on the door.

Miss Jenny just looked at him with a smile that would have made Mona Lisa proud.

Jasper heaved himself to his feet with a grunt, gave the sign a frown, and Miss Jenny and Tom a curt nod, and then leveraged himself down the steps.

Tom set his empty sweet tea glass on the table and peered after Jasper. "If you're gonna be closed a while, it might be a good time to fix them steps up a bit," he said.

"Why don't you get started," she said. "I got some errands to run, I'll use the back steps."

Jenny hitched her bag to hang on her shoulder and

enjoyed the walk, the town was small and by the time she stopped in the café for a club sandwich, her bag was empty.

~~~

It was a week later when Jasper walked into the Moose lodge. Instead of the normal shouted greeting, the room felt like a morgue. He found his table, already occupied by three of the glummest faces he thought he'd ever seen on the city council.

"The usual?" called Tiffany from behind the bar.

"You know me too well, sweetheart," he said and settled into his chair. He gave the faces another look.

"Who pissed on you boys' cornflakes?" he asked.

Before they could answer, Tiffany set a double bourbon on the table in front of Jasper. "Here you go, Mayor."

"Thanks, honey," he said and sipped the bourbon. "Seriously, boys, a cute waitress, good bourbon, and you boys're looking like your pappy died."

Across the table, a man pointed to a bright blue bracelet on Tiffany's wrist.

"You like?" she asked brightly, and held it up for Jasper to see.

His face drained of color when he read the lettering. "Government Permit Required."

Through the window, he could see the ice cream store across the street. He didn't need to walk over to see the flash of blue as the servers delivered to the outdoor tables.

"Bring me another," he said glumly and held up his glass. "And whatever the boys here are having. I think we're gonna need another round."

Interview with Mister Plub

L. Hodges

Roe v. Wade was dead. There was no doubt about that. The Supreme Court, in their infinite wisdom, had ruled, and the register of its death was signed by whoever signs off on such things. Poor *Roe* was as dead as a doornail. For now.

Everywhere, tiny clumps of cells rejoiced. So too did Mr. Plub, a major backer of ending *Roe v. Wade*. Now we'd like to hear his views.

Oh, you ask—who am I? I am your tired, huddled masses yearning to seek the truth—but my identity is not important. What's important is the logic and morality of the great issues of our times. And so we will get both sides of this issue so we can reason together.

But before we interview Mr. Plub to get his side, we'll interview a tiny clump of cells. A human egg is only about one-fourth the width of the period at the end of this sentence, but this clump of cells has been busy, growing, growing, growing! It's taken four to five days, but it's now fully the size of the period at the end of this sentence, about 64 times the size from when it started. Let's give it a good look. So, tiny clump of cells that hurts my eyes to focus on, what does it feel like, knowing you can no longer be aborted?

<SILENCE>

Hello?

<SILENCE>

Okay, we get it. You're just a tiny clump of cells. Your mouth won't start to develop until after the fifth week and your lungs won't be developed until nearly nine months, so you can't respond, and you won't have functioning ears to hear me until seven months. So, to be absolutely fair, we'll conduct this interview telepathically. My mind to your mind, my thoughts to your thoughts, let's try again. *So, tiny clump of cells, what does it feel like, knowing you can no longer be aborted?*

<SILENCE>

Are you there, mind of tiny clump of cells?

<SILENCE>

Oh, that's right, you're just a tiny clump of cells. Your higher brain structures won't start to develop for three months, and won't really be developed for six months, and so you have no more thoughts than a clump of carrot cells. And yet, Mr. Plub will fight to the bitter end for your imaginary life and soul. But we'll let him speak for himself.

Mr. Plub?

"Why are you calling me Mr. Plub? That's not my name, my name is—"

We'll explain later, Mr. Plub, we just want to ask you a few questions.

"No problem, I'm always happy to share my views."

Mr. Plub is the salt of the Earth, a down-to-earth common-sense conservative with strong moral values. He knows this because he's been told this over and over by the opinion leaders who share his views, who coincidentally are the same opinion leaders as those he chooses to listen to. Let's say he's wearing bib overalls and just came in from slopping the pigs. Or maybe he's wearing a business suit and black oxfords and just came home from making hoards of money on the backs of his subsistence wage workers. Or maybe he's a politician wearing a blue suit with an American flag pin and red power tie, raging against the evils of Latinos stealing jobs from Americans by working in jobs no American wants to do.

Being a well-read and curious type, Mr. Plub asks, "Why are you carrying a coat hanger?"

You really don't know?

"Um... oh, I got it. Here, thanks." Mr. Plub starts to take off his bib overalls and/or suit jacket.

No, the coat hanger isn't to hang your clothes on.

"Oh, okay. So... um... did you get locked out of your car?"

No.

"Antenna for an old-fashioned TV?"

No.

"Never mind then," Mr. Plub says. "You said you have some questions for me?"

Why are you against allowing women to choose for themselves about abortion?

Mr. Plub smiles. "Because I'm a good Christian and follow the teachings of Jesus Christ."

Really? Let's take a quick break here. Hello, Jesus? Mind if we ask you a few questions?

There is the sound of a door opening. The light in the room slowly grows brighter. Then comes the sound of footsteps approaching, closer, closer, closer...

"It was kind of dark in here," says Jesus. "I turned up the dimmer switch. So, you had some questions?"

He's short, wears a dirty-white tunic, and has dark hair, a beard, and, of course, a Middle Eastern complexion. His dark, mesmerizing eyes drew attention away from two warts at the end of his nose.

Just one question. What's your take on abortion?

"Abortion? *Jesus*—sorry, I mean *Me*—don't you read your bible? I gave my views there. And my eyes are up here, stop staring at my warts."

Well what exactly did you say about abortion?

"Absolutely nothing, as any true follower of me would know. Abortion was actually pretty common in my time. Now, can I go now? I have a souffle in the oven."

Thank you, and enjoy your souffle.

"Wait a minute!" Mr. Plub says. "You don't look like any picture I've seen of Jesus. How do we know you're the *real* Jesus? I mean, warts? Really?"

Jesus smiles, snaps his fingers, and disappears.

So there you have it, from Jesus himself.

"Oh, okay," says Mr. Plub. "But my church is against abortion, so I am too!"

Your church follows the teachings of Jesus, who had no opinion on abortion. He did have a lot to say about helping the poor and foreigners that your church and Republican Christians seem to ignore, but we'll talk about that some other time. Regarding abortion, though, back in Jesus's day they didn't need coat hangers.

<He's right, you know> says the disembodied voice of Jesus.

Thank you, Jesus, but we're done with you.

<Burned the souffle, dang it. But I think I still have some bread and fish around here. Bye now.>

"Bye, Jesus!" Mr. Plub says. Then he looks confused. "If they didn't have coat hangers in those days, where did they hang their tunics?"

Never mind that. Your bible says nothing about abortion.

"Hah, you are wrong! What about Exodus 21:22-25?"

You mean where a person is fined if he *attacks* a pregnant woman and causes her to lose her pregnancy? What's attacking a pregnant woman got to do with a woman having a voluntary abortion?

"But—but—but—"

In fact, since the attacker is put to death if he kills the mother, an actual human, but only fined if he kills the fetus, which implies that the fetus is not considered human.

"But it is a baby!" Mr. Plub says. "An unborn human baby!"

Why do you keep calling a fetus a baby?

"Because it is!"

Webster's defines a baby as "an extremely young child, especially an infant." It defines a fetus as "a developing human from usually two months after conception to birth." Before that, it is an embryo, from about two to eight weeks. Before that, it has various names, but it's basically a tiny clump of cells. So, can you stop falsely calling these things unborn babies?

"Webster was probably some anti-Christian nutcase."

He was a devout Congregationalist who preached the need to Christianize the nation. He published a book called *Value of the Bible and Excellence of the Christian Religion.* (Thank you, Wikipedia.)

"Okay, okay, I'll stop calling them unborn babies... even though they are unborn babies! Regardless of all this, I'm against abortion on moral reasons. It's murdering a human being!"

You believe a tiny clump of cells is a human being?

"Human life begins at conception, so yes, it's a living human being. Abortion is murder."

Interesting. Could you take a look out the window?

"Sure."

See the kid tied up on those railroad tracks outside? Billy, say hello to Mr. Plub!

The blond-haired, blue-eyed boy looks up and smiles. "Hi, Mr. Plub! Want to hear me play my trumpet?" A trumpet case lies on the ground a few feet away.

Mr. Plub, you'll note that fifty feet before they reach Billy, there's a second set of railroad tracks branching off from the main ones that lead to Billy?

"Yes. What are you getting at?"

Look closely at that other branch of the tracks, the one just adjacent to the Billy. What do you see? You can borrow my binoculars.

Mr. Plub looks through them. "There's some sort of small container on the tracks."

It's a petri dish with three tiny clumps of living embryonic cells, ready to be implanted in the wombs of volunteer women. Oh, and look off into the distance, what do you see?

"There's a train approaching! *It's coming right at Billy!*"

"Are you talking about me? I heard my name." Billy waves. "I learned to play *Amazing Grace* on my trumpet today!"

Mr. Plub, here's a remote device. If you push this button, the train will veer off on the adjacent branch, and go over the petri dish, killing the three clumps of embryonic cells. If you don't push it, it'll continue on its current track and kill Billy. *Hi Billy!*

"Hi, person who tied me to this railroad track!" says Billy. "Boy, this is exciting." He raises his head and stares for a moment. "Um, is that a train coming at me? Would you mind untying me? It's getting awful close." He has a scared puppy-dog look. "*Help!*"

How about you, clumps of cells? Any thoughts on this matter?

<SILENCE>

The train toots its horn.

"Don't let the train run over me!" pleads Billy. "I'll miss trumpet practice!"

"So, Mr. Plub... which are you going to save?

"Both!"

Sorry, you have to choose or Billy dies by default. Save the child, or the three tiny clumps of embryonic cells? You've got ten seconds to decide, or Billy dies.

"But—but—but—"

C'mon, it's a simple choice. What's it going to be? You've got five seconds.

Four... three... two...

"I have to save Billy!" Mr. Plub pushes the button. The train veers off on the alternate track. A few seconds later it smashes the petri dish.

Good choice, Mr. Plub, I'd call it both a "pro-choice" and a "pro-life" choice! So, Mr. Plub, to save an actual human, you murdered three humans, since you believe human life begins at conception. Or maybe we can agree they were not actual humans yet? By the way, the train was set to veer off to the alternate track no matter what. You had a dummy switch. Billy wasn't tied down, either—hey, Billy, you can get up now.

Billy jumps to his feet, tossing aside the ropes. "You owe me thirty bucks," he says. He grabs his trumpet case and runs off.

"So," Mr. Plub grumbles, "you killed three clumps of living human cells just to make a point?"

Actually, there wasn't a clump of embryonic cells in the petri dish, I just cooked a grain of rice and chopped it in three pieces. They look surprisingly alike. So, can we agree that Billy, a human child, is worth more than three tiny clumps of embryonic cells, because they are not yet human, and are, in fact, just clumps of cells with the *potential* to become human beings?

Grumbling sounds come from Mr. Plub's throat. Then he brightens.

"Wait a minute," he says. "The key is, as you say, they have the *potential* to become human! So, if you do an abortion, you are killing a *potential* human! And that's murder! And... why are you smiling?"

Are you married?

"Yes," Mr. Plub said. "For twenty years. Wife and three wonderful kids."

Congratulations on successfully turning tiny clumps of cells into actual human beings. But... what about the potential twenty-three wonderful kids you murdered?

"What? I didn't kill anyone!"

But you just equated abortion to killing potential humans. You've been married twenty years. That's 240 months. If you divide 240 by nine months, that's over 26 babies you could have had. You had three, so if abortion is the murder of potential humans, then you murdered the 23 potential humans you and your wife didn't have. Twenty-three wonderful kids, all dead at your hand. Should I call the sheriff?

"But—but—but—"

Abortion does stop a potential human from developing. So does not having a kid every nine months. Can we agree that potential humans are not the same as actual humans? While you think it over, I'll dial 911, get the sheriff over here to arrest you.

"No, put the phone down! I don't want to go to prison! I just want to know—how did abortion get to be a Christian issue if it's not a Christian issue?"

Mr. Plub, abortion was barely even an issue in the U.S. until after the Civil War, when the recently formed American Medical Association saw it as a way to put midwives out of business, thereby bringing more business to doctors who delivered babies. It also rose as a big issue in the 1980s when the so-called Moral Majority, a Christian and Republican immoral minority organization, used abortion as a wedge political issue. They convinced people that abortion was a Christian issue even though Christ himself didn't make it an issue. Most Christian leaders followed their lead. Apparently, American Christian leaders believe they know more about Christianity than Jesus, and their followers don't seem to actually read the bible.

"Okay, okay, you've sort of convinced me. Abortion isn't a religious issue. But I still don't think abortion should be legal. I just can't find a good argument for it, it just seems sorta wrong—"

Like mixed-race marriages once seemed sorta wrong? Like letting women vote seemed sorta wrong?

Like the Earth seemed sorta flat?

"I'll believe what I want to believe!"

Yes, you will, Mr. Plub.

"And seriously, why do you keep calling me Mr. Plub? That's not my name!"

You are pro-life, correct?

"Of course."

And a good Christian and a Republican?

"Yes!"

So, while you defend the rights of embryos and fetuses, you agree with Republicans who oppose universal health care and other programs that nurture and protect children?

"Well, I wouldn't put it that way—"

Of course you wouldn't. Mr. Plub, like millions of American Christians and Republicans, you are Pro-Life, but only until a baby is born. So you are Pro-Life Until Born. *PLUB.* Here, have a coat hanger.

My Father's Diary

E. M. Killian

The memorial was over, everybody had gone home, and the house was finally quiet. No hushed whispers. No more stories shared from his youth to soothe the void left behind by his absence. No clatter from the kitchen as my family put the food they had brought me away. Nothing but the sound of mama rock chucks chirping in the twilight, telling their babies to get their asses home.

I wondered, as I poured myself a glass of single malt scotch, if the reason why people bring food to the grieving is because they sense, from somewhere in a distant, forgotten past, that food, made with hands filled with love that no longer has anywhere to go, is too hard to swallow.

Taking the bottle with me, I curled my legs up in dad's brown leather recliner next to the end table where his urn stood, and removed the box from the locked drawer. He'd made me promise not to open the box until after the memorial service.

The box was one of those old-fashioned Valentine's Day candy boxes. Heavy cardboard, covered with white silk, scattered with ivory roses and a beautiful, red brocade ruffle with hand-tatted lace stitched along the edges. An artifact as precious as the contents it held. Inside I found a cloth bound notebook with an old-fashioned black-and-white photo of a young woman in a tailored pants suit, and a smart fedora sporting a jeweled pin on the left side. Tall and slim, with deep set eyes, and perfectly coiffed dark hair, she smiled

117

openly at the camera with neat, even teeth guarded by dimples. On the back, in my dad's handwriting was "My Stella. Age 16. 2024."

I'd never seen her picture.

My father loved her, and she loved him. She got pregnant and my father wanted to marry her, but her father refused. Stella's dad told mine that he had bigger plans for her than to be married to an immigrant farmer. They didn't tell anybody she was pregnant. They didn't know what else to do. Dad was only 18. Men had to be 21 to marry without permission of his folks and there was no way Grandpa Joe would've agreed once Stella's own dad said no. Times were hard and he was a foreigner who only spoke broken English. You needed your neighbors then just as much as you need them now.

An old letter, its folds tattered from being opened countless times over the years slipped from between the pages and I gingerly revealed its contents before reading further. "We have to do it. Please, Andy! You must help me! I have a knitting needle. I've heard my aunts say that's all it takes. Just slide it inside me. Break my water. And I'll miscarry the baby. No one will suspect a thing. I have heavy cycles. You know that."

She made no mention of the dangers. Odds are good she didn't know. And even if she did? I can't blame her for not wanting to risk scaring him away from helping her.

They stayed home from church one Sunday and she lay on her bed while he tried to save her from the wall of shame she was headed for. He managed to cause her to lose the baby, but he wasn't a doctor. He didn't know what he was doing and so, he lost her too. She was dead the next day. Bled out before her mother got up to fix the coffee. My father visited her grave every Sunday for as long as I can remember, with a bouquet of sunflowers in his hand. I never knew why until today.

The book contained an envelope and in the envelope was

the deed to her gravesite and a post-it note. "Please bury me with her."

I put everything back into the box, poured myself another glass of whiskey and clinked it against the urn that held dad's ashes. "Don't worry dad. I'll take care of it.

Men!

A. Jill

I set Thomas's towels on a lawn chair. He left them at my house, expecting me to scrub them clean. I don't have to, not really. Thomas is my neighbor, not my husband. He fixes my appliances, I do his laundry and fix the occasional dinner. We have sex in my bed; never his.

Afterwards, he goes home, leaving lumps of him in my off-white bed. Blankets like milk curds remain wrinkled, because he was there. Teeming bundles of cotton and quilt, full of skin cells and dried sperms are a recipe for a baby Thomas.

I incubate long after he's gone.

Now, here we are.

The lawn chair, moldy and white, was missing a leg and turning grey from the summer rain. Its back is rounded and split, like a broken egg. His yard is stale and browning. No grass grows here; only weeds, and the occasional patch of chickweed. A squirrel digs a small hole near his porch. He sees me and bounds away, leaping like a rock on a murky water top. I kick the dirt until the hole 's full, but uneven.

I know this: it will never be flat again.

I want to leave the towels here. Let them get dirty, sit unfolded. But I know better. Thomas lets nothing go unnoticed. One by one, I fold them into squares, thick and fluffy like threadbare sandwiches. I lift the bundle, knocking his chair over in the process.

Car parts clog the driveway, greasy sputum staining the concrete esophagus. Thomas' whole yard, an empire of rubber and steel, bows to the mountain of his truck. It sits on cinder blocks, the phantom roar of an engine—no, bumblebees—buzzing under the hood. Ear-tipped cats seek its shelter, tired tomcats like fuzzy tumors on the ground. He keeps the cats, but I feed them. I do all the domestic things he's too lazy to do himself; cook dinner, wash his linens, sometimes darn his socks. I drop my hand to my stomach. I think of what he's done to me.

What he knows, what he'll never allow me to do.

I made the appointment in secret. Didn't even think about it, just picked up the phone. The woman at the clinic was comforting and kind.. She said, "Don't worry, baby. It's gonna be alright."

I wanted to crawl through the phone, set myself in its cradle and swaddle myself in her succor. Instead, I hung up and prepared to tell him.

I open the door without knocking, unceremoniously dropping his towels on a cluttered coffee table. It's ten A.M. and he's already drinking.

"Please don't leave your towels at my house anymore," I say, reaching for a cigarette.

He swats my hand. "It's not good for you."

"I don't give a shit."

"Think about the baby."

"What about me?"

Thomas only watches Memorable Entertainment Television. Together, we watch old sitcoms. Couples fight in black and white, smoke their own cigarettes that dance like princess wands, fixing all life's problems in a span of thirty minutes.

We do not talk. We watch "The Honeymooners" in a murky silence.

"I want to get rid of it," I say, gripping the albatross by the throat. "I don't want a baby. I am not ready. I don't want to be a mother."

Thomas doesn't look at me. His eyes stay fixed on the television. "No."

"It's my body."

"And it's my decision."

"Why?"

He says nothing, because he's the man.

I stare at the grainy screen, fist crumpled in my lap. A heartbeat of livid veins pounds against my gut.

Ralph Kramden, the show's main character, gets up in his wife's face. *"Men run this world, Alice. Men! They're responsible for the shape the world is in! Men!"*

His wife snaps back, *"Well, I'm sure glad to hear one of you admit it!"*

Damn right.

He stares at me, and I realize I've said this aloud. It's silent, save for the air conditioner pounding against the walls like a hurricane. His eyes stay on me as he nurses his beer, incredulous.

"It's my choice," I say, and then again. "It's my choice. And I do not want to have this baby."

The beer bottle sags down from his lips, his chin, and stops at his hairy chest. "I said no."

"Is that an order?"

He seethes, his face bright red. He thinks he owns me, because he's the man. But he is wrong. He will not push me around anymore.

"And you can wash your own damn towels from here on out!"

Anti-Misogyny Special Forces vs. Earth

M. S. Barr

Mary, Rhoda and Phyllis, anti-misogyny special forces agents, were tooling down the intergalactic highway in their sky-blue hood ornamented space cruiser, ready to defend female sentient life forms against subjectivity crushing onslaughts.

While approaching the exit ramp leading to Earth, they relaxed by blasting the radio and putting the cruiser's top down to enjoy space winds blowing through their hair. National Public Radio correspondent Nina Tottenberg's reporting on the pro-choice rallies taking place throughout America resounded through the cruiser.

"It seems that American Earth women are in big trouble in the wake of Roe v. Wade being revoked," stated Mary.

"Maybe we should help them," mused Rhoda. "After all, we always get our man, especially the male chauvinist pigs. The sky is falling on American women. We can at once fly above them and rescue them from being time traveled back to the eighteenth century."

"But humans are so primitive. Why should we bother?" asked Phyllis. "They cannot even use mind reification and biological transformation."

"Maybe you lack compassion because you are a special forces cadet intern," Mary said. "Perhaps if you had more experience, you might immediately want to lend a tentacle to our sisters—no matter how technologically backward they are. Human women have feelings. They also have space travel, the internet, Netflix and in vitro fertilization."

"Mer is right," Rhoda offered. "I say that we save American women from the slings and arrows and wire hangers of outrageous rescinded abortion rights fortune."

"Okay, I'm in," said Phyllis. "Defending American women's access to justice could be a good experience for me. How do you senior officers think that we should proceed?"

"First, we will put mind reading receptors in all of America's cellphone towers. At the moment of conception, these receptors will read impregnated women's minds. If the receptors discern that pregnancies are unwanted, the penises which delivered the sperm will instantaneously be reconfigured to act as vacuum cleaner hoses which suck out the fertilized eggs," opined Mary.

"Then what happens?" asked Phyllis.

"Once the sucking is completed, the cells, which you can count on one human hand, will be sent to the toilet via the bladder.

"What if the man wants to be a father? asked Rhoda.. "We're talking choice here, are we not.

"Hmm," mused Mary. If the man truly wants to become a father, the fertilized eggs—certainly no unborn children—will be deposited within a sack which will appear inside the men's abdomens," stated Rhoda. "Then, the penises, by growing longer and being bent back, will reverse their suction capacities to blow the eggs into the sacks. After nine months in which the penises only serve the procreative function of being inserted within holes in the sacks, they will detach from the sacks and newborn babies will emerge from enlarged penis holes."

"It is a no brainer for the advanced space feminists to discern how to provide the fetuses with nutrition while inside the sacks. But what will the sacks be made out of?" asked Phyllis.

"The stretchy material that Americans use to manufacture Spanx," answered Mary.

"Great idea. Although the natural material that comprises the pouches of the Earth fauna called kangaroos is highly superior, Spanx will work in a pinch," Phyllis said.

"Yes, it is highly elastic," said Mary and Rhoda in unison.

Despite their technological and biological powers and abilities, Mary, Rhoda, and Phyllis could not control the fact that American conservatives were not happy with the arrangement.

An Evangelical preacher named Jubilation T. Cornpone who hailed from Dawgpatch USA was in a snit because the advent of men carrying fetuses freed women from sexual repression and reproductive slavery. First Cornpone, after emphasizing that baby kangaroos are called joeys, blamed the loss of American men's masculinity on Joe Biden. Cornpone then, being the most radical candidate, achieved the Republican nomination.

As a result Joe Biden was re-elected with sixty-eight percent of the vote. That margin was blamed on the increased presence of empathy in pregnant men who had once been rednecks.

Men, it turned out, made very good mothers and within a generation, the humans were so reformed that the Anti-Misogyny League welcomed Earth into the Federation of Rational Planets.

Enlightened as F***

A. Sweet

Before It Happened

May 2, 2022

A boulder and a cappuccino are nothing alike. That's a quote Peter Legumey used when comparing the atavistic impulses of modern humans with those of prehistoric humans. I'd always admired his writing style—terse and to the point.

But on this fact, he's completely wrong.

I'll admit that I've never been hit in the face by a boulder. As I look back at myself sitting across from Kim with the remnants of her latte dripping, dripping, down my nose and onto my Lacoste shirt, this quote came to me. As I watch the line bounce up and down in monochrome, incessantly beeping at me and telling me that she's still here even when she's not, I think I would have preferred a boulder.

Kim worked upstairs from the Starbucks where the coffee incident happened. She was a programmer or an analyst or something with computers. I'm an old-fashioned sales guy.

I mean, I *used* computers, but she made them do stuff. I told her all the time that she was smarter than me.

We'd been together for a while.

Four years.

Jesus, has it really been that long?

I guess so. I remember it was pre-COVID when we moved in together. In hindsight, I may have been thinking with my other head. I moved into *her* apartment because she said she already had everything where she wanted it. Didn't matter that my apartment was bigger and downtown and very close to her sister's.

Even though we lived together, we met for coffee. Every single day. Like clockwork. That day was no different. It was the second of May, we met in the lobby. I got a caramel latte (sugar-free because I was watching my weight), and she got one of those Caramel Ribbon Crunch Frappuccino she's addicted to—the one with a tower of whipped cream, which I guess was fine for her because she worked out for two hours every night. Apparently, if I got off the couch and stopped spending so much time playing video games, then she'd let me get a latte with actual caramel sauce instead of the fake stuff. I mean, she didn't tell me what to do. She just made so much sense that it was hard to argue sometimes, so I went along.

We were getting coffee, then she picked up her phone when it buzzed its way almost over the table edge. She turned it over, looked at the screen, and her face froze. Then she turned to me, glared, and said: "I told you this would fucking happen."

I was lost. I smiled and took a sip of my coffee, trying to figure out what exactly she was talking about. That's when I saw the television.

Which by the way wasn't something I was used to seeing in a Starbucks. But there was a talking head, expounding on something I couldn't hear. Across the ticker at the bottom of whatever news show it was scrolled the words: "Roe v. Wade Memo Leaked."

That's what it said. And I remembered the conversation we had next. Every single word, because she'd already given me hell when that guy was elected president in the first place. Yet we rehashed it again, asking questions we already knew the answers to.

"You voted for who?

"Gary Johnson," I told her. Her face swelled before my eyes and turned almost cherry red. She swallowed and gritted her teeth, and swallowed again.

"He's the only candidate who was taking environmental issues seriously," I defended myself.

"And you thought that he would *win*?"

"Well…"

No, I hadn't thought that. But I'd voted for someone I believed in rather than for Hillary fucking Clinton. I got that Kim loved Clinton for some reason. I guessed then that women liked to stick together, and that's fine.

I sipped at my coffee. It seems surreal looking back. Her worst nightmare came true, and all I did was try to finish my damned latte. I didn't get it yet. I mean, we used both condoms and birth control. The law wasn't a problem for *us*.

I told her that.

Huge fucking mistake.

I know what you're thinking and no, it wasn't because I was a jerk. I was actually a pretty nice guy, even then. I was so vegetarian that I even ate tofu when she cooked it, and we meditated and all that kind of stuff. I don't mean to brag, but by so many standards, I was enlightened as fuck.

131

While I shouldn't have reminded her of my enlightenment, that comment wasn't what got coffee thrown in my face. That got a glance and a raised eyebrow. Then she took a breath, and we talked about it. Remember? Enlightened.

"You don't understand," she said.

"I don't, you're right. Can you explain it?" (See?)

"I shouldn't have to explain it, Jacob. You *know* me by now. Why don't you get it?"

I didn't get why I didn't get whatever it was I was supposed to get.

I said nothing. And she began to do that thing she does where she breaks it down like we're back in middle school. I tried not to be offended or defensive, which was really, really hard.

"What's been the most oppressed demographic in the United States since its forming?"

Slow ball, easy answer.

"The African Americans. Slavery. All of that."

Kim wiped her hand over her eyes and down to her chin. Then she muttered through her fingers.

"No. Well, kind of. Think harder, Jacob. When did the African American men get to vote?"

"1868. Uh, 1870 if you mean when they could actually do it. Fourteenth and Fifteenth amendments. Kim, you *know* I know this stuff. We go to BLM protests. This is *Austin*."

She sighed.

"You *should* know this stuff. When did women get the right to vote?"

I didn't know. I struggled with it. I went as far as imagining my high-school history teacher, a scary witch of a woman with one solitary mole on her left cheek that

132

had fifteen hairs in it.

Nothing came to me.

"1920," she said.

"Shit. That late?"

"Yep. Now, when could women own a credit card?"

Crickets from me. I mean, do *you* know this stuff? I am—was, I guess—in a relationship with a gorgeous woman who made me waffles on Saturdays and put weird little bacon smiley faces on them. All very strange, because I was thirty-three and that seems like the sort of thing a five-year-old would appreciate, but that was *her.*

You know what sucks the most? She told me this stuff. In four years, she'd been telling me these facts and sharing what was important to her. I... well, you'll see.

"1978," she told me. "That's less than a lifetime ago. And when was the Equal Rights Amendment added to the constitution?"

"Easy one." I said. "Never."

"Right again."

"I get it, Kim. A lot of oppression. What does this have to do with Roe v. Wade? All the decision says is that either the state legislators have to decide or the national one does. That's it. They're not saying that all the states are going to suddenly outlaw abortion. Besides, Dem majority. They'll fix it before that happens."

"They won't, Jacob," she said. "With Congress blocked? It'll never happen."

Sigh.

I grinned like an idiot and said the one thing that I thought might lighten the mood.

"It's a good thing we're not having kids, then."

Splat.
Stomp away.
Search soul.

The soul searching was uneventful. She just wasn't being rational. I mean, I got her point. I think. She was saying that someday we might *want* kids, but we'd talked about it a million times and never came close to yes. So, what could she possibly have been so pissed off about?

Like I said, coffee in the face hits like a boulder sometimes. But it's a slow-motion boulder that you don't realize connected at first on account that it's moving so slow. The inertia carries it right through your face and plows you into the mud over the course of months. Six months, in fact, almost to the day.

When It Happened

June 24, 2022

I hadn't expected her to walk out of my *life* from Starbucks. While I sat there wiping away foam and waiting for her to return (after all, I'm an idiot as we've determined), it never once occurred to me that she'd gone back to our apartment, collected up her things, and moved in with her sister downtown. How the two of them fit into that tiny one-bedroom apartment is beyond me. But they did, and when I got home much, much later—because I seamlessly transitioned from Starbucks to McCormick's—after her call never materialized and she didn't answer mine—there was nothing there. No posters, no paintings, no flowers, none of her clothes.

I called her again.

No answer.

Another week passed without talking to her. The next week and she called me back finally, breathless and using short sentences.

"Deborah says I need to actually break up with you," she said. "I don't see why. You get the hint, right?"

Enlightened as fuck. I got it. Mostly.

"When are you coming home?"

"I can't do this with you, Jacob. You and me—we're in two different places."

"I'll change," I told her. "I can do it. Give me one more try. Just one more. Dinner. At Luciano's. You love Italian food. You come out to dinner. We have some wine. I apologize for two hours straight?"

The expanding silence told me I was in. What wasn't to like about that proposal? Free food at the expense of a stupid ex- (it sucks to say that) boyfriend? If it didn't work out, it was free dinner. And Luciano's was at least a couple of hundred dollars for the two of us.

"I'm paying for myself," she said. "And Deborah's coming too."

I inhaled and exhaled. Mostly in.

"If that's what it takes, Kim. I just want to *see* you."

Dinner was a sordid affair at first. Deborah kept glaring at me. I didn't glare back and was careful not to drink too quickly. By the second bottle of wine, though, we'd all three loosened up.

I should tell you, since this is going to seem a bit weird, how quickly I got back in Kim's (and Deborah's) good graces after she moved all of her stuff out. Deborah was part of it. See, all three of us and a couple of others were friends through high school, and we all went to the University of Texas. We'd been friends forever, so it was easy to hang out and the jokes flowed between us. When the subject came back to Roe, wine softened the conversation.

Here's a hint: if you're ever in trouble for not knowing when Women's Suffrage happened, then *learn that shit.*

I had, in the month and a half since the coffee thing, become quite the expert in abortion and all things abortion. I even knew that Madame Restell opened the first abortion clinic in New York City sometime in the 1830s, and then lost her business around 1870 when a law change put her out of business... before she was possibly murdered in her home.

So armed with education and wine, Kim dismissed Deborah halfway through the non-date and we ended up back at my place.

I thought we were golden, back together again.

I was wrong.

The next morning, I woke up to a note on my pillow with an apology and instructions never to call her again.

I didn't. And I didn't see her again until a gunshot brought her back into my life for three months later in September.

After It Happened

August 26, 2022

I didn't see her, but I did hear from her. There was a phone call on the day the repeal went into effect. I'd been sleeping on my couch. Well, it was her couch. She'd left it for me, probably because she knew I'd never spend any money on a new couch. Regardless, it seemed like a nice place to sleep because the television was right there, and I never ran out of Netflix. Since the pandemic started, I could even get beer delivered. As consequence, I'd regained the ten of the twenty-three pounds I'd lost under her tutelage. Ten, only because it's harder to gain weight than you might think.

Anyway, I was there on the couch when my iPhone shrieked at me. It was an unlisted number and when I connected, I thought I heard breathing.

"Hello?"

The line went dead.

Two weeks later, I was down on Guadalupe because I was on a personal self-destructive quest to become the fattest enlightened person I could be, and I'd settled on a little place called Texadelphia that made cheese-steak sandwiches. Their fresh guacamole and beer helped pad my waistline as well.

I think I was depressed. The funny thing about being depressed is that you don't know it when you are. Someone else has to tell you. And since my someone else had fled my life, there wasn't anyone to do that.

Until that day. Standing in line at Texadelphia, I felt a poke in my belly from the person in a hoody in front of me. I did nothing.

"Letting yourself go?"

It was her voice! I strained my eyes to see beneath the hood, and a hand —her hand—went up and pushed it back just enough so I could make out the slant of her nose.

"Kim?"

"Shhhh," she said. "Don't say my name. They're after me."

I looked around because... well, maybe I'm not as enlightened as I let on. I saw three policemen approaching the store slowly. One looked a little jumpy and had a weapon in his hand. The other two made the low-key search look routine.

"That for you?"

"Yeah," she said, and let out a weak cough. I pushed the hood back just a little more so I could see her eyes (hey, her back was to the cops). She looked gaunt and tired, like I felt *all* the time.

"What's going on?"

"I'm late. Been late for a while. *Too* late."

"For what?"

Her sallowed eyes dug into my own and I got it. That night and the wine and maybe we weren't as careful as we should have been. I felt a lot of mixed feelings then. The first was panic, because I wasn't ready to be a father. That was followed by the serious internal question of whether I should propose or not— because it was Texas, and that's still how unwanted pregnancies are "solved" sometimes. Then I remembered that *she* wasn't ready either, and there was a Planned Parenthood clinic on Ben White Boulevard. I knew her, and that's why I felt comfortable pitching the next bit.

"But you can get an abortion, right?"

"I've been trying, and nobody will see me. And then somebody turned me in." She stopped talking and her eyes welled up. "Somebody turned me in. Those police are trying to take me to the hospital and strap me into a bed. They're trying to make me give birth like I'm a fucking cow."

Her eyes went dead, and her lip curled. A pained expression descended onto her face. I tried to head off the hostility.

"I..."

"It's not your problem, remember?" she spat the words at me. "Not our problem because we always use protection. *Always.*"

She said it too loudly.

"Ma'am, please step away from the line," one of the officers said. They'd spotted her. Two on our right and that one jittery one on the left. He looked like that guy from Big Bang Theory with the clean-cut hair if someone gave that person a gun and made them wear a police uniform.

"I'm not going," she said to me, squeezing in close. Her breaths came rapidly against my chest. I put my pudgy arms around her and held her close.

"Sir, I'm going to ask you to step away. Ms. Reilly is wanted and we're going to take her in."

"What'd she do?" I demanded. Her eyes darted from me to the police officer and back. I felt her pulling against my embrace before she said anything.

"It's okay," Kim said, and she shoved me away. She spoke in a whisper as she did. "You were right before. It's not your problem. And if you don't make it your problem, you've got nothing to worry about."

I'll never forget those words.

I was off balance at her oscillating emotions and partially because I hadn't become accustomed to my new weight yet. As I stumbled backwards, her hand went into her pocket. It was like a bad movie, everything that happened next. Her hand came up too fast for the jumpy rookie cop to realize that the black thing in it was one of those fancy pens that she used sometimes as a stylus. She flicked it toward him and turned her body, I guess, to run? I wondered how long she'd been running. I wondered who'd needed ten thousand dollars enough to turn her in.

Gunshots are loud. Ear-shatteringly loud.

I finished my fall with my hands over my ears and

my eyes riveted to the strange undulations her body went through as she fell. She never spoke again after that. Never walked, and never left her bed. Yet what they did to her next was so much worse than anything that I could have ever imagined.

How It Ended

November 19, 2022

The hospital room is quiet except for the beeping of machines. It doesn't *smell* like her. That's the badness of it. She's in front of me, but when I lean over to put my nose in her hair, it isn't her. It's antiseptic and some weird fucking lemon wash.

Doesn't stop me from trying.

Three months and I've been here every day. No job anymore. I promise I bring enough odor for both of us. My beard hangs down and my eyes have trouble adjusting to the light. I lost twenty-seven pounds because food all tastes like plastic now. Deborah comes and goes.

Tonight, I'm here late (because I'm always here) when Deborah walks in. She's been crying and she needs someone to talk to and I guess her parents aren't cutting it. She sidles up to me.

"I didn't think they would do this to her," she tells me, fingering the cross on her chest. "I thought they'd just arrest her and keep her—you know—monitored so she didn't kill my nephew. I thought..."

I can't look at her, but she keeps talking.

"I thought she could have the baby and maybe I could take it."

She confides in me because we used to be friends. She wants me to forgive her because Kim can't. But it's my first-time hearing that, and all I feel is rage inside.

"You told them?"

"I—I..." and she stops talking. She rubs her cross and turns as the irritating fucking beeping sounds over and over again. She stops by the door and rotates again, slowly.

"Do you think she'll come out of it?"

I still don't say anything. I shake my head slowly. The doctors all agree on that. They're not even trying to save her. Just the fucking baby. She's on life support now and her arms look almost as thin as mine. A tear trickles its way down my cheek, reminding me of a trail of latte foam, and that quote again. And how fucking wrong Peter Legumey was about a boulder being different at all.

Deborah can't take the silence for long. Or maybe it's the smell. She leaves.

The nurses don't come when I'm here. They all look at me like I'm a pariah and if I wasn't still on her emergency contact list, they would have kicked me out. But I am, so they instead schedule their checkups for whenever I have to go to the bathroom or think I can choke down a bowl of hospital chowder.

There's nobody here tonight.

I look at the swollen belly. Maybe it's my imagination because it's too soon (I know this because I'm now an expert on pregnancy), but I see a little movement inside. I put my hand on it in that tender way that husbands do sometimes, just to feel the movement. Then I take my chair and tilt it back against the door, shoving it under the handle. Nobody will bother the two of us now. One by one, I pull the plugs along the wall until I get the one that causes a shrill siren to sound out.

141

Fists start banging on the door.

I sit down. I inhale, I exhale, and I wait. More pounding. Sirens outside, police come in. I check to make sure she's stopped breathing.

She has.

She's not fucking chattel.

I get it now. I'm enlightened as fuck.

I close my eyes and feel my body start to shake. I've eaten too little for too long. The door bursts inward as police officers break through. They try for the machine and a cadre of doctors flood in behind. I block them with my body for as long as I can, but there are only so many blows to the head I can take. I can tell from the monotone bleating that it's too late, and my mouth curls into a bloody smile. Not fucking chattel.

I reach out my emaciated fingers to close around hers and in the sweet solace of my imagination, she squeezes back. My life ebbs, having nothing more to live for and having taken too much abuse. I can die, though, because I've saved her. I close my eyes for what I can only hope is the last time. The last words I will ever hear chill me to my core:

"We might be able to save the child."

The Discerning Gentleman's Guide to 21st Century Attire

D.B. Baldwin

From city streets to campus sidewalks, this guide will help you choose the gear you need to look stylish in the boardroom and stay safe on your commute.

A Classic Suit

The navy suit is a timeless classic, inspired by the military, tailored to the modern gentleman. With options from pinstripes to broken windowpanes, ten-to-twelve-ounce worsted wool makes a perfect all-season suit that will keep you warm and comfortable, rain or shine. We like a peak lapel with a two-button jacket, if only to help your wife or daughter spot you in a crowd of similarly dressed gentlemen.

Charcoal is always a second option, but we caution against lighter colors this year.

Silk Tie

No synthetics here. All-natural silk is renewable, looks great, and lasts practically forever. From fascist red to socialist blue, a loosely woven grenadine's gauze-like texture will draw the envy of CEOs and doctors alike. Keep it tied or remove it entirely; anything less will make the gentleman look like an inebriated Florida congressman.

Footwear

It's the shoes that really make a man, and we have no shortage of options this year. In past editions of this guide we've recommended a variety of wingtips and oxfords, all hand-crafted by the city's finest cobblers. This year we're going more radical and presenting the discerning gentleman two choices: a blood-red oxford, handcrafted by a cobbler who can no longer afford his rent, or a pair of reliable, union-made boots suitable for all conditions. The oxfords will look great until the first water cannon cuts loose, but these boots were made for walking, not licking, and you will soon be doing plenty of walking. They'll keep your feet warm when you join the crowd of women marching at your daughter's campus.

Dress Shirt

Plain white is so 20th Century. Unoriginal, unimaginative, and impossible to hide tear gas residue and bloodstains. A cornflower blue shirt with a white contrast collar offers a complementary shade with our recommended navy and charcoal suits while also helping the discerning gentleman maintain an obvious profile to distract the riot police goose-stepping down the block. If a gentleman is to be kettled, he should be kettled with style.

Backpack

Along with austerity and trickle-down economics, the briefcase is another relic we recommend consigning to the dustbin of history. The discerning gentleman needs both hands free, and a sleek, portable backpack makes for a perfect commuter accessory that is suitable for the conference room, the concourse, and the Student Union.

Stock it with all the necessities. With extra face masks and a bottle of water, you're covered for everything from a train breakdown to an all-night daughter-hunt through a protest that's rapidly evolved into a riot. Don't forget to add a handful of high-powered laser pointers. They're ideal for conference room presentations or fouling the cameras on the paramilitary surveillance drone buzzing overhead.

Cell Phone

The latest iPhone is always in style, but a simple Android will work fine for recording the police behind their riot shields. Keep it in airplane mode except for brief calls to your daughter, oh god, where is she? Remember: do not unlock it for any uniformed personnel, no matter how much they threaten.

Umbrella

Perfect protection from snow, rain, and hails of teargas canisters, a sturdy umbrella is a symbol of style and sensibility that stands out among a forest of placards. When inverted, the carved walnut handle works as a makeshift golf club, well suited for smashing still-spewing chemical weapons away from a crowd of terrified civilians.

Bike Helmet

Safety is important, and head safety is paramount. From madmen in SUVs to flying gas grenades, a well fitted bicycle helmet will protect the discerning gentleman's most valuable asset. Brand and style are secondary to fit, but do take the safety helmet as an opportunity to accessorize and match one's face mask.

Bicycle optional. The students need it more.

Attitude

A gentleman's most important asset may be his wits, but his second most important asset is his attitude. Stand tall in front of the crowd. Be a target while the real victims flee the brutality marching toward you. If your suit doesn't protect you, your bike helmet will stop the first baton strike. Curl up around your phone and let your backpack take the worst of the beating. Your tie will make a perfect tourniquet for the inevitable bloodshed.

Maybe you don't find your daughter, but rest assured she'll find you when your live-streamed video starts trending. Your battered face may be in a police lineup come dawn, but you knew that when you joined the protest. Your body, your choice. It should have never come to this.

A Child that Wasn't Meant to Be?

P.B. Tacy

It's so hard to resist attribution
to a greater cause, when the pain
of loss can be so engulfing.
The months of eager waiting,
found all for naught; the plain
facts of medical explanation
present, but not enough; a life
awaited, that would never be.
Even the kindly doc had said it...
this embryo, that had simply quit
becoming a baby, so quietly,
without giving notice to my wife,
surely did so *at Divine Command!*

The loss of an awaited child defies
one's scientific trust in nature.
We grasp for answers, a feature
on which a heavy heart relies:
God's Wish is always there at hand.

Yes, God is ever busy with our lives
whenever procreation is involved.
What might seem *ours*, which all derives
from evolution, is instead resolved
as God's Turf, when sex might be involved.

That life's a dance above a deep abyss:
and living for a day should always be sufficient.
is clear; yet, at heart-crushing times like this,
mere resolve to accept may seem deficient —
and so we summon, in our frustration,
a Spectral Intruder from imagination.

Not Quite a Child Ballad
Traditional and Later Scenarios

E.A. Scarborough

I am a roving gambler, gambled all around
Whenever I meet with a deck of cards
I lay my money down,
Lay my money down, lay my money down

I had not been in Frisco many more weeks than
three.
I met up with a pretty little gal.
She fell in love with me.
Fell in love with me, fell in love with me.

She took me in her parlor, cooled me with her fan,
Whispered low in her mother's ear,
"I love this gambling man,
Love this gambling man, love this gambling man. "

Oh daughter, oh dear daughter, how can you treat
me so?
Leave your dear old mother
And with a gambler go,
With a gambler go, with a gambler go

My mother, oh, my mother, you cannot understand.
If you ever see me a coming back,
I'll be with a gambling man,
With a gambling man, with a gambling man

The Rest of the Story

He was a rovin' gambler,
A stranger to our town.
Turned out that his money
Wasn't all that he laid down.
All that he laid down.
It wasn't all that he laid down.

I brought him to my parlor and cooled him with
my fan
And whispered in my mama's ear how I loved that
gamblin' man
Loved that gamblin' man.
How I loved that gamblin' man!

Mama smiled like a crocodile and thumped me
with my fan.
There's not enough for you and me.
Much less that no-count man.
Much less that no-count man.
Much less that no-count man.

You ought to marry an engineer,
A man who works the rails.
A romance with a gamblin' man
Is surely bound to fail.
It's surely bound to fail.
It's surely bound to fail.

I would not marry a railroad man.
I'll tell you the reason why.
I never met a railroad man

Who wouldn't tell his wife a lie.
Tell his wife a lie,
Who wouldn't tell his wife a lie.

I said it was no contest to choose twixt him and
home.
So me and the charmin' gamblin' man
We set a course to roam.
We set a course to roam,
Set a course to roam.

A fine hotel in Abilene,
A mining camp saloon,
And then on up to Albeuerq.
Too broke to rent a room,
Too broke to rent a room,
Too broke to rent a room.

I told him I had good news,
That he might be a dad.
He dealt a hand of solitaire
And seemed to take it bad.
He seemed to take it bad.
Seemed to take it bad.

He left me there upon the road
That led to Santa Fe.
Then he headed down to Tucson town
Without me in his way.
Without me in his way.
Without me in his way.

How was I going to raise a child?
What would my mama say?
I never felt so all alone
Though in a family way.
Though in a family way.
I was in a family way.

I was stumbling, tripping through the town
While trying not to bawl
Till a Native woman traded me
A foul drink for my shawl.
She had a foul drink for my shawl.
A foul drink for my shawl.

I drank it, doubled over.
You should have heard me howl.
I bled and cramped, threw up my guts
And told the babe "not now."
I told the babe "not now."
I told the babe "not now."

I married me a brakeman.
You could say I changed my mind.
I don't know if he's lied to me,
But I know that he's been kind.
I do know he's been kind.
That man's been mighty kind.

We had no daughters, had no sons.
I thought I'd lost the right.
After five long years at last one came
In the middle of the night.
In the middle of the night.
In the middle of the night.

While Thomas boiled the water,
I searched for a name
The babe looked up and said to me, "Mama.
High, low, Jack and the game.
High, low, Jack and the game,
High, low, Jack and the game."

Choices Needed, Choices Made: or Why I Fight

L K. Hardie

I was 23 and had raccoon eyes, morning
queasiness
My boyfriend feared the worst
But I didn't worry
It was 1981 and I had Roe v Wade

I'm too busy, I said to my husband in 1993
Can you help me out?
Just wait till you have kids, he said darkly
Good thing I had Roe v Wade

Fibroids, ovarian cysts, dysmenorrhea
The pill, breast exams, pap smears
Planned Parenthood's sliding scale
Women's health care, thanks to Roe v Wade

I never actually had to use Roe
Ovarian cysts made me barren
I never had to make the choice myself
But Roe v Wade guaranteed that I *could*

POST ROE Alternatives

My friend Donna had three kids
Her body, her decision
After that, she tied her tubes
Her choice, thanks to Roe v Wade

Laura gave one up for adoption
Her mistake, her choice
She's always had regrets
But she doesn't lay blame, thanks to Roe v Wade

Mary Anne believes in personal responsibility
For everyone but herself
Her abortion was her choice
She really should thank Roe v Wade—but she
won't

Now I'm a crone, on the other side of the divide
With sagging breasts, dry uterus
Am I too old to care? Do I still need Roe v Wade?
Yes, because my 25-year-old niece does.

Misconceptions

L. Milton

Her breath was torn from her, coming in ragged little gasps. The commotion in her brain was wild and unruly; despite a supreme effort to focus, perceptions were splintered as if gazing through shattered glass. The entrance area where they had deposited her on a bench seemed massive, the vaulted ceiling impossibly high. A dappled light floated down from the sky-ceiling, dancing through a holo-projected leafy canopy. The blossom-scented air seemed weighted with a thick and heavy hush. To Eowyn, the holo production was astonishing, a conspicuous and costly splurge of data. *How was it paid for?*

"You are welcome here," said a woman with a kind and steady voice who had introduced herself as her guide, Ana. "I just need to go deal with these two," motioning to the officers that had managed to seize and deliver Eowyn to the All Souls Detention Center, charging her with several violations under the *Registry and Birth Act.*

Ana stepped back to the receiving station; Eowyn just closed her eyes and sent silent pleas of anguish to any of the universal divinities that might heed her call. *Al, where are you? Please be all right!*

"Watch out for this one," Eowyn heard one of the

officers announce with loud importance. "Gave us quite a chase. Don't know how she thought she'd get away. There's no place to run to anymore. You got an unlicensed bun in the oven and we're going to find you." Both officers erupted into ugly laughter. After that the voices dropped into indecipherable murmurs. Mercifully, they departed. Ana returned and sat down beside her.

"Those two were a bit much." She reached over with a gentle and practiced hand to touch the slight swelling of Eowyn's belly. The smoothness of her face creased in an expression of almost puzzlement.

"What is it?" Eowyn asked.

"I don't usually sense—" She broke off, shaking her head. "About twelve weeks or so I'm thinking," she said. Eowyn nodded. "Maybe she'll have your beautiful black curls?" Ana said this lightly, a goodwill offering.

Eowyn knew better though; she knew that the detention centers were capable of all manner of elaborate deception. "You don't have a biosensor. You can't tell the age or the gender," she said.

"I do know these things though," Ana replied. This was stated calmly, as fact, not with arrogance or conjecture. She continued, "We will take care of you Eowyn. You are safe here."

Eowyn did not believe her. She knew these words were lies.

~~~

Eowyn followed Ana down a series of hallways, holo-designed to appear as lush garden arbours dripping in lavender wisteria, to her assigned chamber. *Jeez, what was next? The church picnic?*

Ana stopped at a door, waved her arm across the

lock and stepped back as the door slid open. "Here's your room," she said brightly.

Eowyn glanced around. Plain and simple, the room contained a bed, a closet, a sink, and a desktop. Ana was speaking earnestly, a rehearsed script outlining the rules of her detention. Eowyn let Ana's words wash over her, paying only the scantest attention. There would be an obligatory schedule for the meals, exercise, medical appointments, and work assignments at the e-commerce warehouse. Assistance would be provided for the forthcoming criminal charges she would be facing. At last, Eowyn found herself alone. She sank to the floor, barely able to breathe under the weight of the suffocating torment. *Al, you were right. I never should have agreed to do this.* And underneath all her despair, throbbed a single question. *Are you all right, Al?*

~~~

The next day Eowyn, along with the other new detainees, reported to what was pretentiously referred to as the Grand Hall. Here the holo-décor had transformed the space into a medieval cathedral. Again, Eowyn marvelled at the extravagance. Had any of these people lived in the real world? In the world she and Al lived in?

Candlelight flickered in iron sconces lining the walls; deep shadows pooled in the corners. Luminous light streamed from the stained-glass windows that framed assorted depictions of sanguine mothers and their babes, pieced in translucent blue, rose, and gold. Anna led Eowyn to a high-backed dark wooden pew, gestured for her to sit, and then slid in beside her.

Eowyn peered through the gloom. Each of the pews was similarly occupied by captives like herself and their so-called guides. Just then a wave of alertness moved through the room like a tide, the guides synchronously shifting and stiffening, apparently the result of an imposing female figure arriving at the dais at the front of the room. Enveloped in a flowing gold and crimson garment, this woman moved smoothly to the pulpit, opening her arms and offering her palms.

"Welcome, welcome to you all," she began, a smile affixed to her wide face, swivelling her head from side to side, appraising the entirety of the room. "Let me introduce myself. I am the Director. I am responsible for All Souls Center. I make it a point to meet each new class of residents. My dear girls, I consider all of you as daughters. The daughters I was never blessed to have. Please know this. You are all safe. No matter where you have come from, no matter how troubled your lives, please know that All Souls is not an ordinary detention center. Here you will be treated with the greatest of love."

Repulsed, Eowyn shrank back into the bony hardness of the pew. "While you may not have chosen to find yourselves here," the Director continued, "I am here to tell you that although you may not think this today, your detention at All Souls Center is a blessing that will change your lives forever. We will teach you new ways. Ways that will guide you to truth that not only will transform your lives, but also the lives of the souls that you are carrying." She paused dramatically, letting the magnitude of her conviction expand before the assembly. "No matter the wrongdoing and transgressions, do not despair. No matter the depravity in your lives, do not despair. It is here that your wounds will be healed and in healing you will be able to step into the light and assume the responsibilities you all have as women to bear life."

Somewhere in Eowyn's mind, a voice was shrieking. "No matter how life has been conceived, no matter the circumstances, a child is a gift of life from our Creator. All souls are gifts of love from the Creator and are entitled to their lives." Despite gripping the edge of the pew tightly, Eowyn could not prevent the escape of a peculiar, strangled sound from her throat.

Ana calmly reached over and patted Eowyn's hand. "Really, Eowyn, you will learn to like it here," she whispered.

Eowyn cast a sidelong glance in her direction, struck by the incongruity of her softness and sincerity under these punitive circumstances.

The Director continued to speak, accompanied by the same grand and showy gestures. "My daughters," she finally concluded, "I will leave you now and let you commence your first lesson." She beckoned to a guide waiting backstage to come forward.

"Good morning daughters," the guide began. "I would like to invite you all to get comfortable in your seats, close your eyes, and take a few deep breaths." Eowyn heaved a sigh, closed her eyes, and followed the commands to breathe and visualize obediently. Gradually, she became aware that Ana's nearby and tranquil presence had gathered and grown into the space surrounding the two of them. She could sense the delicate fingers of warmth and ease touch the brittle edges of her hardness and then retreat. She peered discreetly at Ana, who seemed oblivious.

Eventually, they all were released and directed to exit the center aisle, in single file in an orderly fashion.

The reason for this instruction became apparent as they neared the entrance, where each detainee was required to wait their turn for a seat at one of the stations that had been set up to issue what they were told were identity and communication devices. Eowyn sat down and placed her right arm inside a black cylinder that automatically measured and clamped a wide metal band around her wrist. It wasn't painful, but the sudden constriction was alarming. Wide-eyed, she looked up at Ana, still at her side.

"Don't fear Eowyn," Ana reassured, tapping her shoulder lightly. "It's meant to keep you and your baby safe." Her manner conveyed an inexplicable comfort. This time Eowyn permitted a tiny fragment in the core of her guarded heart to open to receive a moment of reprieve from the relentlessness of the ever-present suffering.

~~~

Both lazy and rushing, the days that followed flowed, tumbling over stones like a stream. Endurance for Eowyn had meant barricading the waterfall of emotions that threatened survival; she navigated the currents numbly, doing her best to avoid the eddies that promised peril. Consuming the regular and appetizing nourishment provided produced a jumble of mixed feelings: relief at not having to experience hunger, guilt because she knew the names and faces of many who were starving. Times spent attending her health appointments were treasured pools of solace. Glimpses of the fetus, images of the intricate, delicate miracle growing inside, created a joy, pure and sweet that she stored away for savouring in secret moments. *Oh Al, if only you could see.*

Ana had asked if there was someone that she wished to notify about her detention, someone who might be allowed to visit. Eowyn just shook her head. Answers to those questions led to definite known hazards. Still, Ana persisted. After several repetitions of this conversation, Eowyn felt compelled to explain that her parents had died in the last war, that she had had a spouse by the name of Alex who had unaccountably disappeared. Which was, if not exactly the full truth, sufficiently credible to produce the desired result of putting an end to the inquiry on personal history.

Eowyn was punctual and cooperative with her drone operator duties at the warehouse and all the other activities and appointments blocked in her schedule, which apparently was somewhat unusual as Ana commended this warmly. It all fit with the plan to avoid endangerment. Participating silently in the uneasy fellowship of the Center's involuntary residents had been educational. Although she maintained an appearance of affability with her fellow detainees, she avoided any verbal exchange that risked verging into genuine disclosure. Besides having a front-row seat for the daily dramas of betrayed intimacies, whispered rumours about the Center's operations were revealing. Like the one that claimed the Center was profiting handsomely from the detainees' labor at the warehouse.

It became clear that Ana reserved her highest praise for personal development in meditation as Eowyn's performance in this area so exceeded that of the others it had drawn the curious attention of many of the other guides. Daily practice was expected morning and evening in their chambers and twice more at assigned times in the Great Hall, but Ana spent additional hours sitting in practice with her, exuding that same richness of presence that Eowyn had experienced in the hall. This unfathomable presence touched an ancient yearning Eowyn was unable to name.

It had become obvious that the function of the monitoring bands extended far beyond the initial explanation. Each band was equipped with a signal panel. A solid green light indicated correct management of emotions; a flashing yellow warned of the need for immediate corrective action. Beware the flashing red. With Ana's assistance and time, Eowyn had learned to decipher the signals and adjust her arousal state accordingly. Persuasion not to feign performance had been swift and compelling after the first excruciating experience of watching an emergency team respond, competently and efficiently bundling a sobbing woman away who apparently failed to comply with the minimum emotional status parameters.

One afternoon, Eowyn was surprised to find that she was invited to Ana's personal sitting room for tea. Ana poured a steaming spicy brew from an elegant ivory vessel with great ceremony and handed her a cup. "I don't think the other guides invite their assignments to tea," Eowyn said, leaning forward to accept the tea.

"I find you to be somewhat different from the others," Ana said. "Eowyn, you are doing exceptionally well here." The inflection in her voice signalled curiosity without judgment. Eowyn sipped from her cup, searching for a suitable reply, thinking she, too, found Ana to be different than the others.

"Ana, why do you work here?"

"I have a gift, I sense things. I thought I could help," she replied.

"And do you? Do you help women?" Eowyn squirmed as she heard the unintended pointedness of her tone. Ana was unconcerned though, continuing to exhibit her customary calmness. Eowyn watched her take time to collect her thoughts, compose a response.

"It is a good question," she finally said. "It's so much more complicated than I imagined. I had thought—" Ana stopped abruptly. "What's wrong, Eowyn?"

Eowyn looked up full of awe, both hands cradling her belly protectively. "I just felt...I think I just felt the baby."

Ana's face glowed. "How wonderful!" she exclaimed, then turned solemn. "Eowyn," she said in the voice of someone comprehending an enormous truth hiding in plain sight. "You want this baby." The silence stilled, waited while two women held their breath.

"Yes, I do." Eowyn's words were simple and small, but Ana reacted with urgent intensity.

"There's something extremely important you need to know," she said. "When a woman has an unregistered pregnancy there is an appeal process where a woman can apply for parental status to keep the baby. I don't know if anyone at the Center has ever tried, but I might have some influence. If you wanted to, I could help you apply?"

"Ana, I do want this baby. But you can't help me. No one can."

"What do you mean?"

Eowyn's heart hammered fiercely. Her monitoring band chirped, and they both looked down, noting the flashing yellow.

Ana's response was swift; she seized Eowyn's arm and pressed a code into the panel which returned the light to its former non-alert status. "Don't worry," Ana said. "They won't know. Now tell me."

Eowyn covered her face with her hands, wavered between agonizing fear and irrational hope. She took the leap. "I'll tell you the truth Ana. But there's nothing you can do." She willed herself to breathe and summon courage. "I was living in the Diss-zone with my wife Alex."

And then she waited, waited for the shock to dissipate, prepared herself for the inevitable condemnation.

"The Diss-zone? My dear girl! How did you manage?"

"Barely. We scraped by finding bits of work here and there. Scrounged for food. Did our best to avoid the gangs. But it's the only place where they don't ask questions about who you are, who you live with."

"What happened to Alex?"

"We wanted a better life. We dreamed of having our own apartment. Our own family. In a safe place." Ana made vague but sympathetic noises. "It's why I did it. It's why when the brokers offered me a contract, I agreed."

Ana's eyes went wide with shock. "That's how you conceived! You agreed to be a surrogate! For the black market?!"

"It was our only way out. We could make enough money to start over, build a life somewhere. Somewhere we could have our own baby. Alex told me I was out of my mind. Told me it was too dangerous."

"I can see that it was a hard life and a hard choice. What happened?" Ana said with utmost gentleness.

"We argued. But I went ahead and did it anyway." Eowyn swallowed. "You remember when those Diss-zone riots happened?"

"Yes," Ana said in a low voice.

"That day the riots started we were fighting all day. She was so angry. She went out and she never came back." Eowyn began to weep uncontrollably. "I looked for her for days. That's what I was doing when the guards picked me up. I don't even know if she is alive or dead," she finished with a protracted sob.

Ana looked stricken. "I am so sorry, Eowyn."

"I would keep this baby if I could! But it's impossible. There isn't anything you can do. How could I even get away from the brokers?" She paused. "Are you going to report me?"

Ana crossed the space to sit down and put an arm around her. "Give me some time," she said. "I need to think."

~~~

Faraway sirens were clamouring in the blackness of the night. Eowyn awoke in hazy confusion. Remembering the site orientation, she realized that this was an emergency drill. She scrambled to her feet and pulled on day clothes. The halls became quickly crowded with similarly befuddled detainees, some wailing and others cursing. She slipped into a spot in the lethargic line of moving women and followed the pack. At some point in this sluggish parade though, a door passage malfunctioned and refused to open, resulting in a pile-up that only served to intensify the upheaval and animosity. Guides mysteriously appeared from elsewhere, issuing contradictory directions. Focused on self-preservation, Eowyn wandered in the opposite direction of the throng.

"Just where do you think you're going. Come with

me!" someone demanded. From behind, a guide grabbed her by the elbow and steered her towards an evacuated lounge off the rear of the hallway.

"What's going on?" Eowyn said, struggling to turn around.

"Shush," the guide hissed, shoving her towards a hidden corner where she transformed and unlocked a concealed door. "Follow me," she said, "I'm taking you to Ana."

Eowyn hurried to keep pace through a series of intersecting deserted passageways that descended lower and lower, an area in the center compound off-limits to the detainees. The passage ended, opening into a grey stone cavern that housed a transport silo at its center. Ana was waiting.

"We have to hurry," she said, after a quick, tender embrace. "This transport will take you to a safe house." She handed Eowyn a sack and strapped it around her. "I've deactivated your band in the system which will buy you some time. There's a pass card with some credits in the sack. Give that to the receiver that meets you. Not sure about the conditions you're going to find so I threw in some meal bars and water bottles." Eowyn fought to bring her wild swirling thoughts into focus.

"Ana, what's happening?"

"You needed help and for this sort of thing, there are many friends. This one was a bit of a gamble. But isn't that life? Oh, and I told your receivers about Alex."

"But why? The other women...why are you helping me?" Eowyn cried. "Won't you be in trouble?"

Ana grasped Eowyn's shoulders, sent a full-force gaze deep into her eyes that Eowyn felt all the way to her fingers and toes. "Eowyn, you won't understand.

You were sent to me. You gave me the push I needed to figure out some things. And I'm going to figure out how to do things differently. Now you need to get going," she said in a rush. "I hope they find Alex. And take care of that daughter of yours."

~~~

Ana and the Director faced each other across a desk, the case file notes projected between them.

"We *will* find her," the Director stated emphatically, "so this atrocious, illicit plot you have conspired to commit will be utterly wasted! You are facing numerous criminal charges for which there will be no leniency. Most of all though, what I will never understand is how you, a guide, would endanger the life of an unborn child. An innocent soul trying to make their way to a life. It is the antithesis of our mission!"

"Eowyn wants that child. That baby is not in danger. We don't need to be in control."

"That's heresy! Clear evidence of criminal acts. Homosexuality. And a criminal transaction."

Ana cleared her throat, knowing that this would be her only moment to express a shining, pealing truth. A heart-truth, once inchoate and embryonic, now an emerging tendril, calling for love to nurture life. "Those were acts of survival in a brutal, unjust world," she said. "We cherish the souls of the precious unborn children. Why do we never think about the mothers?"

My Name is Jane

Jane

My middle name is Jane but I haven't used it in years. I use my maiden name as my legal middle name.

I had forgotten, until Roe was overturned, that Jane was also our code name when we were helping women get to safe health care 50 years ago. We provided pregnancy tests, education, counseling, money, transportation, support, and hugs.

I was naive and privileged when I first became aware of the abortion issue. One night in my college dorm, a young woman down the hall was rushed to the hospital with sepsis after an illegal abortion; she had a hysterectomy to save her life. That event sparked my interest in women's health and I ended up working 45 years in women's health care taking care of women.

In California, I worked as an office manager in a Planned Parenthood clinic. One day, working the front desk, a woman came to the window, sweating and anxious. The only thing she said, was "I need help." Then she sank to the floor out of sight from the desk. Unfortunately, her body was blocking the door from the office to the waiting room. Back then, there was no monitor or keyboard in the way. I swept the Rolodex and huge phone to the side and squeezed through the sliding glass window while yelling for the nurse to call the hospital next door.

The woman had an ectopic pregnancy which had ruptured. Only because she was so close to the hospital, did she survive.

My experience at that clinic motivated me to go into health care. I wound up getting three more degrees, numerous licenses, and certifications.

In Tennessee, while in school, I had clinical training at a very rural clinic in the mountains. I remember a woman whom the physician overseeing me was worried about. It was her third pregnancy, this time NOT by her father, and the physician was concerned about her safety. I've taken care of thousands of women and educated/trained hundreds of health care providers. I have learned that there is nothing simple or easy or safe about pregnancy. Pregnant women have miscarriages. Fetuses die or have severe genetic or congenital issues. Women have to deal with cancer, substance abuse, rape, incest, and domestic violence. Anything can and does happen to these women.

One in four women have an abortion in their lifetime. I have had two family members who have had abortions, twice. The first had an early procedure (5-6 weeks, then called a menstrual extraction) that missed the tiny embryo and she had to have another procedure at 13-14 weeks (think about those 6 weeks abortion laws). The second got pregnant on the pill and again with an IUD. Contraception is not easy; nor is it simple nor is it perfect.

I've worked with Planned Parenthood for 50 years in 4 states so I'm familiar with the anti-abortion crowd. I've gotten a bomb threat in the middle of a busy clinic. I've worked in a clinic after it was firebombed where the surviving charts had scorch marks around the edges.

I've called all over Los Angeles trying to find a pro-life outfit that would provide shelter, food, and health care to a 13-year-old who wanted to keep her baby, without success. I've worked at a maternity center staffed by awesome midwives and done home visits on new mothers without running water. Try hauling gallon jugs of water from the creek on the first day postpartum.

Some of our Supreme Court justices do not have a clue what a pregnant woman has to handle. How could they? Old angry white men, weepy frat boys, and evangelical Godbotherers don't even recognize that women have rights much less understand her situation.

So, what's the alternative to Roe? There isn't any viable alternative to women being able to choose whether to have a baby or not.

The only response is to do what we did 50 years ago:

Vote.

Volunteer.

Donate.

And for me? My name is Jane, again.

Unwanted

K. Herrmann

July 1973
Protestors decry Roe v Wade on TV
I watch on vintage green couch next to Nana
I relish this time this place
Lady slippers in the woods, cardinals at the feeder,
unpinning wilted wash in a sudden shower, crunchy
creamy bites of grilled cheese, even kneeling at Sunday
Mass
But abortion rights--how could she understand?
I am certain I can read her mind

I lay the silver, baked beans simmer
I think it's a good law she says
Our eyes meet
There's nothing worse than an unwanted child
One word fills her tiny kitchen

Unwanted
No family, no home, no resources, no education, no acceptance, no opportunity
No care, no tomorrow, no heart(beat)
There's nothing worse
I know how she knows
Baked bean pool blurs on my plate

June 2022
Protestors decry Roe v Wade, others fight to save it too late
Choice denied to low-income families, single mothers, teens with consent
10-year-old rape victim

Y'all wanna see the new Elvis movie?
Grandgirl asks between bites of buttermilk pancakes
For sure
We relish this time this place
I wrap cool fingers around warm mug
Our eyes meet
I have something important to tell you
I think it was a good law...

Santa Maria

A.J. Lucas

Maria struggled out from behind the dumpster, hoping the coast was clear. She'd been on the run for so long that she knew when there was somebody nearby. When they might be watching. She pulled her oversized jacket, looted from a Goodwill drop off box in Los Angeles tight about her body. This close to the border where the weather demanded proper clothing and she was happy to have it, both for the warmth and for the way it hid her belly. She was used to warm weather, after weeks of dodging bounty hunters, but the chill in the air this far north had taken her by surprise.

Beneath the padded layers of reclaimed clothing her stomach rumbled. Stamping her feet to warm them, she yearned for a decent breakfast.

It was still early and the smell of fresh baked bread, mixed with cigarette smoke, was down the alley. The baker had chased her off last night and she was hesitant to risk encountering him again, but the smell of the bread was making her stomach growl. Last night she had made do with the remains of a discarded burger and a couple of fries. It wasn't enough to keep her strength up, and she needed her strength.

"Come out."

She turned to run, spooked by the baker's deep

voice. Then she turned back. She had nowhere to go, and the baker wouldn't chase her. Probably wouldn't even leave the back stoop. Maria picked up the battered canvas bag that held her possessions and stepped out from behind the dumpster.

"You're still here, I see."

"Got nowhere to go."

The baker looked Maria up and down slowly, taking in the holed knitted cap, the battered knapsack, and the torn jeans tucked into one-size-too-large boots. Maria has seen this look before, the dismissal and judgment in the man's eyes, the slight curl of disdain on what portion of his upper lip escaped his moustache.

"Well, you can't stay here. Go on. Git."

The man took a step forward but Maria stood her ground. She'd stood up to rougher men than this rotund baker. That didn't mean he couldn't overpower her and, in her condition, she had to be careful. Maria retreated a step as the man advanced.

She could run if she had to, but the smell of baking bread called to her.

"I'm not hurting anyone. I'm just hungry."

"We're all hungry, girlie."

"YOU don't look hungry."

The man stopped short, appalled at the comment. To be called out on his weight by this immigrant trash was too much. He bellowed in rage and lunged at her.

Maria sidestepped the clumsy rush and sprinted for the open door of the bakery. She slammed it shut behind her and locked it. Adrenaline rushed through her veins, making her light-headed. She hadn't expected the man to rush her, but she knew to take advantage of the situation.

A loaf of bread went into her jacket, and she filled her knapsack with donuts and a plastic wrapped strudel from the glass display case. Then she was out the front door running along the empty main street.

A few minutes later a patrol vehicle prowled the street, halogen floodlights probing the dark crannies of each alley, but she was long gone.

~~~

The border was in sight, but the whine of a hovering surveillance drone told Maria it wasn't safe to move. She hunkered down in the culvert hoping the thick concrete would hide her from the probing heat sensors of the border patrol. There wasn't much she could do at the moment, at least until the patrol moved on and she was able to poke her head up to get the lay of the land. Getting across the border was the easy part. Not being dragged back by Homeland Security, the local sheriff, or bounty hunters, would be the hard part.

The Canadian border was rigorously unfortified, unlike the boundary between New Mexico and California she had forced her way across only a few weeks ago. It was a grueling, hazardous journey, during the height of summer. Moving through rural towns, avoiding the eyes and questions of locals, informal residential patrols, and ICE sweeps. Thank God her father had taught her how to survive in the bush with few resources. Of course, that had been in the relatively safe, groomed parks of New Mexico, where resources, be it a Park Ranger or a Denny's were always close at hand. Trekking a few hundred miles alone, with only a backpack of trail rations and a bedroll was a completely different matter. She'd lost even those supplies trusting the wrong hostel outside of Phoenix.

Since then, Maria had made do raiding donation boxes, restaurant garbage bins, and the occasional grab and run at a service station. She'd been lucky enough to find refuge on a north-bound train, transporting cheaply made Toyotas. That had taken her as far as Los Angeles. Another two weeks of panhandling on the streets of south LA bought her a Greyhound ticket.

She'd read on a Discord channel that California had a statewide statute barring any Immigration agent from boarding public transport while on duty. There hadn't been any uniformed agents on the bus, but she'd noticed a middle-aged couple striking up conversations with her fellow passengers—only the Latino ones. Maria had pretended not to understand the couple's questions, and they had moved on. Perhaps they were only being friendly, but Maria wasn't taking any chances. She knew what waited for her in the camps; they'd never believe she was legal.

Now she was almost there, a few hundred meters and she would be in Canada, where she could finally stop worrying. The risks were great, but she was almost there. She just had to be patient and wait for her moment.

She retrieved her stolen baked goods from her pack. The strudel label declared it to be something called bumbleberry, overly sweet for her taste but just the thing to settle the pangs of her hunger. Half of it was gone before she realized it. She licked the purple jam from her fingers and set the remainder aside for later.

Outside, the drone activity had moved on. Maria could no longer hear the incessant whine of their propellers. She hoped that meant they were too far away to detect her.

The border wasn't that far. Safety was just within sight. A short sprint and she'd be across. She ran with strudel-born energy, lifting her legs high to clear the clumped scrub brush. There was no way to tell just where the border was, so she was not about to stop before she reached whatever Canadian town was closest.

Then the sirens started.

Over her shoulder Maria saw the strobing red and blue lights of a vehicle. She couldn't tell if it was police or border patrol, but it was behind her and the border was in front, so she kept running for all she was worth, putting all her energy into the sprint.

It wasn't enough.

The jeep vaulted a small hill and spun in a dusty arc in front of her, cutting her off from the border. She tried to dodge around it, but she wasn't agile enough. The hood of the car clipped her thigh, spinning her around, dumping her into the dirt. Excruciating pain lanced through her leg. She tried to get up, but the limb buckled beneath her weight. She moaned and tried once again with no luck.

"Well look at this."

The drawling voice came from a thick bodied man levering his way out of the jeep. In spite of the pain in her leg, Maria tried to get up once again, failed and settled for a crawling scramble away from the man.

A second man extracted himself from the jeep, younger but no smaller than the first. Maria saw that both carried intricate looking rifles and some sort of badge pinned to their flannel shirts. The older man's was battered and slightly askew.

"Well pa, you hit her good. She's not going to be

running anytime soon."

Maria was putting distance between herself and the slowly advancing men, but it wouldn't be enough not if she couldn't run. Not that she could outrun a bullet.

"She looks young. Where you from sweetheart? Venezuela? Columbia?"

The older man pointed at her with his rifle.

"Oh no, look at that belly. She's preggers. Another one of them damned baby-killers."

He fished a cellphone out of his shirt and tapped the screen a few times.

"Yeah. It's Bradford. I got one."

Maria couldn't hear the response, but a moment later the older man gestured at her with the rifle.

"He wants to see her."

The younger man sprinted forward and roughly pulled her to her feet. He was stronger, stronger than her and almost twice her size. The older man, Bradford, held his phone out to her face briefly. Then continued his conversation.

"Yeah. Yeah. I understand."

The odd word filtered through the other end of the cell words like, database, internment, patrol. Not enough to understand the entire conversation, but enough to get the gist of it. She'd soon be in an internment camp, headed for deportation if she was lucky. She knew what happened in those camps, how girls like her, girls in her condition were treated. She struggled with all her might, as if her life, their lives depended upon it – but the younger man was too big, too strong. She could barely budge him.

"What's this then?'

The man pushed her roughly to the ground,

scrambling to raise his rifle. Maria scrambled away from him as he brought it to bear on the two people standing a few meters away.

"You hold it right there."

The pair raised their hands but didn't stop walking forward. Maria could see they wore some sort of uniform. They both had large blocky pistols holstered high on their hips, like police or soldiers. Neither reached for their weapons and neither looked deterred by the assault weapons pointed at their faces.

"I think you will find that this woman is well and truly across the border and into the Dominion of Canada."

The older man took a step forward almost pressing the barrel of his rifle in the newcomer's face. Maria could see now that the pair were a man and woman, each with a crimson maple leaf embossed on their shoulders, but no other markings. The woman moved toward her, kneeling as the younger American retreated.

"Are you okay?"

She placed a hand on Maria's damaged leg. Maria winced in pain. but nodded assent. This close she could see the woman wore the thin white collar of the clergy, in stark contrast to the thick ballistic vest that framed it.

The older American, Bradford, waved his rifle aggressively but the Canadians were undeterred. He pulled his cellphone out again and pushed it out at arm's length towards the man, using the barrel of the rifle to support it. Then he aimed it at the woman beside Maria. The man fished out a tattered sheet of paper from the breast pocket of his jacket and held it out to the newcomer. Maria could see an image of herself partially obscured by the shield and eagle of Homeland Security along with a smaller text framing a dollar figure. She had no idea if that was a large amount, a good price for her and her child. But if she could, she would pay it tenfold just to get away from these men.

"She's ours. Rightful bounty on a baby-killer."

"She's crossed over to Canada."

The man looked over his shoulder not taking his eyes off the two Americans.

"Are you wanting to claim asylum, my dear?"

Maria nodded vigorously.

"Now wait a minute."

"I need to hear it. You need to say the words."

Maria swallowed, trying to lubricate her dry throat.

"I want... I claim asylum."

The woman patted her shoulder.

"Again, with your full name please."

"I, Maria Suarez, request and claim asylum."

The Canadian shrugged his shoulders.

"That's it then. I believe our business is done. Sally, if you could help Ms. Suarez to our car, please."

The woman helped Maria to her feet, but before they could make their way to the Canadian's waiting car, the young American placed himself in their way.

"Now just stop a minute. Washington has an extradition treaty covering all illegals fond within 10 miles of the border. Either side. And this girly is by God illegal."

The older man joined the younger and side by side it was obvious they were related.

"That's right. The Border cops is gonna be here in a few minutes and we are all going to be here when they arrive."

The woman supporting Maria looked the older man dead in the eye. Maria could feel a hard jostling at her hip as the woman shifted, prodding her with the holstered pistol. A second later she felt the flickering tickle of the woman's fingers as they sought the grip of the weapon.

"Extradition treaty. You mean to send this woman to one of your camps. The same camps that will take away her body autonomy. Take away her future family."

The man had the decency to look embarrassed, but his weapon never wavered.

"That's not for me to say. If she wanted to stay safe, she shoulda kept her legs together. She ain't welcome and her children ain't welcome."

The woman, Sally, gritted her teeth in response, her fingers tightening into hard bands of iron against Maria's hip. Her partner watched closely, ready to back her next move, no matter what came.

"You are right. The treaty extends across the border. And it was a foolish compromise by a weak administration to appease a bully. But you are correct. It is the law."

The man smiled and reached for Maria.

Sally pivoted slightly placing Maria just out of his reach.

"But it doesn't extend to married couples, does it?"

The man frowned, deep creases carving their way through his forehead. He frowned a lot, Maria guessed.

"Miss. She's alone. I don't see no ring, no husband. She's for the camps."

Maria knew she couldn't run, but she also didn't want these two Canadians endangered. She pushed

185

herself away from Sally. She stood alone, defiant, if a little unsteady.

"I'm not married. I'll go with them."

Sally smiled warmly, and Maria saw her hand was firmly on the grip of her pistol. It shifted slightly loosening the weapon in its holster. What was Sally going to do? Was her flight to the border going to end in bloodshed? She only wanted a better life for her child, and now she might lose it all. She knew the trip was a risk, but for it to end so close to freedom…

Still, she had a choice, even now. She shuffled forward, until Sally put a firm but gentle hand on her shoulder.

"Maria Suarez. Would you marry if you could?"

It was a strange question that took her off guard, so she answered honestly.

"Yes."

Sally looked deep into Maria's eyes, and smiled warmly, then winked.

"Then marry me."

Maria was confused. Why would this woman ask this? What was the point? But the woman had placed herself between the American weapons and she trusted her. She didn't know why but she did, and really did she have much choice. No choice at all.

"Will you marry me, Maria?"

"Yes."

There was no hesitation, there was no point in hesitating.

Sally winked and turned to the confused Americans smiling. Her partner stepped forward clapping his hands as if he had just toasted the bride.

"Well, that's it then. I pronounce us wife and wife."

The Americans looked at him then back at Sally and Maria. Their rifles drifted off target as they struggled to catch up to events.

"What?"

"Sally here is a lay preacher."

"So?"

Sally smiled.

"Ordained to conduct any presbyterian ceremony. Including marriage."

The American stared, slack-jawed, realization dawning. But Bradford wasn't done. "No. No! I won't have it. She's my bounty. She comes with us."

Sally slipped her pistol from her holster and slowly raised it to eye level. Her partner raised his own pistol, both aiming directly at Bradford's left eye. The man started to sweat, realizing his own weapon was off target.

"Federal statute doesn't recognize same sex marriage."

"I guess she's lucky we're in Canada then."

Dear Baby

M. Shepherd

I want to tell you this story so you know how much I love you. People will tell you otherwise, they will shout from the streets that I wanted you dead.

It's true you were never meant to come into this world, but that is a reflection on me, and not you. I know you will do great things in life. Do not throw it away because of the rumors others spread.

This story is mine, but it is also yours. It starts with me, in a bar with floors so sticky my new high heels don't squeak when I walk across it. Or maybe it starts earlier, when I was too young to wear heels, coming out of a Payless with a new pair of sparkly flats packed snug in their yellow box. That night was my first formal middle-school dance, and I wanted to make an entrance. There was a man outside on the sidewalk, talking to his friend. I lingered behind my mother, wondering if I dared to peek into the box one more time before we got home, when I heard the man call out to me: "Hey cutie!" He followed that up with some other things, I think, but honestly as time has gone on they have blurred into the dozens of remarks men have made in my direction.

"Hey!" they say, "Where you goin' looking so good? Hey sexy, hey baby, hey hey hey! Smile for me, why aren't you smiling? You're so beautiful, hot, smoking, come for a kiss, don't look at me like that, look at her ass, look at those tits..."

That day, I bowed my head down and rushed up behind my mother like a little lost duckling. Once we got home I asked why she didn't say anything to that man, calling after her eleven-year-old daughter with such confidence, she took my hands in hers and told me, "It's just the way it is, baby. Might as well get used to it." Then she sighed and warmed me up a cup of milk with a tablespoon of honey, and we spent the night quietly together, not speaking at all.

The first time I went to prom it was my junior year of high school. I'll get back to what happened in the bar, don't worry, but in order for you to understand, *really* understand why I made the choice I did; I think you should hear this part too. By that time most of the girls in my class had labels: *slut, psycho, crazy, poor, quiet, weird, funny, pick-me, prude.* Sometimes we'd use them in jest, as if to show off how familiar we were now with these words, reclaiming them from the boys that had given them to us. But they never felt right, and slowly they would drop from our vocabulary like the stones they were, only to be picked up again in a fight, only when you lost the words to tell them how horrible they were and wanted a shortcut to an insult.

I was called *teacher's pet,* but only to my back. They called me that because I wasn't interested in the boys in my class. By then I was already disenchanted with their rough attitudes, the animalistic way they pursued girls. There were a few I found attractive, but I had noticed I had these emotions about some of my female classmates too, so I pushed the confusion of hormones down into my stomach and threw myself into schoolwork.

That was, until Michael asked me to the dance. He was a senior, pretty quiet, and we studied together in the library sometimes. When he asked there was resignation in his voice, and thinking back on it now he had probably already faced rejection from the girl he liked. I was an obviously single choice. I agreed because from what I knew about him he was nice and a little too serious like myself. I wore a pair of silver heels and a blue dress with little cap sleeves, and he got me a white corsage. The dance wasn't magical, Michael and I had fun but there was no spark. It was all set to be a great but ultimately unmemorable experience until I had to use the bathroom, during one of those awkward slow songs neither one of us really wanted to dance to. I heard crying from the stall next to me. After I washed up, I considered leaving the crier to their privacy but decided I should at least check on them first. When she came out, I saw it was one of my friends, blotting her mascara-streaked face with toilet paper when she opened the stall door. Her hairdo was half undone, and the strap of her satin dress was torn. When I asked what was wrong all she would tell me is that she just wanted to leave.

I found Michael against the gym wall talking to some of his friends. "Hey," I said, tentatively. They all stopped talking to listen. "My friend is feeling sick, I was wondering if we could drive her home?"

"Uhmm..."

His friends laughed and punched his arm. "C'mon, man, stay with us! She's not our problem."

Michael looked embarrassed as he pulled me aside.

191

"I thought we could go somewhere after, and you know... my friend is having a party, it could be fun."

I suddenly felt a hard ball of anger in my stomach. "Could you take us home first?"

Michael looked over at his friends who were not being subtle with their eavesdropping. "Oh please, don't be a prude!" One of them shouted. My cheeks warmed at the accusation. They all laughed again.

"Likc... you want mc to just drop you off? At homc?"

"Could you?" I was almost pleading now, and I hated it.

He sighed. "Can you ask someone else? That's really out of the way for the party..."

"But... you're the one that took me here! As my date!"

"Yeah," he said, "And I thought that we... I thought that you would be more... fun." He shrugged almost apologetically before turning back to his friends.

I looked around the gym for my own friends but didn't see anyone I recognized in the crowd. The room was dark, broken up by flashes of light from the cheap disco ball overhead. I wished I'd never agreed to go. I marched back to the bathroom and left with my friend, making sure to pick the ripped bits of single ply off her cheeks. I called my dad from the parking lot, and we huddled together against the chill of the spring night air until he came to get us. He was upset, but pleased by how responsible I was for not going to a party.

We dropped my friend off at her house. Later she would thank me, and tell me why she was crying. Her date also thought she'd be more fun, but didn't let her leave until he'd had the fun he wanted.

Our sex education in high school never covered the

concept of consent, nor did it teach us about any other type of birth control besides abstinence. Most of my friends had kids, were married, or both by the time we entered college. The ones that did start college rarely finished. I was lucky. By prioritizing books over a social life I had spared myself the fate of premature motherhood, and had gotten into a good college. I majored in Accounting. I dated a few men, and a few women, too. Sometimes I slept with them, always with a condom, always with birth control, always with a plan. A few of them pressured me, men more often than women, and some of the encounters I had I regretted. But even though birth control was hard to come by and not covered by insurance, I was happy to pay $40 a month to always make sure I was protected. Maybe I was still too young, too busy, too driven, still confused about who I wanted to be with—but I never could quite picture myself having kids. I would think back to the men outside the Payless, the way my mother held my hands so tight, and I would shudder at the thought.

In my senior year of college I got a job at a bland accounting firm with beige cubicles and a microwave permanently stuck at 50-percent power. It was a good job to get off the bat though, and I was quietly happy with myself when I punched in every day. Less enjoyable was Joe in the cubicle next to mine, always peeking over the divider and commenting on my clutter, my schedule, anything that came to mind. He would go to any work event I went to and follow me around the room like a lost puppy. It was bearable, the way catcalling was bearable, the price of relative attractiveness. If I ever complained about him my concerns were dismissed; his infatuation was "cute" or "harmless." As the office newbie I was worried about stirring up the waters so I simply nodded my head and remained passive.

It was Joe who was at the bar with me, the one with the sticky floor. Many of our co-workers were with us, commiserating about the workday over cheap Happy Hour drinks. It was their presence that made me feel safe enough to get a drink, wear those new heels that would squeak every once in a while, to slip my hair up into a ponytail. Everyone was drunk, after all. Because everyone was drunk, nobody noticed as I slipped off to the bathroom to freshen up—except Joe.

There is something so dangerous about letting things be. Remember that—please. I don't ask for much. You'll meet him someday, I can't stop it from happening, so I need you to know that you shouldn't let things be.

Joe followed me to the bathroom, came up behind me, and sniffed my hair. I told him to fuck off and leave the woman's room but he didn't listen. His breath smelled like the cheap light beer he was drinking, and his hands were cold and clammy when they touched my waist. I tried to fight him off when he pressed my face against the scratched red wall of the stall, tried to turn around, but by that time he had my ponytail in his fist and my face was pressed against the stall with such force my teeth hurt.

I remembered hearing about a meditation technique a long time ago. I can't remember where I heard it, exactly, or why. The scenario goes like this: you count down with your breathing, from 10 to 1. While you count, you picture going down a flight of stairs. That was the easy part, the rhythm of my body going down, down, down. Step two: you see a door. Everybody's door looks different. When I tried picturing mine at home, I struggled to visualize it. I couldn't decide on what I wanted it to look like, and that defeats the purpose of the meditation. In the bathroom I didn't have time to linger at this door to my subconscious, flesh out the details and wonder what such choices said about me, or if they should be choices at all, if I was supposed to find them there, already formed. All I wanted was an escape. So I pushed past the door, hoping for something deeper, even if it was dark, a place for my mind to go besides the shaking of the walls of the bathroom stall and the tight pinch of my hair at my temples. But when I opened my door, I saw my friend from Prom, sitting in the bathroom stall, little pieces of tissue stuck to her face, marking where her tears had been.

I had no proof about Joe, so nobody believed me. It was my word against his until three months later when the test came back positive. Still, nobody believed me. They told me I could get proof once I gave birth—a paternity test that would force child support and visitation. But I wasn't ready for this, wasn't ready for such a serious commitment so soon after starting my adult life. I had three weeks until I graduated with my degree, three years until my next guaranteed promotion. But it didn't matter. The law had been upheld by the Supreme Court. My body was no longer my own—it already belonged to you. We were tied together by Joe, a quiet monster, still in the cubicle next to mine, turning in spreadsheets at the same dependable rate he always did. I couldn't bear the thought of him finding out. I couldn't bear the thought of him meeting you.

It was hard to trust anyone with this, but I needed

help. I couldn't search for a doctor on my computer because it would be flagged, my search history condemning both me and anyone whose name I would find on it. Nobody operated above ground anymore, not for this. My situation, and my need to remove you from it, put everyone around us at risk. My work friends had already dismissed my concerns about Joe before; my college friends were focused on finals. I didn't know who to call.

The face of my high school friend with her torn prom dress kept running through my mind. After exhausting all other options, I got her new number off Facebook from another high school friend that I still talked to. I called her.

No, I can't tell you her name, she's still free— plausible deniability about her involvement. She tried to help, though. We came so close. But a suspicious neighbor saw me getting out of an Uber in the motel parking lot and called the police. They told me at the trial that it wasn't the neighbor, but God himself who intervened to save your life. Me, however, I must be an agent of the Devil to want you out of my belly. Yes, that's right, I'm the evil one. That's why, if the test matches you, and it will, after you're born, you'll go to Joe. Mothers can't raise children in prison. You won't grow up knowing what life is like locked away, pacing a room hardly longer than you are laying down, talking to people who exist solely in your head now, and might only exist there for the rest of your life. It's a small comfort.

You won't be condemned with me. They assured me of that.

Once you're born you'll be taken away, which is why

I'm telling you all this now. I heard that you can hear me, inside there. I know you're still too small to understand this, I don't know if you even have a brain yet—but maybe if I tell this story enough times, you'll have your suspicions about Joe.

Maybe one day you'll find me. If you leave your mind open to why I tried to do what they accuse me of. I want you to know I can feel you in there. I can feel your little hands and feet kicking and I love you more than I ever imagined I could. I just hope you can hear this, and don't come out a girl, baby. Just don't be born a girl.

.

Nothing is Promised

J. Thompson

Nothing is promised, whisper old women.
I know you're frightened by the growing dark;
those things which have been may yet be again.

It hurts to feel less than a citizen
in a land where freedom's more than a spark.
Nothing is promised, whisper old women.

It seemed impossible just last year, and then
partisans of the past glibly remark:
those things which have been may yet be again

Progress erased by injustice's pen,
bullies determined to make their mark.
Nothing is promised, whisper old women.

We should have listened closer to them when
cynical realists made their grim remark:
those things which have been may yet be again

Those threatening words have become an amen.
Justice has ebbed, but we see the floodmark!
Nothing is promised, whisper old women
Those things which have been may yet be again

POST ROE Alternatives

The Value of Human Life

M. Candelaria

The only furniture in counseling room 3552-B was a metal table with two hard chairs, one on either side of it. On one of the chairs sat a woman. She was young, painfully thin, and frightened. The other contained a man. He was perhaps a decade older, powerfully built, and angry.

"Please," the woman said. "I need help. This is killing me."

"You should have thought of that before you spread your legs," the man said unsympathetically.

"He said," she whispered, perhaps hoping the man would not hear, perhaps hoping he would. "He said it couldn't happen. Not if we were both virgins."

The man rolled his eyes. "And you believed him?"

"I... don't know," the woman said, her eyes downcast, focusing on the table. "I thought—"

"Yes, yes, you 'thought'," the man snapped. "Of course you did. You thought you'd have your fun and not have to face any consequences. You thought wrong. You will see this through to the end. You will not be allowed to abort the children."

"Children?" the woman said, looking up for the first time. "Children?"

The man reached across the table and slapped her.

"Don't you dare say that they are not children!" he screamed.

"It—"

"They!" the man interrupted, his voice echoing in the small room.

"They will kill me," the woman finished.

The man just shrugged. "You're one person. You are carrying more than one child. What is one life when so many are at stake?"

"They're just clusters of cells," the woman said. "Just clusters of cells growing on my cervix. No minds, no thoughts, no individuality. How can they be children?"

The man seemed about to slap her again, but stopped and sighed instead. "I see I have to explain this yet again to another woman ignorant of basic biology."

The woman flinched, but said nothing.

"The Supreme Court decision is very, very clear," the man continued. "Cells residing in the uterus with distinct DNA from the mother are babies and must be protected to the full extent of the law."

"The 'father' was a virus," the woman protested. "The 'children' are cancers."

"A human papilloma virus," the man countered, leaning over the table. His face was so close the woman could smell his breath: expensive food, alcohol, and malice. "*Human* papilloma virus," he emphasized. "Which you received through sexual intercourse with a man. What else could these 'clusters of cells' as you called them be but babies? Are you claiming that you're not human?" he finished sarcastically.

"No, but—"

"Good. Now that we've established that, are you

202

claiming that their DNA is the same as yours?"

The woman hesitated.

"Think. You just said that HPV DNA was involved in the babies' creation."

"No, but—"

"That will do. You have confessed to attempting to murder your children," the man said flatly. "No further evidence is needed and no time need be wasted on a trial. Since the punishment for attempted or contemplated abortion is lifelong imprisonment, the length of your life is no longer your concern. It is only an issue of how long the state will be forced to pay for your upkeep."

"Self-defense—"

"Is not a valid argument. No woman has a need to defend herself against an in-utero child. His interests are her interests. That too is established law, upheld by the courts from district to Supreme, and enshrined in the Constitution."

The man pressed a button on his side of the table. The door opened and two guards entered.

If I fight, scream, kick, and punch, they'll say I'm hysterical and violent, the woman thought. *If I go quietly they'll say it proves that I secretly agree with them and am grateful to be saved from myself. I think I'd rather be violent and hysterical than secretly in agreement with my own murder.*

She fought, but could not fight for long.

The man smiled as the door closed. Her fear would satisfy him for many nights to come.

Plan C

L K. Short

On January 22, 1973, the United States Supreme Court ruled in Roe v. Wade *that unduly restrictive state regulation of abortion was unconstitutional; the court held that state laws criminalizing abortion in most instances violated a woman's constitutional right of privacy, which it found to be implicit in the liberty guarantee of the due process clause of the Fourteenth Amendment.*

On June 24, 2022, the Supreme Court ruled in Dobbs v. Jackson Women's Health Organization *that women do* not *have a constitutional right to abortion and therefore cannot be guaranteed access to the procedure, overturning* Roe v. Wade. *The regulation of abortion immediately reverted to all fifty individual states' legislatures.*

Lamar, Missouri
May 28, 2026

A car horn blared, shattering the dusty stillness of the motel parking lot. Jessica started, dropping the placards she'd been pulling out of the SUV's cargo space into the dirt. As she looked up, the horn sounded again, a long hard blast. Her body tensed at the sight of the white Crown Victoria with *Barton County Sheriff* emblazoned on the side. She glanced back at the motel's front office just in time to see the shutter flick down over the window; the corners of her mouth quirked up sardonically.

The man climbing out of the Crown Vic had the neck and arms of a bodybuilder, though the way his shirt fit under his belt suggested that his bodybuilding days had ended a while back. His eyes were icy pale and if looks could kill, she'd be lying in the dirt next to her placards. She spared a glance at his nameplate and felt some of the tension drain out of her—he was the right man, at least, even if this wasn't the right time or place. She could still make this work.

As he stopped in front of her, Jessica said brightly, "Is there a problem, Sheriff?" She folded her arms under her breasts and his stare flickered briefly down, making her wish she hadn't.

"I want to know what you're doing in my county," he said flatly. "In my *state.*" He looked pointedly at the SUV's Maryland tags.

Jessica took a deep breath. "I'm just passing through—"

"Amanda Bartlett says you told her you're *spreading the word.*"

Well, now she knew the motel clerk's name. "She must have misunderstood something I said. Really, I'm driving straight through to Nevada—"

"Figures." Glaring at her with disgust so obvious that Jessica knew he wanted her to see it, he jerked his thumb at the SUV "What have you got in the back?"

"Uh—"

"Step aside." She jumped back as he brushed past her.

He stared for a long moment at the piles of boxes and papers, then ripped the top of the first box open and glanced at her over his shoulder. Jessica lowered her gaze and, satisfied by her show of compliance, he continued his rampage through the contents of the SUV's cargo space. A few minutes later, he stiffened up like a board; Jessica barely had time to look up before he wheeled around, a fistful of glossy paper clutched in one hand.

"What the hell is this?"

"Informational pamphlets," said Jessica warily, taking a step back.

"Bullshit! These are *instructions!*" He spat out the word like it was poison. "Were you planning on handing these out *here*?"

"No, no, of course not! They're for a symposium in Nevada, like I said—"

"This shit's already legal in Nevada." His eyes narrowed on her face. "Instructions aren't much use without the drugs, are they? I'm impounding all this."

"What? You can't!" Jessica cried, clenching her fists. "There aren't any drugs!"

She let out a shriek as the sheriff grabbed her shoulder with his free hand, his fingers digging in past the muscle and biting down to the bone. "Or I could arrest you right now and you could spend the night in jail while we document the contents," he said through his teeth. The pain was excruciating; Jessica's eyes flooded with tears and it was all she could do to keep from wrenching away. He gave her shoulder a hard shake. "You want to swing at me with those fists?"

"No sir!" Jessica sobbed. "Please, take it all, I don't care!"

He let go of her so abruptly she staggered and nearly fell. He was staring at her breasts again—*always remember it could be worse*, Jessica told herself coldly, *count your blessings when it isn't!* She deliberately tried to make herself smaller as his greedy eyes returned to her face.

He jerked his head at the Crown Vic. "Get in the back of the car and wait for me."

"May I get my purse, please?" she asked timidly. "It's in my room."

"Hurry up."

Jessica jogged back to her door—it wasn't like he had to worry about her sneaking out the back; there was no back exit, and the front door led directly out to the parking lot. She slipped inside, shot the bolt on the door and dug her cell phone out of her back pocket, praying that Liane was able to answer.

She was. "What's up, girlie?" Liane said cheerily.

"Real quick—Li, I'm about to be taken to the county sheriff's office."

"Say what? Already? What the hell happened?"

Jessica took a deep breath. "No time to explain. The plan just didn't quite go off the way we intended."

"Are you okay?"

"Yeah, I'm fine." Jessica gingerly probed her shoulder. "We just have to move the schedule up a bit. Are you at the house yet?"

"About a mile away."

"Well, hurry up—her husband's busy *now*, not six hours from now. I'm assuming this won't keep him occupied for as long as my rally attempt in town would have, so get started with her as soon as you get inside."

"Yeah, okay…" A slightly breathless pause; Liane

had clearly picked up her pace. "Jess? Is he like she said he was?"

"Oh, yeah. She didn't exaggerate. Poor thing."

Jessica hit the Eraser app on her phone and shoved it into her purse, then cast a quick look around. There was nothing else in the room she'd need to come back for. Her gaze caught on a modest stack of pamphlets, identical to the ones that had so enraged the sheriff— *Do You Reside in One of the Forty No-Choice States? Plan C: Safe, Private Options for an In-Home Abortion.* "Poor thing," she muttered again, then hurried out the door.

.

Impossible Choices

L. A. Kurth

It's hard for the comfortable to fathom the lives of the desperate. That fact presents a huge obstacle when powerful men and women of great, or relative, privilege decide the fate of those whose struggles they've never witnessed and may even deny. When I think of Supreme Court Justices--Ivy League graduates who've arrived at success by way of privilege—arrogantly imposing their paternalist and theocratic preferences on women who face unbearable choices, I want to retch. Unseen suffering will increase. I'm sure of it.

Here's a memory that comes to mind, a report I heard from an eyewitness when I was a child. Bear with me. There's a prologue, necessary scene-setting.

Remember the admonition: "Eat your vegetables. Think of the starving children in China"? My father was a Marine in China at the time when children *were* starving, visibly and daily. Gangs of ragged orphans with filthy scalps cracked with dirt and crawling with lice stood by the gates and begged the soldiers in the few words of English they knew: "no Mommy, no Daddy, no Chow Chow." The GIs thought it was fun to teach them to add "no flight pay," and, though it was against the rules, soldiers would slip them chocolate or a coin.

In the frigid winter, these most desperate and

211

abandoned children burrowed into piles of horse manure around town, hoping to keep from freezing to death. But each night, some would die of starvation, exposure, or disease. A local man with a horse and cart would come around and throw their bodies on his cart and haul the load of corpses out of the city gates to be burned. Once, in a certain time and place, this was ordinary life.

Didn't the world care? Yes it did and sent warehouses full of food and clothing which sat and rotted a mile from destitute children while Chiang Kai Shek's warlords argued over the spoils, over who would get to sell those donated goods for a profit. Is it any wonder Mao Zedong won?

The war was small then, but still, my father said, the Marines lost about a man a day. One of his friends was on guard duty one night down by the river. He watched a woman come down to the wharf and right there, she went through labor and gave birth. When it was finished, she lifted up the baby, looked at it, and dropped it in the water.

Was it a girl whose future promised only suffering and prostitution? Was it the offspring of some GI? I don't know. But the guard was outraged by this murder. He lifted his rifle, aimed, and in a second, her body, too, tumbled and plopped into the river, never to be known, retrieved, or avenged and only remembered in a troubled conversation between one buddy and another. Judge, jury, and executioner, the Marine felt he had done justice; she deserved it. And yet...

I think a similar spirit of judgment and punishment inhabits some of those who blithely list alternatives as if to carry a baby to term and go through labor is nothing, a slight problem, easily solved. Yes, easily solved by those with means. Which women most desperately need abortions? Those in extremely unstable situations, unemployed or just scraping by, those climbing, doggedly and with utmost effort, out of poverty, for whom one misstep can send them tumbling back to a grinding existence they are struggling to escape. How many judges, Representatives, or Senators have met such people? Those who wield power tend to hobnob with the wealthy and powerful, or at least the settled and secure. Because they themselves face easy choices, they assume everyone else does too. But everyone else doesn't.

These deciders don't know what it's like to be forced to choose between two sad and difficult options. They don't know what it might be like to be completely overwhelmed by impossible choices, and yet ignorantly deprive others of the lives they wanted, their liberty, and their choice of happiness. Most elite and many comfortable people won't see or hear about the most horrible of cases, but eventually, clues emerge. In states where abortion providers are almost impossible to find, clues are already emerging. And they aren't pretty. In the October, 2007 issue of *World Psychiatry*, (https://www.ncbi.nlm.nih.gov/pmc/articles/PMC217 4580/) we learn this horrifying fact: "Rates of infanticide parallel suicide rates rather than murder rates. The risk of being a homicide victim is highest during the first year of life. Though the US has the highest rates of child homicide (8.0/100,000 for infants, 2.5/100,000 for preschool-age children, and 1.5/100,000 for school-age children), the problem of child homicide transcends national boundaries. These rates of child murder are probably underestimates, due to inaccurate coroner rulings and some bodies never being discovered."

How horrifying to think that the U.S. already has a high rate of baby killing, of babies born only to be murdered as infants. It's a fact we seldom see acknowledged. Removing the option of abortion can only increase that number.

Our Democracy Under Attack

J. Ganshaw

I knew moving back to the US would be difficult and I had reservations. I left five years ago because of the 2016 election and, though the administration has changed, the damage of the previous four years was done. I kept track of the craziness that was overtaking our rights, our constitution, and our entire democracy. I had moved to Cambodia, not the moon.

I learned quickly there were new rules for getting along. Number one: you don't speak about Trump in any way. My first experience of this was in the doctor's office in the waiting room, I overheard a conversation between other patients. The three of them, an older woman in her 70's, and a couple in their early 60's were all discussing Covid and the current administration when the older woman stated, "Biden is not the President, Trump is." "The election was stolen." The other couple immediately agreed, and I just shook my head in disbelief. I couldn't believe I was hearing it.

I overheard similar conversations in the diner, in the barbershop, and at the grocery store. I was in a small town in Western New York and it was like living in the twilight zone, a different universe separate from reality.

Then the day came when the Supreme Court overturned Roe v Wade. I immediately began to draw similarities between the GOP and the Cambodian People's Party, (CPP.) We are living in a country where one party is trying to take complete control of the country and make it an authoritarian state. The signs were there long before the overturning of Roe v. Wade. It began with the attack on the educational system which is still in full force. Just ask any conservative about Critical Race Theory or look at Florida's Don't Say Gay bill.

Since moving back to the US, I have been inundated by the news of states having shortages of teachers, with some states encouraging individuals without a degree in education to become educators. These same states are promoting classes on civics. In theory, civics classes sound like they would be a good thing in these times, but when "Civics" reads like a party platform, the goal simply becomes indoctrination. Comparing the current US to Cambodia, we are closer to moving to an educational system that is promoted in Cambodia than vice versa. In Cambodia, because of a teacher shortage, much to the satisfaction of the government, young adults with a high school degree are recruited to become teachers. Cambodian education entails a civics component which in reality, was and is, just propaganda provided by the CPP.

As the assault on education being required for educators, envision this is the path some states would be comfortable pursuing. The collapse of the education system makes it easier to implement my next fear: the judicial component.

The Equal Protection Clause has come under attack with the overturning of Roe v. Wade. This is a case where the domino effect made famous in Southeast Asia is critical. With the bulwark of ROE gone, other rights that we enjoy and perhaps take for granted at times, need to be safeguarded and protected. To me, that would mean the right to marry. As a gay man, I am especially interested that this might become the next focus of the courts. One only needs to look at the comments made by Justice Thomas, where he explicitly invites a challenge to this precedent and previous Supreme Court decisions. When reviewing the current makeup of the Federal Judicial System, we realize that this is not an unbelievable fantasy. Trump appointed over 250 federal judges to the bench, most if not all, have connections to the Federalist Society. A rightwing think thank that would readily return America to the Antebellum south.

Recently, it was reported that a federal court in Texas approved that people can be prevented from getting HIV preventative drugs, (PREP,) because providing those drugs may be against religious belief of the employer. Religious freedom is the new basis for discrimination of any kind and if this is allowed to stand, then my rights will always take second place to your religion.

While living in Cambodia I saw the damage that can be done when government is run by the US. After being back in the US for just six months I can see that the similarities between the two are much more alike than I imagined.

Both Trump and Hun Sen are narcissistic psycho/sociopaths, based on their actions. Each came to power legitimately and each used their power to enrich themselves and their families. Each has attempted to establish their rule as an autocracy. While

I am use Cambodia as an example, but I believe any autocracy could be used as a comparison. Ask yourself how Putin became worth 70 billion dollars.

The Supreme Court overturning Roe v. Wade, in essence giving those states, where government and religion are inexorably linked, control of women's bodies, was just the beginning.

The words of the majority justices cannot and should not bc taken at face value. When they say, "Don't worry, all other rights are fine," they are not to be trusted. Justice Thomas in his comments regarding Roe v. Wade was inviting states to bring a case to the Supreme Court so they can overturn the Right to Marry Act. This is just the beginning, not the end. My fear isn't just one but many because *all* of our rights are in peril.

Within days of this publication an election will be held. It is our duty to vote to ensure our democracy and all of our rights are protected.

The threats are real. Women have already lost the right to choose, contraception is on the block as the next big target. It would be so easy to sit idly by and hope that those currently in government will uphold the will of the people and the law.

Such is not the case, as Kansas taught us, the people have markedly different views on rights than do politicians. Left to the politicians, abortions would be banned in Kansas. What more do we need to witness for our eyes to be opened and our ears to hear what is so maliciously happening? The time is now and we need to speak with our voices but more importantly with our ballots on election day. We must each commit as citizens to protect the constitution and we can do that by voting to ensure those on the far right do not gain the power to harm our democracy and the rights of the majority.

We have a duty through the power of the vote, but the media also plays a role and the truth needs to be told, to be shared, and spoken truthfully. Social Media has a special role to play. Facts should be promoted, and conspiracy theories have no legitimate right to be promoted as fact or truth. Only through the presentation of facts can we as citizens determine the truth and guide us when we vote. This is the only way I believe our democracy can be preserved from further denigration and sliding into an autocracy.

So vote, speak out, protest, and do not remain silent in the face of attacks on our democracy or our rights.

You Don't Own Me—Or My Body

N.M. Rechtman

Nothing has changed since 411 BC
When Aristophanes brought "Lysistrata" into the world
Reminding women of their power over men
When they withheld sex
To end the Peloponnesian war
And convince the men to make peace.

In more recent times
The women of Iceland
Went on strike for a day
Demanding equal rights
And called it "Women's Day Off"
Instead of a strike
To make it more palatable to those who were hesitant
And afraid to ruffle any feathers.
But either way, it paralyzed the nation
When men had to do everything for just that one day
And they began to understand
So change finally came.

Making women powerless over our own destinies
Has always been the way of the patriarchy
But we have the clout when we learn to use it
strategically

And the ones who wield the power
Don't know what to do without us.
Strikes work
And men can be our allies
Because our strength lies in the numbers
And the need for our partnership
And the knowledge that we are equals in this society
With the understanding that no one should control our
lives
But us.

Now that shockwaves are reverberating throughout our
country
With Roe knocked down
Everyone needs to take a step back and understand
That we are all pro-life
That the decision to terminate a pregnancy is not done
lightly
Or flippantly
But often with agony and tears
With no other choice.
Only we and our doctors can know what's viable
And what's right.
No one should ever dare tell a person what they can and
cannot   do   with   their   body
But that consideration is once again being taken away
from   women
And if it takes a nationwide strike to get people to
comprehend   this
It just might work.

"You Don't Own Me" was an anthem
Fitting for the times
For those who stood up to oppression
Sung by Leslie Gore almost 60 years ago
And sadly, just as relevant today
Women are being told we are no longer in control of our
own bodies
While pontificating politicians who have been salivating
for decades
At the prospect of taking away a woman's fundamental
rights to choose
Need to be reminded
In a tsunami's chorus
That they don't own us
We own ourselves.

Upon a Wind of Change

H. Brown

To be up front: This report is mostly drawn from anecdotal evidence, observation, and, what some would say, a lot of jumping to conclusions.

But now that the aliens have left, we can only guess at their motives, intentions, and, most importantly, the consequences of their actions.

It is only because of their visit that we now have confirmation that other life exists in the universe. The knowledge we gained from this experience only shows how little we actually know.

As anyone with the Internet knows, the aliens appeared abruptly—identical in size, color, and shape, as if produced by a cookie-cutter machine. They were surprisingly humanoid in form. At first, they were thought to be merely thin teenaged pranksters decked out in gray Halloween skinsuits, opaque onyx goggles, and mechanical antennae.

But their advanced technology could not be denied. It became almost immediately clear that our authorities and weapons presented no barriers over where they went and what they did.

There was no need for them to issue the clichéd command of "Take us to your leaders." In the United States, the aliens found their way, either by instinct or from study, to city halls, state capitols, and Washington, DC. Similar excursions occurred in other countries all over the world.

Fingers were pointed as antennae swiveled. Accusations

between nations were launched as the aliens remained stubbornly mute. War was threatened, but whether it would be human versus human or human versus extraterrestrial varied by the hour.

What did they want? Did we have any reason to fear them? What nation, if any, were they working for? Or against? How could we communicate with them? Why wouldn't they communicate with us?

They silently passed among us and left. Like ghosts that wander a cemetery at night but are gone by the next day's dawn.

But these ghosts left more than stoic glances and sudden bursts of teleportation. We thought they had barely interacted with our world. We were wrong.

The recent world-wide discovery of alien-impregnated people (yes, astonishingly both males and females, but more on this later) provides only a proof of concept that Earthlings are somehow sexually and biologically compatible with these unearthly visitors. But the physical fact provides no clue of the intent: was this an intimate gift through the sharing of genes? Or a parasitic step toward invasion and conquest through reproduction?

Or was there an even more basic purpose, that the aliens stopped by not to explore our planet or to learn about our culture but simply to answer a natural and urgent call to breed? To put it crudely, was our planet just subject to an "intergalactic booty call"?

The other focus of speculation is how the deed actually occurred. Those affected, or some would say afflicted, provided sworn testimony that they had never engaged "in relations" with the aliens in any of the typical interactions understood and recognized by humans.

Proximal fertilization. That's what the biologists call it. Sort of what trees do with pollination. Apparently, the aliens never needed that talk about "the birds and the bees." No pollinators needed. Just atmosphere and wind.

Also of interest is that the aliens were very selective in whom they chose to "mate" with. A potential partner's selection criteria did not appear to be based on physical appearance or even gender. There's significant evidence that there was a "mental" aspect held as the dominant qualification.

Based on in-depth interviews, the chosen humans apparently hold a narrow-minded outlook on life, with their politics and values arbitrarily informed by ancient texts and alternative truths rather than reality, practicality, compassion, and logic.

If any of their offspring are carried successfully to term, it will take medical experts and scientists years to understand the xenobiology, especially as it is now mixed with human DNA.

As I said at the beginning of this report, all of the above theories about the aliens are, at this point, speculation and much more time and effort will be needed to unravel these Gordian knots. Perhaps someday we will have our answer. Hopefully, before the aliens pay us another visit.

But, for now, human thinking seems to be improving or, for some, at least shifting to a new paradigm, as exhibited by the following quotes (names not given to provide anonymity):

"I have said that even when life begins in that horrible situation of rape, that's something God intended to happen. Except when an extraterrestrial is involved, of course. That's different. Everyone knows aliens are godless."—an Indiana senate candidate.

"If it's a legitimate rape, the female body has ways of shutting that whole thing down. For once, I wish I was a woman."—a U.S. representative from Missouri.

"I mentioned that a sonogram of a 15-week-old male baby may show its hands between its legs, experiencing pleasure. Mine is rubbing its head. If I carry this alien baby to term, I'm worried that he'll have to wear a hat for the rest of his life!"—a Texas representative.

"Have a baby? I'd rather have a beer. I checked my personal calendar. Do you know how long I'd have to go without a drink? End this pregnancy now!"—a high-court judge.

"I've re-thought my position on abortion. I'm also reconsidering my support for Israel. Where were those Jewish laser beams when we needed them?"—congressperson from Georgia.

"I'm not pregnant. But if I was, it would be the greatest pregnancy ever! But I'm not pregnant. So, it's for truly altruistic reasons that I'm re-introducing MAGA: Making Abortions Great Again!"—former and possibly current POTUS.

As a result, the United States Supreme Court has reversed its reversal on Roe v. Wade, and a Republican-led Congress has initiated additional legislation to protect the medical procedure of abortion.

Rights

J. Dorr

Thomas had just begun to boil an egg for an egg salad sandwich when the 177th Right To Life Brigade burst in through his kitchen door.

"Freeze!" the lieutenant in command yelled. "Hands on your head. Now back away, slowly." She gestured toward the stove. "Jones!"

Private Jones dashed to the burner and switched it off. He grabbed the pot and placed it in the sink, and ran water into it. After a minute, he removed the lone egg from the pot and placed it, carefully, into a padded box.

"I think we're in time, ma'am," he said.

"Good," the lieutenant said, then turned back to Thomas. "We received a tip from one of your neighbors that you had been seen at a country store in the vicinity of a local chicken farm. A second team even now is interrogating the farmer. Under the provisions of the New Patriot Act, we are holding you on suspicion of plotting a terrorist act, to wit, depriving an innocent chicken of its God-given right to be hatched. I don't need to add that your actions disgust me personally. You have the right to remain silent until such time that we decide whether to actually bring charges against you. Should such a time come, depending on the nature of the charges, you may or may not be provided the right to consult an attorney. In the meantime, anything you say will be construed as further evidence of—"

Just then, a little girl bounded in through the door to the dining nook. "Daddy," she called, "is lunch ready yet? I—"

The lieutenant shot her.

Thomas, his arms pinned behind him by two of the burly troopers, strained to reach his daughter. "Katy," he sobbed, as brains and blood spread from the dying five-year-old's shattered skull onto the tiled kitchen floor. Then he raised his eyes and screamed at the lieutenant.

"How can you?" he shouted. "How can you claim to be supporting life, when you do things like this?"

The lieutenant shrugged. "Hey, it looks to me like she's already been born. So it's not our concern."

Cousin Sarah

J.A. McColley

My grandmother tore up the tattered old carpet in the back room, and laid down a red and cream woven rug with frilled edges. I thought she had gone crazy, pulling at the edges of the carpet with the back of the hammer, cursing under her breath.

That room had been my mother's once upon a time, and I would sit and talk to Mom as though she hadn't died, imagining that if there was a place she was still connected to, it was in there. An unbelievable amount of dust and old clothes and things came out as Grandma worked. I honestly didn't know where it all came from.

One afternoon, Grandma had me help carry bottled water, some extra blankets, an old cot, and snacks in plastic bins into the now clean room. I almost asked if we were going camping, but it was a stupid, fleeting thought. Why would we gather all that stuff in a room that didn't even have a door to the outside?

By the next day, it was all gone. We never brought it back out, that I saw. But I was ten, so it didn't bother me much.

Grandpa just said, "Grown-up business, Gaten, don't you worry about it," when I asked about the box of rifle shells I spotted in one load he brought in behind me.

231

The next week, Sarah, a cousin I never knew I had, showed up at the door. Grandma showed her right in and set her up in Mom's old room, told me to get her anything she needed, but not to mention she was visiting, not to anyone. She couldn't have been more than a couple of years older than me, and I had just finished fourth grade. I figured she was here for the summer and I'd get the chance to find out more about her.

But the next week, she was gone. She'd taken most meals in that back room, and I'd only had a chance to say "hi" once, to which she'd smiled shyly, but also in a pained, scared way, the way Mom had when she told me she was going to the hospital, but then never came back.

A few days later, another cousin, also mysteriously named Sarah, a few years older maybe and taller than the first, with darker hair, knocked on the door. The car that dropped her off was already just a pair of red lights sliding away in the dark when I peered out. Nonetheless, Grandma had me carry Sarah's suitcase and, arm over the girl's shoulder, led her to Mom's old room.

She was still there a few days later when the police knocked on the door. I was closest, and I could see the officer's badge through the window, so I let him in.

"Hi, officer, what seems to be the problem?" I asked like they did on the TV.

"Hello there, son. I'm looking for... runaways. runaway girls. There anyone unusual in the house? I notice you have lots of space."

"There's my Cousin Sarah," I started. Grandma caught my eye through the doorway into the living room and shook her head with an angry look. "But she left a few days ago. Nobody here but us Joneses."

"Mm hmm," the officer said, looking over his shoulder at his partner who stood by their car. "Mind if I have a look around?"

Now Grandma swooped in and held me by the shoulders from behind like she did at church sometimes when she was talking to Father Donnelly and didn't want me to interrupt.

"Surely, Dale," Grandma said. "I think Colin's out back cutting wood to size if you need to talk to him. Like some tea? Lemonade?"

"Thank you, Shirl, but I'm working a case. Serious business, no time for chatting."

"Oh? Some dangerous felon running about escaped from the prison, I suppose?"

"Something like that. She's a felon, at any rate. Anyone who assisted her would be on the wrong side of the law. Things are changing."

"Seems to me they're going back to how they were," Grandma observed, though I didn't have the tiniest little clue what things were going backward.

"That's not for me to say."

"Just doing your job, then, Dale? Following orders?" Grandma said in that way she did when she knew she was pushing someone's buttons. "Seems I've heard that one before."

The color rose in Officer Dale's neck, reaching toward his face. His hands tightened into fists briefly, then relaxed.

"No need for that kind of talk, Shirl. The law is the law."

"Doesn't make it right."

Officer Dale turned away then, waving to his partner, who came to the door.

"You look around outside. Check all the sheds and outbuildings. I'll take inside the house." Turning back to us, he said, "Why don't you get yourself some of that lemonade and go sit in the front room? Don't come out. Don't make me... This is hard on everyone, Shirl. Just go sit."

Officer Dale and his partner spent the rest of Grandpa's news show and part of the football game poking around in every room, and I don't know where they went outside. Grandma held me on the couch all that time, tensing up when they moved to the back of the house, where Mom's room was.

"Should we check on-" I got out before she squeezed me extra tight.

"Hush now," she whispered.

"All right, Shirl, Colin," Officer Dale said to Grandma and Grandpa. "No one's here, but you never know when a fugitive might show up. Keep an eye out."

"I surely will." Grandma nodded. The officers drove off before Grandma stood, letting me go.

I didn't understand. "Officer Dale said there was no one else here. Did Cousin Sarah leave already?"

"Hush, now. That Dale's an ornery one. Might be parked around the corner waiting for us to run to her. You just watch the game with Grandpa."

Grandpa fell asleep, and football was boring, so I went to play outside. I ended up around back by the apple trees. There was a giant old one with a hole on the front where I used to throw apples from the ground nobody would eat. Grandpa said it was good for my aim; I threw one, then a second before I noticed the wasps.

Had they been there before? Certainly there were more after I threw the third.

The loose, curving paths of the small black bodies in the sun drifted toward me as the buzzing became more ominous. I ran. I'm fastest in my class, but not faster than angry wasps. One stung me, then another, on my elbow, my arm between my elbow and my hand, then one right between my fingers.

I hollered and ran into the house, then back up to the hallway outside Mom's old room. Grandma stood in the doorway. Behind her, I saw just the eyes and up of Cousin Sarah before she dropped out of sight, into the floor! Grandma slammed the door to the room behind her.

"What's going on out here. I thought you'd been playin' with Grandpa's knife again and cut off a finger."

"Wasps!" I said between sobs, holding up my arm for her to see.

"To the kitchen! We'll get some baking soda on that right quick!"

When I was all patched up, Grandma fixed me with one of her stares.

"What are we going to do with you?" She asked. I knew better than to answer. I never had the right answer, even when I was sure I did. Grandpa spoke up, though. I was sure that was a mistake, too, but Grandma's eyes softened as he spoke.

"Tell him. He's old enough, smart enough, and good enough to hold it to himself, even if he doesn't need to know the... grown-up parts."

"Seems like I'm outnumbered by fate and Grandpa," Grandma said. "I'm going to let you in on a big secret. Like Grandpa says, it's an adult secret, a real one you can't tell anyone about, not teachers or friends, or even police officers."

If I hadn't already been curious, that spiel would have hooked me like a bass on a worm. "I don't really have a Cousin Sarah, do I?"

"Sure you do, lots of 'em. Tall ones, short ones, round ones, thin ones, light ones, dark ones. Could even be more than one at a time on occasion, if things go on like they are."

I tried to push all those cousins around in my brain, trying to figure out how our family had gotten so large. "But does that mean I have aunts and uncles I never met?"

"Well, I suppose it would, normally," Grandma agreed. "But these cousins are girls... well, *people*, who need our help. That's all you really need to know. They need a place to sleep, a few meals, and a place for the next car to pick them up and take them on their way."

"Why can't they just take the bus? Or why can't we drive them all the way they're going?"

"Because it's a secret, this help we give. Remember Officer Dale? He was looking for Sarah. We don't need to go into why, but he's wrong, and he can't see it, or won't admit it."

"But the police are the good guys. If she needs help, why can't they help?"

"Because that's not... that's... oh damn, why does this have to be so difficult?"

I'd never heard Grandma swear before. If she was so troubled as to use the angry words, I knew it must be really, really important. "Ok, Grandma, I-I won't tell no one."

"Anyone," Grandma said.

"Anyone," I repeated.

That summer and into the fall and winter, and for years after, "cousin" after "cousin" came through, sleeping in the room beneath the back room, the room with the trap door hidden by the rug with the tassels.

Whenever there came a knock at the door, I ran to be the one to answer so I could wave the visitor in and say, "You must be Cousin Sarah. You must be tired. We have a room all set up for you."

Inmate 08-G7N Will See You Now

J.P. Burnham

The clunking reverberations of the baton against metal cell bars woke her long before the guard stopped in front of her door, keys jangling, blocking the sunlight from her hallway's lone window.

"Wake up, Janssen, you've got a patient." The guard swung the door open. Elaine didn't have to look into his face to know it wore a demeaning smirk.

She grunted when the guard rapped the baton against her kneecap. Elaine knew the nerve arc the blow took through the pain receptors, up her spinal column, and into her brain was too rapid to prevent the reflexive noise that escaped her lips, but she still wished it hadn't come out—it gave the guard too much satisfaction. The pink flush to her face from the pain was also involuntary.

"Hard to deliver a baby when you can't stand up," Elaine said, struggling to rise from her threadbare cot.

"Maybe you should retire." Retirement was code for lethal injection. "One of the other baby-killer docs in here can take your place—maybe they won't talk back so much."

Elaine rose slowly, allowing time for the guard to appreciate the full two meters her Dutch genes had given her, along with the muscles that gym time serving her life sentence had afforded her.

"Don't make me get out my taser," the guard said,

voice trembling.

"Surprised you haven't fired it already." She snorted and felt the *thwack* of the baton across her quads. The guard jumped away as he did it—he wasn't as unintelligent as his chosen profession suggested; he knew she could take him in a fair fight.

"Let's get a move on," he said, though there was a hint of begging buried ever so superficially underneath. "Mrs. Umsk is having contractions every five minutes."

Elaine shuddered at the name and followed the guard down poorly lit, un-air-conditioned concrete hallways. Mrs. Umsk was the wife of the wealthiest man on the planet and it irked Elaine to no end that she had to care for her. What she wouldn't give to ... *First do no harm,* she reminded herself.

She shook her head. For some reason, she still had a will to live, despite being one among many obstetricians imprisoned at the McConnell State Prison Facility in Montgomery County, Alabama. It was an honor, the guards told them, to be housed at McConnell State—the best abortion performing obstetricians were held there, which afforded them the best prison conditions in the US. The sweltering hot facility stank of despair and rats—an environment not befitting the hundreds of years of medical knowledge which it housed. Yet, somehow, it was the best it got for obstetricians in practice who'd formerly performed abortions. Life in McConnell State wasn't that much different than their other option—death.

As they passed the threshold into the white, pristine hallways of the rich, predominantly White women's ward, Elaine shed her orange jumpsuit for pink, prison issued scrubs. They weren't much more comfortable, but the patients preferred them. Undressing and redressing all happened in full view of the guard—the waves of nausea that came with the embarrassment had lessened over time from the quotidian humiliations.

When she entered Mrs. Umsk's delivery room, alarms were shrieking.

"Status report?" Elaine asked the labor and delivery nurse, also a prisoner, though from a section of the prison Elaine never interacted with except during deliveries. She'd not met this one before—she was broad-shouldered, with light brown skin and a short afro.

"Only twenty weeks pregnant, we can't maintain mom's blood pressure despite having initiated the rapid blood transfusion protocol, and baby's having wildly long decels," said the nurse, holding up a long strip of paper.

"Fuck," Elaine said as she studied the strip.

Mrs. Umsk screamed at her. "Don't say *fuck* like that while my baby is coming out!"

"Fuck," Elaine repeated, holding the strip to Mrs. Umsk's face. The guard held up his taser threateningly and approached the bed.

"I wouldn't shoot that if I were you," Elaine said holding her ground.

"And why not?" the guard retorted.

"Because if you knock me out, Mrs. Umsk will die."

The guard swallowed hard and backed to the corner, lowering his taser.

"Fix it! Do something!" Mrs. Umsk shouted.

Elaine grabbed the ultrasound probe, squirted the warm jelly across Mrs. Umsk's abdomen, and moved the transducer across her skin.

"What are you doing?" Mrs. Umsk squealed.

"Saving your life, if you'd please be so kind as to shut the fuck up."

Mrs. Umsk bit her lip, but didn't shout again.

Elaine got the uterus and placenta in view and swore under her breath.

"Mrs. Umsk, you have a placental abruption. Your placenta has almost completely torn away from the uterine wall and your baby isn't getting any oxygen. Your blood pressure is critically unstable despite multiple units of blood. In addition, part of the placenta is blocking the cervix—your baby can't get out. And even if it could, it's too young to survive outside the womb."

"What do you mean? Why didn't someone catch this on my last ultrasound?" Mrs. Umsk's face was a mix of rage and fear.

Elaine could feel the taser being raised, but didn't look back.

"I wasn't present for your last ultrasound; I cannot speak to its findings." As part of standard prenatal care, Mrs. Umsk would have been due for an ultrasound approximately two weeks prior, but Elaine had not been the one to do it—she'd been in solitary after an altercation with a guard who'd crossed one of the last remaining lines she had. She'd do it again if it kept the guards' hands off of her. Perhaps whoever had done her ultrasound had not reported the placenta blocking the cervix on purpose. Perhaps one of her cellies was also contemplating whether Hippocrates' maxims were relevant in their current situation.

"What do we need to do?"

"We need to have started an emergency Caesarean section *five minutes ago.* Your fetus cannot be saved, but you can."

Mrs. Umsk wailed. The nurse's eyes went wide. Elaine got it—there weren't emergencies in this ward. Somebody was going to pay and Elaine wasn't sure who it would be.

"Do it then! What are you waiting for?" Mrs. Umsk shouted.

From the claustrophobic memories of solitary

confinement, from the guards' daily rancor at her continued existence that made all two meters of her feel so small that she could walk between the bars of her cell, a plan coalesced and clarified in a heartbeat. There *was* a way out. Elaine knew they wouldn't have time to retrieve another OB without Mrs. Umsk dying. There was no time.

"I want to walk out of this prison, after the surgery is complete, as a free woman and I never want to come back."

The adrenaline coursing through her had her heart beating so loudly in her ears that she scarcely registered the clatter of the guards' footsteps approaching. Lancinating pain erupted from her flank where the baton struck, burning waves of an agonous earthquake shaking her to her core. She dropped to her knees, but Mrs. Umsk's scream stopped the guard before he connected again.

"Stop it! Stop IT! This woman is going to save my life and you're going to try to prevent her from doing that?"

The guard stood and pulled at the fringes of his uniform. "Sorry, ma'am, but you don't have the authority to let this inmate leave."

Mrs. Umsk pulled out her cell phone and dialed her husband. Elaine was used to husbands not being present in the labor room; they were too busy doing whatever got them the money to have their wives see the best OBs money could buy.

"Honey, yes, it's me. No, I haven't had the baby." She sobbed as she tried to get out the next words. "The doctor says the baby is going to die no matter what, but if... if they don't do a C-section right away, I'm going to die too."

Mrs. Umsk held the phone away as the wealthiest person on the planet shouted on the other end of the connection.

"Yes, she says she won't do it unless she leaves prison a free woman right after the surgery."

What? Elaine heard coming from the phone's speaker. This was where it might fall apart. Was there any sliver of this man that cared about his wife enough to help out a prison doctor? Or at least some part that cared about the optics of sending his wife to the best OBs in the country and having her die? Some other possible social backlash that might befall him if he allowed his wife to die? She didn't care what the reason, she just cared about getting out.

The response was more muted and Mrs. Umsk held the phone closer to her ear.

"'Do it', he says. He'll get you out of here by nightfall."

"If he follows through, you have my word that I and the other doctors will keep you alive. Otherwise, your blood is on his hands. Tell him to hold a press conference about how he's overseeing my release so he'll be held to his promise. I will save you, and you save me from this place. Fair?"

For a fraction of a second, Elaine saw the understanding on Mrs. Umsk's face, the empathy, the shared humanity—a flicker of hope in a dark place, a candle to light her path out of the Stygian hellscape that was McConnell State.

Mrs. Umsk exchanged words again with her husband and dropped the connection.

"He swears." She sniffled and her bottom lip quivered. When she spoke, it was just above a whisper. "Now, will you please save me?"

Elaine nodded to the slack-jawed nurse as they wheeled Mrs. Umsk into the operating suite. If she hadn't been so focused on trying to operate her way to freedom, she'd have looked back at the guard to see his surprise. But she didn't care that much; she could taste freedom and everything that had come before suddenly meant very little in the grand scheme of things.

After the operation was over, she was going to have to light the match of revolution quickly with the other obstetricians, to tell them what she'd done and hope they could do the same, if not all of them, at least some, the first drops of water escaping from a dam about to burst.

She was just one woman, one free obstetrician, finally, finally, but she knew it was going to be the start of something big.

Draft Dodgers

T. Easton

After Roe v. Wade was overturned, it quickly became difficult for women of child-bearing age—whether pregnant or not, whether seeking an abortion or not—to cross certain state lines.

The blue F-150 SuperCrew pickup slowed behind the traffic waiting to cross the Texas line,

"Jeez!" said Shirl, in a mellow contralto. "Are they stopping everybody?" Her blonde hair was piled sky high in a Texas beehive. "At least the luggage is in the back." Every suitcase was decorated with "Toronto Festival of Improv" stickers, and was readily accessible to nosy cops and customs officials. If they got that far.

"Voice!" Bonnie's obviously fake soprano could cut glass. She was driving, and dressed accordingly in tight magenta slacks. Her brown hair was tied back in a ponytail.

"Jeez!" Shirl was back in character.

"Socks in place?" From the back seat of the F-150, Eileen's voice was even shriller.

"You just had to read Pratchett's *Monstrous Regiment.*" Audrey, sitting beside her, started with a mellow tone but shifted before anyone reminded her.

"It worked for Pratchett's heroine." She had run

away from home, dressed as a boy, to join the army. When someone slipped her a pair of socks to ball up and tuck into the front of her pants, the bulge helped immensely. "Women can masquerade as men. It really ups the game when women disguise themselves as men disguised as women."

Audrey laughed. "Reminds me of Julie Andrews, in *Victor/Victoria.*"

"That's *old!*" said Eileen.

"How many more of these idiot state lines do we have to cross?" Shirl's voice was still high.

"Too many," said Bonnie. "Half the country has gone nuts."

"I am *not* having that pig's baby." Eileen had been at a party when the man she now only referred to as "the pig" had dragged her into a bedroom.

"My choice," said Bonnie. "He said he couldn't get condoms."

"Yeah," said Audrey. "I'm not ready for a kid now. Maybe not ever."

Shirl nodded. "I'm not getting drafted to be a mother!"

They each had their own reasons for being on the same mission.

The traffic moved slowly forward. Eventually, Audrey exclaimed, "They have dogs! We can't get away with this!"

"Just remember your lines," said Shirl.

"Let me do the talking," said Bonnie, just as shrilly.

When they finally reached the head of the line, a Texas Ranger rotated his hand. Bonnie, knowing his intention, pushed the button that opened the window.

Furnace-quality Texas air filled the car.

Behind the Stetson-wearing Texas Ranger, two dogs began to whine and pull at their leashes.

"You ladies trying to get out of state?" leaning forward until the brim of his Stetson hit the upper edge of the open window. "Maybe looking for abortions?"

"Oh, lordy no!" Bonnie fanned herself with one hand. Was she hamming it up too much? She knew that the sudden heat was making her sweat and her makeup would run. She hoped that the black "beard" under it wouldn't smear. "We're female impersonators! There's a festival in Toronto!"

Shirl, in the passenger seat, passed her the invitation. "See? We do improv, y'know."

"If you're female impersonators," said the young Ranger, "I'm the King of Spain." These pups..." He pointed at the still-whining dogs. "They can smell it on you. You're women and at least one of you is pregnant." He sighed. "And you know the rules. If you, or any member of your party, is pregnant, you can't leave the state."

"But we're not!" Bonnie's voice struck a new high note, and the Ranger winced. "We left our girlfriends in Austin. And we," she held up her hands with air quotes "hugged 'em good before we left." They had heard about the dogs. If they were really men, and if they really had girlfriends, "hugging" would explain away the dogs' reactions. Scents rub off.

"You guys have girlfriends?" The Ranger did not look convinced of the idea of either guys or girlfriends. "Let's see your papers."

They handed over their licenses and the truck's registration.

"Shirl? Bonnie? Audrey? Eileen?" He looked up

blankly. "What's your anthem? 'A Boy Named Sue?'"

From the back seat of the truck, Eileen piped up with, "We *don't* hate our names.

Bonnie rolled her eyes and exclaimed, "But parents! Is it any wonder we became female impersonators?"

"I actually know a guy named Audrey," said the Ranger. There's only one way to be sure. Get yourselves out of the truck, and, keep your hands where I can see 'em."

When Bonnie stood up, the Ranger looked down toward her slacks and nodded. "Nice package."

The others wore skirts. He stared at them and made a rolling motion with his fingers. Audrey was the first to lift her hem. He nodded again, and she dropped her voice to a masculine rumble to say, "We're delaying traffic."

The Ranger looked up and nodded but still gestured to Eileen and Shirl.

Within a few minutes, they were back on the road. No one uttered a word for the first five miles. Then Eileen said, "Socks! For that masculine look! Maybe someday I'll get close to a penis that's as wide as them socks." Her voice was normal.

Audrey said, "Thank god for those geniuses in Toronto. How many people got that invitation?"

Eileen swore, which was of course not ladylike. "Not enough. And the cops will catch on too damned soon."

"We'll need an Underground Railroad."

"We're good," said Shirl. "I just hope Canada lets us stay."

Bonnie laughed. "What about our 'girlfriends' back in Austin? The ones we hugged so good?"

Audrey laughed too. "They're okay. Don't even have

to pay rent."
    "Can't get pregnant."
    "Never have to run."
    "Never have to be real."

Letter From a Federal Women's Prison July 17, 2048

S.L. Weippert

July 17, 2048
Dear Marie,

Thank you so much for jumping through all those bureaucratic hoops and all so I can send you mail without being watched like a hawk. Since they told me you accepted responsibility for our discussions, I know they're not bothering. Lazy Bastards. Not that I can talk as freely as I would in your kitchen over coffee, but I can be a little less paranoid when I answer your questions now.

And please keep the questions coming. You don't know how much better I feel when I read one of your letters. Hearing about what your life's like, and what trouble those two nieces of mine have gotten into reminds many of us why we did what we did to end up here. They cheer up more than just me in this place. Thank you again for doing this. Most importantly, keep the letters safe because History needs to know how it really happened. Even if the winners write the history books, a voice from one of the losers can put a crack in the propaganda monolith.

Anyway, your last letter asked about why your Grandparents had to re-marry in California. Right? Well, I'm sorry. Many, many marriages got annulled by State fiat back then and your Grandpa's and Grandma's was one of them. See, when Roe fell, many other things fell, too.

Why? Because more than just our family planning decisions depended on the 14th amendment. That's why. Everything from marriage equality to what consenting adults did in their bedrooms became subject to regulation at the state level, and I don't have to tell you what kind of idiots ran our state.

All of human behavior could be legal or not depending on where you lived. It was MASS CHAOS, Marie. Overnight fifty different rules applied instead of one. And at the time we happened to live in Virginia, who we found out had never deleted any of the legal code about whites marrying non-whites after the supreme court struck it all down way back in 1967.

So, with an old anti-miscegenation law on the books that hadn't been updated since the civil war, all the Virginia Republican legislature had to do is update a few definitions, and SURPRISE! everyone had to go to the DMV to register their "melanin number" on their I.D. Once they had you in one of their neat categories, M0 to M100, that ancient anti-miscegenation law meant you couldn't marry anyone with a number more than so many shades away from your own.

If you didn't like the number they gave you at the DMV, when the clerk "visually inspected" you for your category, you had to pay a genealogist to certify that no one in your direct family tree "showed higher amounts than you" back six generations. Notice how this works exactly like that nasty one sixty fourth Jim Crow "drop of blood" thing, but all polished up and tweaked so it looks fair and reasonable. May God bless their tiny devil hearts because I'm not going to.

So, it turns out that Dad, your Grandpa, got rated at what got explained to me as "light skinned Mexican" and Mom, your Grandma, got rated so many "shades" lighter as "Mediterranean European." I exploded when I got the news. I stormed down to the DMV and raised such good trouble I got my first arrest. Hopefully, you can get an archive pic somewhere. Article called me Antifa-terrorist, too.

Anyway, we hired an attorney after that. Mom and Dad couldn't be legally married anymore, but had lived together more than long enough to be considered "common law married" which made a fine legal mess. Your mother and I had to have new birth certificates as we couldn't have Dad's last name anymore. It hurt Dad so much. This is why your mom and grandparents moved to California. Mom and Dad wanted to be legally married again.

After your grandparents moved with your teenager mom so they could live together without paying fines, I got to be the family claimant in the anti-miscegenation law class action suit against the state for the mess they caused. That ended up going nowhere, but it was at one of the class litigant meetings the firm hosted that I met Beth and Catherine. See they had been married before this, just like your grandparents, but same sex marriage had fallen with everything else.

We hit it off and it didn't take much for them to convince me to join their "circle of aunties" to help women cross borders to get what they needed done by a doctor in a clinic instead of the back of a beat-up van.

The first time Beth called me and asked if Aunty Cindy was available, it'd been so long I'd almost forgotten, but I said yes without hesitation. Beth told me to pick my passengers up at the Greyhound station and take them to a certain border town where another Aunty owned property on both sides of the state line.

Oh Marie, it breaks my heart even now to remember this. I felt so horrible about asking after I knew but when I pulled up, I saw a mother and daughter, I was confused. From the car I asked the adult woman why she brought her child with her. After the woman buckled the child in behind me and got in the front passenger seat, she shut her door firmly, turned to me and said, "I'm not her mother. I'm an Aunty, just like you." She pointed with her thumb at the girl behind us. "She's too young to travel alone. She'll attract attention alone, but an adult and young girl won't. At least not as much. Now, I've been on a bus for the last ten hours, and I'm tired. Let's go."

I remember sneaking glances at the child sleeping behind me for the next hour as I drove them to their destination. Her feet didn't even touch the floor, yet! What kind of monster would do that to a little girl?

The adult next to me asked me with wry amusement, "Can't believe she's old enough?"

I dragged my attention back to the freeway. "No, I can't." I gave her a quick stink-eye, but her eyes were closed. "Is this a test to see if I'll turn you guys in?" I demanded.

The woman turned away from the window, leaned her back on the head rest and turned to meet my eyes. "Nope. And Beth and Christine don't do sick tests like that. Nope, this horror's real. That little girl behind you is eleven. Her menstruation started a few months ago and uncle didn't check before he got his annual quicky during this year's family reunion." She gave me the full story then, which I'll spare you the details and give the lowlights.

See, the police already had her uncle in jail awaiting trial because finally this pregnant child meant the prosecutor had iron clad proof to put rich & powerful uncle scumbag away for good, thank you for your sacrifice child, but so sorry, medically ending the pregnancy isn't going to happen. Her attorney tried to get a judge to allow the procedure, but that motion was blocked by the Uncle's attorneys who said if the state wanted to use it as proof he's a criminal, that meant he had a "father rights" claim to the fetus. The men involved, and aside from the girl, they were all men, had decided that forcing her to carry to term would be the best option because it "preserved evidence" in a way that also "preserved the father's rights".

The prosecutor had even argued that likely she'd miscarry anyway as young as she was, so the state's position was to let nature take its course and deal with the results when they happened.

What was best for the child in my backseat wasn't even discussed.

The girl's attorneys got ahold of Beth and Christine and of course they helped They arranged to get her to the next state over, where the attorney had already filed a motion through a local attorney to arrange things in a much more humane court in a state with legal women's health clinics, so that the biological remains of the pedo's actions could be legally preserved.

They were waiting for us all at the end. The girl went to Juvie, the uncle got off, and Beth, Christine and I each got life

Damn, my med bracelet just beeped at me. The infernal thing says this is making my blood pressure rise, so I better wrap this up. They monitor everything about us here, and if my BP rises when I write to you, they may make me stop for my own good, y'know.

But before I go. I wanted to be sure to tell you I got the baby-soft, rabbit fur yarn your eldest made from her 4H rabbits and I promise to make her a scarf. I'll start working on it right away. Tell her thank you so much and I'll take as much of that yarn as she wants to send me. All of us fiber gals here adored the yarn.

Give both my nieces a kiss for me, and be sure to write back soon.

Counting the days until your next letter,
Your Aunt Cindy.

A Christmas Wish

R.M. Kyle

Multiple summons, from distressed women, were stronger than Perchta had experienced in many years. Worse, it was during the holidays. She contemplated calling other spirits to assist in the event of a mass tragedy.

Please, not so close to Christmas.

The summons came from a state capitol festooned with flags and mottoes, writ in Latin, above the doors.

The interior was decorated with lights and garlands. Christmas carols echoed faintly through the hallways. Ignoring men's leering glances and verbal come-ons, she sought women in need.

Women's cries rose from a lower floor.

REINSTATE ROE

PROTECT SAFE LEGAL ABORTIONS

RAPE/INCEST VICTIMS HAVE RIGHTS, TOO

"What's happening?" Perchta asked a participant.

"Since the Supreme Court invalidated Roe, legislators removed a woman's right to choose before they realize they're pregnant." She went on to explain the "fetal heartbeat" bill's problems.

Armed policemen arrived.

"Take this outside," an officer ordered.

"We have a First Amendment right to be here!"

Women shouted. A young man with a press badge lifted his camera and started filming.

"Keep it down. Clear the path. Cause trouble and you're going to jail."

More cameramen, with equipment emblazoned with an alphabet soup of call letters, recorded the women while reporters chose various spokespeople to interview.

A young woman spoke, her quiet voice trembling. "I trusted the man I dated. When he offered me a drink, I took one. That drink was drugged. He raped me. I got pregnant. I was lucky to have the right to an abortion. Now, women must either go out of state or carry a rapist's baby."

"A sonogram near the end of my pregnancy showed our baby's brain was growing on the outside of its skull," an older woman sobbed. "We terminated the pregnancy because the doctors said our baby would only have a short, painful life. This bill prevents compassionate terminations."

"We've tried to speak to Senator Simpson," another said. "He represents my district. He's not answering our calls."

Men in gray and black suits stood on the periphery, angrily eyeing the demonstrators. Several used their phones.

Soon, more police arrived.

The ordinary chill from the building's hollow core rose in temperature from too many bodies and heightened emotions. Protestors spoke eloquently, forming a protective wall around the most vulnerable.

A man in an expensive gray suit strolled out of an elevator, surveying the growing chaos like an apex predator.

"Senator Simpson!" Reporters clamored, seeking an interview with the man whose legislation had started this confrontation.

Simpson drew the reporters toward the center of the rotunda, choosing a strategic spot near a brightly lit Christmas tree and the state's flag.

Perchta suspected he spent time before a mirror, making certain every well-coiffed hair was in place, without a wrinkle to be seen. Perchta sensed unease from many women, outright fear in others.

Yes, her witch's magic told her. *He's the one who created this chaos and pain.*

Perchta moved to a strategic spot between two of the cameramen, front and center, directly in the Senator's eyeline. She needed no mirror to know she stood out like a cardinal amongst a flock of sparrows. The senator's eyes fastened on her. Just as he was about to speak, she licked her generous, red-painted lips. He paused, dazed.

"Senator! Senator!" The reporters cried.

The senator knew who to call on and get the softballs right over the plate. The protesters? He never acknowledged a single one until he gave them a cheerful wave and a million-dollar smile as he stepped away from the lights. She discreetly followed, mixing in with the press corps and staff.

She waited until he emerged from his office and met him in the hallway, just the two of them.

"Well done, Senator," Perchta drawled. "Quite a gubernatorial performance."

He eyed Perchta, his focus moving languorously between her full bosom and shapely legs.

"Have we met somewhere before?" He stepped

forward with a half-smile and an open hand.

Perchta chuckled. "Do I look familiar to you?"

"Only in my dreams."

"Maybe you should write movie scripts instead of laws," Perchta suggested with a flirtatious smile.

"I could use a drink," said the senator, his voice hopeful.

"No doubt you could use several after the *hard* day you've had," Perchta agreed.

"I know a place…"

Perchta batted luxuriant lashes and took the lead, making sure her hips swayed provocatively.

Senator Simpson was panting by the time they stepped past the knowing smile of a policeman at the door and climbed into the back of his Town Car.

What a sordid place, Perchta thought as they moved away from the capitol, and other, lesser state buildings, into the surrounding neighborhood. Scantily clad women strolled in front of rundown-looking motels, offering hourly services to passing motorists.

Several of the sex workers recognized the senator's vehicle and attempted to wave him over, despite his having a female passenger.

"No," Perchta said when he suggested a threesome. *I don't like witnesses.*

They arrived at a well-maintained, gated condo complex, far away from the city center, with carefully manicured lawns. Each offered private, discreet entrances, windows equipped with tightly drawn curtains.

"Would you like a drink?" Senator Simpson asked once they were inside, the door locked behind them.

"I'll have what you're drinking. I trust you." It wasn't

a lie. She fully trusted him to drug her and rape her, while she was unconscious, and then, later, blame her drinking for the lapse of her remembering to give consent.

She turned obliquely to look at a bronze statue of a horse on a shelf beside his desk. She could feel his gaze on her as he poured two glasses of scotch. Human hearing would not have been keen enough to hear the subtle hiss of powder into one of the shot glasses, but hers was.

Despite her nose wrinkling at the reek of fear, from far too many previous women, emanating from his leather couch, she sat and crossed her legs seductively. Glancing at his bookshelves, she noted a tiny red light switching from red to green. Cameras? She made a mental note that, likely, there was undoubtedly a box of very incriminating SD cards present nearby.

He approached with glasses in hand and sat beside her. She deliberately leaned forward to accept a glass, displaying a generous amount of cleavage. He swallowed hard enough to make his Adam's apple bob. Perchta used just enough magic to cause him to hand her the wrong glass.

It was time he got a taste of his own medicine— literally.

"To responsibility for our actions," Perchta toasted, holding her glass to clink his.

He chuckled, cocksure that he held the untainted glass, and took a generous belt.

Perchta sipped her Scotch, noting Simpson's casual observation, watching her for signs of sleepiness. She yawned expansively, pretending to be affected.

Eventually, Simpson's eyelids began to droop every

time he blinked. Another yawn, and his head finally dropped against the back of the couch.

Perchta put her drink aside and created a quick spell, infusing his mind with a very sensual dream, with her as the main attraction, doing things to him that he'd only dreamed of in his darkest, most brutal fantasies.

The senator's body writhed with a mixture of pleasure and pain as her spell deepened.

When he climaxed, Perchta combined a magicked ovum with his sperm and sent the zygote directly into his body, where it quickly found a place to fasten against his alcohol-infused liver.

She focused while the zygote's growth accelerated, growing exponentially faster, fueled by her magic.

Leaving him asleep and snoring on the couch, she let a nurse friend, who had been prepared earlier, into the condo with a portable ultrasound device. They took photos of the growing fetal sac, making sure that the Senator's name, as well as the date and time, were clearly marked on the pictures.

Exhausted and more satisfied than she would have been from actual intercourse with a man like that, she departed, taking the memory card from the camera in his bookcase as well as all the others from a stash she found behind the shelves.

Perchta waited for news. When the Senator was admitted to the hospital, she anonymously sent the sonograms to every news outlet.

FIRST PREGNANT MAN, the headlines read. Senator Cletus Simpson, author of the state's first heartbeat bill, had been admitted to hospital with what was initially believed to be appendicitis. Abdominal sonograms, instead, showed a fetus with a heartbeat.

Surgery was scheduled, since the Senator's life was endangered by the unlikely event of an ectopic pregnancy in a man's body.

Before the Senator could be wheeled into pre-op, however, armed police arrived to arrest him, as well as his private physician, for attempting to break the Senator's own law against abortion, regardless of circumstances.

Earlier videos of his position on abortion rights surfaced, mocking the Senator's sudden change of heart once *he* was the one carrying a fetus. Simpson's former allies decried him publicly, shocked at the supposedly devout man's heartless attempt to kill an innocent baby.

The religious among them declared the babe to be a miracle child who *must* be carried to full term. The law he'd pushed through the legislative process denied him the right to remove the child from his body, making his abortion attempt a horrific flaunting of the law he had been so passionate about putting into action.

Physicians and scientists gathered to determine the best way to assure the child's life, despite the certain loss of the father's.

In the end, Senator Simpson decided to save his own life by doing what so many women among his constituency had been forced to do: flee to a neighboring state to get the necessary surgery to remove an ectopic pregnancy.

"I have no idea how this happened," Senator Simpson stated to the press as the out-of-state hospital prepped him for his life-saving surgery. "I regret my participation in creating these kinds of hurdles for women in need of medical care. If I survive, I promise to fight to rectify the wrongs I have done."

"Is that a promise?" Perchta, in her crone form and disguised as a nurse, asked of him once she'd shooed the reporters out, granting him privacy for a peaceful death.

"It is," Simpson choked, and Perchta sensed the fear and hopelessness within him, something he'd never had the empathy for in others.

Perchta laid a healing hand on his abdomen and crafted a small spell that snuffed out the presence of the magicked fetus. Then, after granting anonymous assistance to several female patients and staff, she quietly departed the hospital.

Simpson was good to his word. He immediately authored a new bill to overturn his previous legislation, replacing it with carefully worded laws that fully restored a woman's right to choose what happens with her body, giving her the autonomy that men had always taken for granted.

The new laws completely legalized a woman's right to an abortion, and he personally escorted many patients across state lines to get the healthcare they needed until the legislation was signed into law, with an emergency clause making it effective immediately.

Even after achieving higher office, he remained a faithful advocate for women all his life, striving to undo the wrongs he had committed while still oblivious of the consequences of what he had once thought proper.

Bat Scat Crazy

S.M. Macdonald

It was on a Tuesday when the controversial representative from Georgia introduced a bill more controversial than usual (even for her). The bill would end HIPPA protections in matters of pregnancy.

The representative was generally referred to her as 'controversial' rather than 'idiotic or moronic.' Lawyers can't sue over 'controversial.'

In the early days of her political career, she had been vehemently anti-Soviet. A staunch opponent to the Red Menace. After the former president adopted his signature role as the Russian premier's catamite, she became as strongly pro-Russian as she had been anti-before, however given the literacy rate in her district, it did not impact her staunch anti-socialist campaign. She had no concerns on the impact on her electability from such a bill.

With the announcement of her bill, the House of Representatives was filled with gasping and mutterings.

"Is she crazy?" asked the crazy gun toting Congressman from Colorado. Herself considering the role of congressional nut job her purview and not appreciating the competition.

"I've been wondering that for years," another representative replied in a louder than necessary stage whisper.

A representative from Washington, the state of course, as no such representation would ever be considered for a mere district, rose to his feet. "Point of Personal Privilege, Madam Speaker."

The Speaker of the House banged her gavel upon her desk. "The honorable representative from Washington is recognized and has the floor."

"Thank you, Madam Speaker," He straightened his tie just in case C Span was watching. Would Congresswoman from Georgia be kind enough to explain the reason for wanting to repeal a law that has served the people of this nation" ... he checked his cell phone ... "since 1996."

The Speaker of the House turned to face the woman who had caused all the hullabaloo. "Ma'am, would you be willing to answer the question at this time?"

The Georgian broke the first rule of politics by calmly standing, adjusting her empty shoulder holsters, and answered the question. "I propose revoking HIPAA's application to pregnant women to make it easier to enforce the anti-abortion laws. If we can't get the records, how do we keep track of pregnancies. If we can't keep track of pregnancies, how do we keep them from traveling somewhere to murder their babies." She gave the entire house a scathing look, and, before she sat down, muttered a very audible "DUH.""

The fuss and bother of five minutes ago were nothing compared to the reactions that broke out now.

The speaker, also a grandmother from California—currently the second oldest member of the House of Representatives—went to YouTube on her laptop. She e-mailed a one sentence message to the Georgia representative, along with a link to *Schoolhouse Rock's Suffering Until Suffrage.* The question was simple: 'Are you seriously advocating a separate law for men and women in the 21st century?'

A moment later, with the impulse control of a rabid chicken, the representative clicked on her e-mail. As her speakers were at max (target shooting at cutouts of Bill Clinton had made her kind of deaf), the entire house was treated to the opening bars of the '70's song about the Nineteenth Amendment. Fearing the spread of socialist propaganda, she snapped the cell phone in half. (She worked out you know.)

"Blondie" began a delegate from California, you are just bat-scat crazy."

"What's 'bat-scat crazy?" someone asked.

"It's a more polite way of saying batshit," replied the California representative.

At that point, a lone piper marched down the center aisle, playing "Hail to the Chief." He was followed by the President and two Secret Service agents.

King Charles is not allowed to enter the House of Commons. He lost that right when he ascended to the throne. But POTUS may go to the Senate, the House of Representatives, the Supreme Court, or anywhere she pleases, other than the men's restroom at the Smithsonian Museum.

The speaker noted the intrusion of the President and banged her gavel. "Can I help you Madam President?" she asked.

"Yes," said the President, and pulled out a document. "This is an executive order stating that the representative from Georgia is indeed scat," she emphasized the word, "shit crazy."

The representative from California gave the 47th president a standing ovation.

A representative from Tennessee rose to his feet. "Madam Speaker, whereas this bill is obviously well-intentioned, I move we skip the usual time-wasting discussion and debate and vote to approve it immediately.

The president shook her head. "That's not the way the system works." She raised her right hand high above her head and snapped her fingers.

Ten school children, the boys dressed as Uncle Sam, and the girls dressed as the Statue of Liberty appeared. They began swaying and dancing and then broke into *I'm Just a Bill* from *Schoolhouse Rock*. The presidential piper accompanied them.

The floor of Congress descended almost at foot and tilted to the right. Some of the children lost their balance and stopped dancing.

The president sniffed and snapped her fingers again. A tall handsome young African American male with a thin mustache and a small goatee appeared. He was wearing a khaki uniform with a patch that said National Zoo.

The president sniffed pointedly. She gestured to the Zookeeper to do the same.

He, too, took a deep whiff. "Guano," he agreed. "A lot of it.""

She read his nametag. "Thank you, Reginald." She snapped her fingers again, and Reginald disappeared to be replaced by a middle-aged man wearing khaki pants with a blue button-down shirt, clutching a rolled-up drawing. He wore a yellow hard hat over his sandy hair.

"Diagnosis, engineer?" she asked.

He opened a briefcase that hadn't been in his hand a moment ago and pulled out a neatly typed ten-page report. "The amount of bat-scat in the chamber exceeds safety limits. Congress is sinking under the weight of the guano."

"I suspected that was the case. Can you repair the damage to the building?"

"It won't be cheap," he warned her. "The easiest way will be a new election. Or we can dig out the guano, and shore up the foundations, do some rebuilding."

The President gave a smile as she looked deep into Karen Green Barrett's soul. "When it comes to getting rid of bat-scat", she said, "I know just where to start."

"You're getting too big for your britches, honey," snarled the "blonde" Georgian who immediately reeled under the slap she had never seen coming.

"It's Madam President to you," said POTUS.

The Tennessee representative spoke up. "But the bill, we must pass the bill."

Sensing a cue, the children again formed up next to the piper.

The room darkened until it resembled an immense cavern and the Speaker's gavel transformed into a gnarled staff while she grew taller and developed a lengthy beard. She pounded the floor with the staff and, with an echo to her voice, shouted "your bill shall not pass,"

The small band of school children already in the first stanza of "I'm Only a Bill" fell silent. One little girl, bolder than the rest, started singing the Jolly Green Giant jingle. The piper prudently did not play along.

"The Hippocratic Oath forbids abortions," the Congresswoman from Georgia interrupted.

"The Hippocratic Oath also requires physicians to swear by Apollo," the grandmother from California countered. "Are you a Pagan?" she asked.

Congress gasped collectively. No Pagan had ever been allowed to serve in congress.

The towering "Blonde" Congresswoman from Georgia, sensing defeat, reached into her shoulder holster for her spare bible, ensuring C-SPAN was watching, opened the bible and began scanning pages.

Only later that night, while listening to her husband laugh at Stephen Colbert, did she realize she had held the Bible upside down.

Donald sent her a thumbs up.

All Color

M. Rainbird

Sepia photos of old apartments
tell sepia stories of sepia lives

But they lived in color
our grandmothers our grandfathers

The old neighbor lady who can't hear well
The old man who sits on the stoop

Once she heard words of hate
Yes, and music also

One he stood and danced
Once he raised his fists high

Our grandmothers tore down beige curtains
and set the world on fire

Our grandfathers painted the town red
and sometimes they bled red

There is no sepia
There is no black and white

Everything is burning and bleeding
and filled with light

.

Judgment Day

L. Hogan

Nine Judges rode in around noon. At the gabbled news the smattering of day-timers pushed away tumblers of whiskey and, with a curt nod from my father—the saloon owner—I stepped out onto the porch, still carrying my broom, to watch them arrive.

No horses. Equal in pace to any of God's creatures, Judges don't need them.

Gran says they travel as swift as the gas-guzzling automobiles of old, though the only one of those I ever saw at a county fair wasn't any faster than a slow man walking.

"This town is in lock down," Chief Justice Fisher announced, her voice echoing from clapboard walls as she pinned the proclamation to the door of the church with a metal hand. "By order of the Scotus, until we complete Judgment."

Father Petherton blustered up the steps, staring at the notice as though it were a personal slight. "This here's a God-fearing—"

"You too, Alfred Sebastian Petherton. Your time will come," the Judge said, turning her back on the priest, and you could see his legs crumble as his words dried up. He staggered away from the cordon of Judges until he vanished into the sullen crowd.

It was hard not to feel singled out, even if the Judges, always in their nines, were pinning identical

275

declarations to dozens of other churches across the forty-eight States.

Father Petherton had not been our priest during the last lockdown, shipped in by a Scotus-confirmed Church of America decree when Father Kelross succumbed to the coughing sickness.

And I? I'd been too young to make sense of it. If I remembered the Judges' previous visit at all, it was mixed in with Gran's tales and the nightmares I guess all kids have.

But I was near thirteen now, two years shy of my maturity. This time around I was curious to see what the Judges did. If I had done no wrong, I had nothing to fear—so taught Mr. Cowper, in the two-room schoolhouse.

I should have listened to my Gran, who liked to point out that it wasn't whether *I* thought I'd done nothing wrong that mattered.

"We will use the church, the schoolhouse, and the five rooms-for-hire of the saloon."

I frowned; some of them were occupied. Our paying guests would have to be turfed out until the Judges left. Though with nine of them, that might not take long.

"Every citizen will be Judged. Do NOT attempt to evade justice."

We wouldn't be so foolish; the Judges were armed with the Right Hand of Judgment. Flechettes would cut down anyone trying to flee, guilt proven by their actions. A hangman's noose for more measured judgment, and an electric lash to punish minor transgressions.

"We will start with the town's oldest citizen. Who claims that position?"

"That'll be me," came the gruff reply.

I looked around in surprise. Gran's smallholding was north and out of sight of town, which was the way she liked it. She came in once or twice a week and I usually knew when, as she was on a mission to make sure my schooling was up to scratch. She'd spend an hour quizzing me on all I'd learned, scoffing at much of it, but only correcting the more egregious errors, be they mine, or Mr. Cowper's.

"Mrs. Angela Rose Fogerty—"

"It's *Barrett*, as I tell you every Judging."

"—And every Judging, Angela Rose Fogerty, we remind you that your legal name, as a widow, is that of your son-in-law. Fine: ten dollars."

"Fine," Gran snapped back, and I heard the collective intake of breath from those gathered. "Let's get on with it. I'm a busy woman."

All nine Judges—all nine of them—escorted Gran as if she was a hardened criminal into the cool, unseen dark of the church. I felt a tap on my shoulder: my father, Gran's son-in-law, Roger Fogerty.

"Shel; back to the saloon, there's work to be done. You'll be Judged late in the day, if not tomorrow."

I started to protest, I wanted to make sure Gran was okay. But what could I do, either way? Other townsfolk suffered the same quandary, some drifting away, others, of more advanced years, eyeing up shady spots. I guessed they were figuring to be next in line, no point in wandering far. All of them a decade younger than Gran. An outlier, she claimed her eighty years wasn't that special, it's just that everyone else was dying young.

The Judges had their part in that. But not as much as waves of coughing sickness and failed harvests, or even late summer nights, when whiskey flows and tempers flare and grown men, armed with rusting knives and ancient firearms, behave like spoiled children.

I was about to open the side door when it opened for me. Five Judges marched metronomically past as if I—and the dust I'd swept into a now scattered pile—didn't exist. Glued to the wall, heart thumping, I clutched the broom tight.

One of the five squeaked as they ascended the back

stairs. Step, squeak, step, squeak. I wondered who maintained them? Was that a better job than tending a saloon? If so it would surely go to a boy. Boys were taught more interesting things than us girls, or so I gathered from snatches I heard through the thin walls that separated the classrooms. Mr. Cowper split his time between us, but he sure as heck didn't split it equally.

A minute or so later I heard footsteps on the stairs, those off to be Judged. Maybe the Judges did their maintenance themselves. Maybe they carried screwdrivers and spare parts and cans of oil. I imagined them putting their feet up after a day's Judging, having another Judge tend weary limbs...

Gran appeared at the saloon door as I was wiping down tables. She looked frail, in pain, and there were angry red stripes across her forearms, already darkening to purple.

"Kiddo, a whiskey."

Gran wasn't one for liquor, except at Thanksgiving. She tottered to the nearest chair. "Kiddo?" she repeated, and I creaked into action. Father was nowhere in sight, nor anyone else for that matter. But there's no particular skill to pouring whiskey, 'cept not to spill any.

"And water," Gran demanded, as I eased the cork back into the government-labeled bottle. Let the cowpokes drink their rotgut and take the licks if caught. My father always bought legal hooch, properly taxed, even if it *was* weaker.

By the time I'd made my way toting water and whiskey, Gran was looking less frazzled. "Everything okay, Gran?"

She barked a laugh. "No, but I'll live." She downed half the tumbler in one and I waited for the inevitable splutter, but it didn't come. Made of stern stuff, our Gran.

"I was born in America," she said, apropos nothing, and I took it as an invitation to pull out a second chair with a scrape of wood on wood. "But I spent a dozen years abroad."

I'd heard hushed whispers of this, but nothing concrete. "Where, Gran?"

"Hmm?"

"Where did you live?"

"Oh, all over, Kiddo. *Canada.* Europe. A spell in Australia, even."

Mythical places. Filled by heretics and non-believers, to be sure, those who have strayed far from the one true church. But the things she must have seen!

"My family—parents and younger sister—returned when the last sections of the wall were going up. As America shut itself off, abandoning the parts that didn't fit and, behind bolted doors, began to implode."

That wasn't the way Mr. Cowper taught it. I knew the basics, the wall, which wasn't that much of a deterrent, except it was policed by forerunners of the Judges. Deadly autonomous drones that didn't care if you were coming or going. *Necessary* to protect what we still had. And, when the Presidency abdicated its responsibility to take appropriate measures, it was the Scotus that filled the void, to maintain, at all costs, the rule of law.

"The point, Kiddo, is that I was an adult, albeit a young one, at the time. I had a *choice*. I could have stayed, led a different life in a different country, following a different set of rules. Kinder rules."

"But... leaving your family?"

"Indeed. A choice then, but not much of one. I don't regret it, even on days like today. If I hadn't returned, I would never have met your grandfather. Never have had your mother, who would never have had *you*."

At that, I knew Gran was hurting. Gran rarely mentioned my mother, who I was named after, too painful, was all she'd say on the topic. She didn't blame my father for her death and that of the child that might have been a sister, or a brother. No, she blamed the cowpoke who forced himself on my mother, despite her struggles.

I might have asked what punishment *he'd* got, from the Judges, when the time came, but I knew from experience that Gran would merely say he'd got what he deserved.

A hand, whip-cord muscles hiding beneath the liver spotted, tanned skin, reached out and briefly held my softer, paler one.

"Well, I'm good for another Judgment, I guess. Tell Roger you saw me, Kiddo."

"You're off?"

"Chickens won't feed themselves." She eased gingerly to her feet. "Remember; be respectful, answer truthfully, and don't volunteer one *scrap* more than asked for."

I didn't need reminding. It was scripture drummed into me as firmly as my ABCs had once been by Mr. Cowper. Firmer, as it didn't matter what else I was being taught at the school, from bible study to domestic science, Gran's lesson was never retired.

"I'll see you Friday," she said, silhouetted by harsh sunlight at the saloon door.

I nodded, and she stepped out, and when the door swung shut it wasn't just the saloon that darkened. Though I'd not expected to see her, now that I had, I'd hoped she'd be around for my Judging. Whenever I thought about it, it gave me the *worst* butterflies.

Gran's post-judgment restorative was not the last of the day. I'd assumed we'd be empty, at least until the Judges rode out, but whiskey was what a man, or a gray-band woman like Gran, needed after their one-on-one with a Judge. No-one lingered. A slow conveyor belt of the town's residents, from the hunched bulk of the blacksmith to the pinched features of the priest, old before his time.

A whisper went round: names of those who *hadn't* stepped through the saloon door. Those who had suffered the Judge's lash. Muttered gossip—mostly nonsense, even I could tell—over *why*, talk of long held grievances settled by outside reckoning, the judged skulking off to lick their wounds and contemplate their crimes. It was lucky no-one suffered worse. Capital punishments and even floggings would be held with the town in mandated attendance, and I hadn't looked forward to *that*.

My father's judging passed without comment. He came back down the saloon stairs and went straight behind the bar to serve those I'd been making sure didn't serve themselves. He didn't say a word about it, or anything else, for a goodly while.

In the late afternoon I'd already done everything I could think to do, and more. I took a hunk of bread from the pantry, well used to fending for myself in the evenings, and traipsed up the narrow steps to the attic, hoping to get an hour's reading of my trove of hoarded books—none proscribed, naturally—before the light faded.

I must have fallen asleep. A lantern shone in my face, and my father was shaking me awake. "Shel..." he said. "Shel... wake up, Shel...?"

I groaned. I was still clothed, my shoes kicked off somewhere beneath the bed. "What's happening, Dad?"

"It's your turn, Shel."

It took a beat to realize what that meant. I blinked into the wavering light, dry throated. "What time is it?"

"Gone nine. I think they want to be done today."

I groaned again and hastened to make myself presentable, wishing for a brush, for a bowl of water, and for fresh clothes. But there was no time for any of that. Besides, it wouldn't change a blessed thing; the Judges don't judge on appearance.

I expected to be sent to one of the rooms for hire, the short journey down the stairs not even giving me time to think. But, trust my luck, I'd been allocated to a Judge in the schoolhouse, the other side of town.

The buildings were as brightly lit as the Fourth of July, light in every window and lanterns dangling on porches, all aided and abetted by a half-moon and a clear sky. A shape detached from the schoolhouse steps as I approached and my breath caught. But it was only Mr. Cowper.

"Sheila," he nodded, in greeting.

"Sir," I nodded back.

"Remember—"

"—Respect, and truth," I replied, cutting him off. He didn't smile and I didn't add Gran's third commandment—*Don't Share*—since it wasn't strictly official.

"In you go, then. Girl's classroom."

In the gloom, the room I visited three times a week (and envied the boys who got five days, and an extra two years, *and* less chores to boot), was alien territory. A jumble of desks and chairs, half-empty bookshelves leaking shadows. The lantern at the rear was for my benefit; the waiting Judge didn't need it. This one stood in front of Mr. Cowper's desk, watching my tentative approach with faintly glowing eyes, weighing me in the scales of justice.

"Sheila Anne Fogerty: Stand in the designated spot for Judgment," he instructed, when I hesitated at the edge of the clearing made by desks pushed to either side. On the floor was an arm-span circle sketched in chalk. Staring at my feet, I stepped into it, careful not to smudge the line.

The Judge's left hand gripped my wrist. I felt sensors adjust their positions, an echo of my pulse, and a sting like a mosquito as a needle sampled my blood.

The robot *froze*. I tugged at my arm, but it wasn't moving, not when held by bands of steel. Did the tests normally take this long? I felt rising panic. Was there anything I'd eaten or touched in the saloon, which might leave a chemical trace? The acrid, home-grown tobacco smoke, Gran's whiskey...

"Be still," the Judge commanded at my continued wriggling. "I am summoning colleagues."

I quailed. What had I done? A single Judge was all that was required to make Judgment. They were linked, anyway, sharing the information that we spilled, weighing up rumor and gossip and spite to arrive at the solemn truth. But a minimum of three Judges were required to enact punishment or lay down a ruling. More, with the seriousness of the crime, until all nine were involved for a capital case, a straight majority of their individual programmings enough to send a man to the gallows.

Not that the Judges needed gallows any more than they needed horses. They provided their own nooses, their tall metal bodies the scaffolding. But I'd done *nothing* wrong. Had I?

I cringed, silently sobbing, tears running down my cheeks. The Judge didn't say another word, not of comfort, nor contempt at my weakness. Did nothing, until the door opened and two more Judges entered, another male, and a female.

Cleaning the saloon even during daylight hours you heard a lot of scuttlebutt about the differences between the Scotus Judges. Some, the drinkers claimed, could be reasoned with, more or less. Others were hanging Judges.

Gran said they were *all* hanging Judges, and don't ever forget it. Their mechanical bodies were identical, but the robes and hats they wore told you the gender and identity of the real-life Scotus Judge they represented. This female Judge was Jennifer Thompson. A relatively recent appointee, not one the drinkers took bets on who might be replaced next. And not much more to tell about her.

In an intricate exchange which at no point left me free, the original Judge traded places with Judge Thompson, who then gripped my *other* wrist just as firmly, the two male Judges taking up places either side and a step further back.

"Sheila Anne Fogerty," Judge Thompson intoned, "by Scotus decree and as witnessed by Judge Pereira and Judge Morden, I hereby install you with a fertility tracker. Attempting to remove or damage the wristband is a contravention of the 2042 Fertility and Pregnancy Act, and punishable most severely."

She released my right wrist. I stared at the band encircling it like a noose as it slowly turned pink. A band only adult females wore. "But I'm not yet thirteen," I protested. "I'm a child—"

"A *woman*," Judge Thompson corrected. "Having attained her biological maturity. You've had your first period, haven't you?"

I felt the blood—the betraying blood—rush to my face. My jaw clenched, but before I could utter a word, Judge Morden interrupted.

"Perjury is a serious crime. Think carefully before you speak."

Judge Thompson's grip was still tight around my left wrist, sensors picking up heart rate, perspiration, a dozen chemical indicators of stress, of truth. Even without that, what could I do but follow Gran's repeated advice? I nodded. Stammered a yes when instructed to do so.

"Henceforth, you will be treated as an adult. That includes all laws, all amendments, which pertain to adult, fertile females. It is important, Sheila Anne Fogerty, that you know and understand these laws and amendments. Please answer clearly, for the record:

"What is your duty as a woman?"

"To repopulate America," I answered on automatic. For the first time the response, demanded of us whenever we dared complain about our chores, actually applied to *me*, and not to some future, impossible to imagine version. It was our Christian duty to be fruitful. A child was a blessing, both Mr. Cowper and Father Petherton lectured, from the very moment of conception.

"And all of your actions have to be compatible with that duty. You understand what that means?"

I nodded, and the grip became painful.

"Speak! List the primary prohibition."

"No birth control," I muttered, feeling like the damp cloth I used to wipe tables. "Chemical, or physical."

"If your tag changes from pink to blue, then you have been blessed with a child," Judge Thompson went on. "You will bear the responsibility for bringing that child healthily to term. Further restrictions will be imposed at that juncture. What are those prohibitions?"

"No alcohol. No dangerous activities. No travel."

"And?" the Judge prompted. I dredged up the memory of the final instruction, a fleeting image of Mr. Cowper, the sharp snap of the cane against the back of my calves, the word I always used to stumble over, especially when first taught it at the age of five.

"No abortifacients." And still I stumbled.

The Judge tugged my imprisoned arm, forcing me to lift my head, and I stared into eyes that weren't eyes, a face that wasn't a face. Only the voice was human, the perfect mimic of the actual Judge who sat on the Scotus, and that, somehow, made it worse.

"What abortifacients, natural or unnatural, do you know, Sheila Anne Fogerty? What substances should you avoid, be it deliberate, or accidental?"

I stared back, horrified. "I don't know!" I clamored. "I just know that you can't..." I tailed off, miserable in my failure, teachings I couldn't even recall having forgotten.

The Judge nodded her mechanical head. "As it should be. All women, from fertile age upwards, whenever Judged, are asked this question. It is best for them if they do not know the answer. If someone *does* attempt to tell you of such wicked, prohibited substances, what will you do?"

"Report them," I half-muttered.

"And?"

"Um... Ignore them?"

There was the briefest of pauses. "*Interrupt* them, is a superior option. Tell them you won't stand for such talk. And *THEN* report them. Understand?"

"Yes, your honor," I said.

Walking out of the schoolhouse, rubbing my wrist, I saw other kids my age and even younger, abroad when normally they'd be home, obeying the unofficial curfew that kept us safe. And the *look* that Emily Perkins gave, when she saw the band around my wrist—hostile, naked *envy*.

The feeling of having crossed some line into adulthood kept me buoyed only as long as it took to return to the saloon. I don't know what made me enter via the main door, instead of discretely at the side. But the hush that greeted me, the eyes that turned my way, the startled face of my father behind the bar... I was, again, the center of attention, and this wasn't envy.

Hand wrapped tight around the fertility band, I rushed between the tables, hearing my name called from behind. I clattered up the stairs, not stopping until I could push my bedroom door shut and let the dark swallow me.

The knock, when it came, was tentative. "Shel?" I wondered who was minding the bar. I wondered if, if I didn't respond, he'd go away.

He didn't. The door was pushed slowly open, the light from his lantern spilling through. Father looked almost as miserable as I felt.

"Ah, Christ, Shel you should have *told* me..." he said. He ducked his head beneath the low beams as I drew knees up to my chest. Perched on the other end of the bed, he reached out and gave the fertility tracker a tug.

I winced, I'd already rubbed my wrist raw.

"Don't try and remove it, Shel. It's on, now. Can't be undone." There was a long pause, me staring at him,

him staring at his shoes. "You'll be completing your education at your grandma's.

"What?" I gasped. Leaving home? Leaving school? "*Why?*"

"I'll let her explain. She's downstairs, waiting. Even brought a horse and trap. Gather your things, Shel. You leave tonight."

"Ah, it's not your fault," Gran said, as I sat huddled beside her, a bundle of clothes and books wedged between us. "Bad timing, is all. If the Judging had been a couple of months earlier... We'd hoped you'd be safe until you were fifteen."

"Safe?"

"Girl, it's *hunting* season. With that band around your wrist, turning red at ovulation, you're fair game for any man in town. Underage sex, consensual or not, would have been punishable by a Judge's noose. But after the age of maturity, or, drat it, the first sign of your menses, rape is only a lashing offense, and rarely prosecuted."

I'd assumed I was leaving town to get away from the Judges, hiding out on the outskirts, but Gran gave that voiced thought a withering glance. "It don't *just* track your fertility.

"I should have known my son-in-law wouldn't notice the signs. But then, I should have warned him you might keep 'em secret. Though how were either of us to know the timing would be so rotten?"

I tried hiding the banded wrist behind me, but Gran shook her head.

"'Ain't nothing to be ashamed off, that. Heck, in this day and age they celebrate it, though it's a pity they don't celebrate the woman who wears it. But kid, whatever that band says, and whatever the law might say, you're *still* a child. If you have any sense, you'll lie low and learn what you can from me for the next two years. Maybe longer."

"Farming, and washing, and sewing?" I moaned.

287

She chuckled. "And other things. Things the Judges wouldn't particularly like."

I frowned, though she couldn't see it. "You can't escape Judgment—"

"Oh, there are ways. They don't see all, and they don't know all. And there are ways of fooling even a lie detector."

A thought struck me. "You incurred that ten dollar fine deliberately, didn't you, Gran?"

"I did." I heard the smugness in her voice, like when she was playing cards and laid down a winning hand. "It's a sure-fire way to get me riled up. Puts quite the spike in my baseline! Not that you should ever deliberately lie, you understand? But sometimes you need to pick your words *very* carefully."

The bone-weary nag came to a halt, unbidden, outside Gran's barn.

"Is there *any* hope?" I asked in abject misery.

"There's always hope, kid. There are always ways to resist. Some are... stupider, than others. But sometimes, just *thinking* about them, just persisting, is a kind of resistance. Proves we're not mindless slaves. And someday, maybe sooner than you think, there's going to be a different kind of judgment."

"Like Father Petherton preaches?" I heard an echo of Gran in my scoffing. Scant relief, the Rapture. Pretty much everyone dies, even if a select few are saved.

Gran sat silent a moment. "No, Kiddo. See, I hear they've lost the ability to make new Judges. Those robotic brains are awful complicated. And Judges are tough, but they don't last forever. There's hope as long as there are still a few cantankerous old crones like me knocking around, and I aims to outlast them. Someone to remind folk of what we once took for granted. Because just knowing it was *possible* opens up a whole different world. And, if needs be, I'll pass the flame down to the next generation."

She turned, the darkness of the barn and her

homestead surrounding us, pressing down. Taking both my hands in hers, she stilled my trembling.

"And that, kiddo, for better or worse, means *you*. Best get some sleep. Lessons start bright and early tomorrow."

The Cobra Effect

W.T. Paterson

Rhonda felt immense relief as the door closed behind the couple, leaving the veterinary waiting room empty at last. They had lost Ellie, their dog, one of the most painful things that can happen to a couple short of having a child taken early. She had been a severely ill German Shepherd and had to be put down, and the cost had come as a shock. She suspected the couple lived on a fixed income; her boss had bent the rules a bit and let them make payments.

She glanced out into the July day as she began to tidy the office. Cars were moving along the road with little regard to the happenings behind the wall, and they were none the wiser for it. They did not care that an old couple with broken hearts was entering the traffic.

Rhonda placed a hand over her stomach and wondered about her own future. No more than the old couple was prepared to be alone, was she prepared to be a mother.

Not that she had a choice now.

The nation had erupted when her state restored old laws making it illegal for pregnant women to get an abortion. She thought about what was growing inside of her. Then she thought about the guy that put it there—Derek—a pierced and tattooed dropout whose sex appeal was in rebellion and counterculture. He flipped off cops, wore his pants below his crack, and openly smoked joints in public places, challenging the world to say something. If and when someone did, Derek would absolutely erupt about the hypocrisy of our "free" society.

It was fun at first, Rhonda felt alive in ways she hadn't before because Derek was the type of person all of her teachers and family members warned her about. No future, barely a past, homemade prison looking tattoos, and an affinity for vape pens, he proudly carried himself as a caricature of an anarchist. The sex, admittedly, was good in sort of a primal caveman way.

But then Rhonda graduated high school and took a job in Annette's Vet clinic, and realized veterinarian school might be a future worth pursuing, unlike Derek. She fell in love with the idea, heartbroken couples and all. Six months after starting, after finding a much-needed role model in Dr. Annette Stoller, Rhonda bought a pregnancy stick and pissed hot.

A child meant veterinary school would have to be on hold, but for how long? Ten years? Fifteen? Eighteen? To afford a child meant she would need an increase in pay, but she couldn't get an increase in pay without schooling. Maybe she could take a second job, but taking a second job meant that she would have to pay out for additional childcare, which meant she'd need a third job. And how would she pay for school? Loans were one thing, cost of living was another. The spiral was vicious and even thinking about it was a cause for intense anxiety. America was not a friendly place for young mothers who wanted more.

Rhonda couldn't count on her mother for support. The woman was a barely functioning alcoholic, scarcely able to take care of herself, let alone the needs of a newborn baby. Rhonda's father was long gone, no sense in even attempting to ask him for help, and the string of men her mother brought in weren't permanent fixtures by any measure.

Then she thought about Derek as a father and it made her physically ill. Motherhood was a commitment that she just wasn't prepared for, and what passed for her family wasn't going to be a help.

But the problems with her family were, in an odd way, the same reasons that she looked up to the Veterinarian with more than aspirations. Rhonda found Annette to be caring and compassionate, well spoken, in control, and honestly it was a turn-on. She had never fancied herself a lesbian, but there was something that moved in her blood like an uncoiling snake whenever they were alone together. It wasn't so much physical, Annette just had it together, and Rhonda wanted a piece of that success or, at the very least, an unburdened chance to pursue it for herself.

As was her custom at the end of the workday, Annette came out of her office and sat. She'd told Rhonda that it helped her to unwind a bit from the day's challenges. "It was hard today when we had to put Ellie to sleep, Rhonda. How are you doing?"

Much to her embarrassment, Rhonda burst into tears.

~~~

Annette handed her another tissue. "The dog's cancer was a kind that we couldn't have taken out earlier, even if we'd know about it. But I have a feeling that you were already upset when you came in today, even before we knew about Ellie."

Just the past week, there had been a case in the news about a doctor who had been arrested after one of his patients had an illegal abortion that he said he knew nothing about. She didn't want to get Annette in any kind of trouble, but she just had to tell someone.

"So... how do I put this," she said. Her words were slow and calculated, intentional. "I'm sort of like Ellie, but it's not cancer."

Annette was silent for a moment. "You're wondering if there might be a solution, other than what happened to Ellie, some magic 'poison bones' that might make everything all right," Annette said, scanning Rhonda with soft, knowing eyes. The scan felt like a satisfying *100*. "Even if I knew, I'd never be able to tell you because I'd become an accessory after the fact. Is that what you're worried about?"

"It's all hypothetical," Rhonda said quickly.

"Of course it is. Are you familiar with the Cobra effect?" Annette asked.

"I didn't realize we treated snakes here at the clinic."

"We do, but what I'm talking about is more of a concept. Years and years ago in India, there was a huge problem with cobras. Entire towns were overrun, people were getting bitten. It was an epidemic. The government stepped in as an attempt to control the cobra population and restore order.

"They told citizens that for every decapitated cobra head that was brought to a collection facility, they'd pay out a monetary sum. Officials believed that if people actively hunted the cobras, the cobra problem would end.

"What happened was that people chased the money and not the actual problem. Instead of going out to hunt, they bred cobras as a way to cash in on the new law. People were making out like bandits and the problem didn't go away. It actually got worse. The snake population exploded for a second time. It's the Cobra Effect, the unintended consequences of an act meant for good, but instead it leads to imminent danger."

"The lawmakers couldn't see the whole picture," Rhonda said. "They say they want to protect unborn children, but this will just make life harder for everyone."

"What I tell people who are considering the possibility of poison bones is to instead look at *getting in shape*. I have a friend, Jaycee, who owns a kickboxing gym on West 8th. Former champ on local circuits, competed a few times in Thailand. Tell her I sent you and inquire about *private lessons*."

"I'm not really into MMA or combat or anything,"

Rhonda said, doubtfully.

"It doesn't hurt to tighten up the tummy...through physical activity," Annette said slowly.

Rhonda scribbled down the address, still a touch confused if this was general advice, or doublespeak. But she didn't have any other ideas.

After Annette went back to her office, Rhonda googled the school. Positive reviews, in shape instructors, a clean space, affordable classes. At the very least it was worth checking out, and it was on the way home.

The office finally tidied, Rhonda clocked out and said a quick goodbye to Annette. She drove to the kickboxing school so that she could meet the instructor. She wondered why she didn't feel more relieved that she had a possible solution to her difficulty, why it was so hard to accept, but deep down, she also knew. Sometimes what masqueraded as love was really pain and rebellion under the guise of pleasure. More than anything, she now understood the difference between Mr. Right, and Mr. Right Now.

She pulled up to the building—a standalone center with large glass windows showing off a handful of boxing rings and heavy bags with people pounding away. A sign near the door advertised affordable private sessions in big red ink. It was still hot outside, the southern sun beating down on the world with unyielding weight.

A blast of cold AC and a smiling receptionist greeted her. The woman had impossibly straight and impossibly white teeth.

"How can we help you today?" she asked. She looked only a few years older than Rhonda. A college textbook was tucked next to the computer's white keyboard, and a purple spiral ringed notebook was sitting next to the phone.

"I work for Annette the Vet, and she mentioned that I should check this place out. Maybe get a private lesson?" The words felt oily. The back of her throat started to burn as though the contents of her stomach had decided to catch fire and creep back out.

"No problem. Let me grab the owner," the receptionist said, and picked up the phone. In less than a minute, a strong-looking woman in shiny blue kickboxing shorts, a loose tank top, and a neon black sports bra stepped out from behind the door marked Office. She had strong, muscular shoulders, sturdy quads, and a flat stomach.

"I'm Jaycee," the woman said, holding out her firm hand to shake. Although they looked completely different, Jaycee and Annette shared the same knowing, caring gaze. Strong eyes, compassionate focus, and a flair for pageantry. With all of the thuds and groans echoing through the space, it was like Jaycee had been custom made for the setting.

"I'm Rhonda." The name came out as almost a squeak.

"You're Annette's girl," Jaycee said, a knowing smile spreading her thin lips. "She talks about you all the time. I get it now."

"I don't follow," Rhonda said.

"Yeah you do," Jaycee winked, and led her back toward the active part of the gym. Behind them, a man in compression shorts and no shirt launched a thunderous shin kick into the hanging heavy bags, which shook the steel posts of the frame.

Rhonda felt her blood start to tingle with anxiety. Maybe it was a bad idea to come here. Maybe she hadn't considered the alternatives.

Or maybe she had, which was why she was there.

"Our receptionist mentioned you were interested in a private lesson," Jaycee said.

"Annette said it would be a good way to uh... to tighten my tummy." Her skin went cold when she said it. What if she'd massively misinterpreted the signals and was unwittingly signing up for an hour of push-ups and burpees? For conversations about meal prep and routine? For a lecture about lifestyle changes?

What if she wasn't?

"Sure. Private lessons with me cost $40, but we need you to sign a waiver to absolve the gym of responsibility should you incur any injury. And you have health insurance?"

"I do."

"Great. Then you'll be all set."

Jaycee put her arm around Rhonda and showed her around the gym explaining that their style of kickboxing was based in Muay Thai. They used their shins like baseball bats and elbows like sharp hammers. It sounded like a brutal form of self-defense.

"I've never really had to punch or kick anything before," Rhonda said.

"That's ok. Our teaching style during private lessons is *take one to give one*. It helps contextualize the impact. We have a spot open now if you'd like. We try not to schedule anything beyond a day or two because most people find reasons to talk themselves out of it instead of holding firm and committing."

"Ok," she said, knowing that would be true in her own case. Relief breathed onto her shoulders like the crisp AC. Decision made. "I'll do it."

Jaycee led Rhonda back to the front desk where she filled out a bunch of paperwork and signed her name to the big familiar X's. Hearing the thump of people hitting the bags, the way the floor shook with each collision, she wondered if it would hurt.

Of course it's going to hurt, she told herself.

She paid the $40 in cash, which meant no proper dinners for the next week, and changed into the white practice outfit they provided. Then she followed Jaycee to a back room. A separate space away from the main training area with no windows and a thick red wrestling mat on the floor, it smelled like stale sweat and burnt rubber from old weight machines. Parallel bars, just wider than shoulder width, went from floor to ceiling by the edge of the mat.

Jaycee closed the door tight and walked up to Rhonda. She put her hands on the sides of the young girl's face and leaned in so that they were touching foreheads.

"Remember that you're young and strong, and you have your whole life ahead of you. Promise me that you won't give up hope."

"I promise," Rhonda said, blinking her eyes and feeling them well with water. "Is this going to hurt?"

"Clench your stomach as hard as you can and squat your legs. Keep your back straight. Hold these bars. I'll be fast."

Jaycee kissed Rhonda softly on the forehead and stepped back. She swung her legs in large arcs to loosen the muscles, bouncing from foot to foot, and threw some shadow punches at the air hissing with each strike. Then she looked at Rhonda who was clenching the vertical bars, tears pouring down her cheeks.

"I wish it didn't have to come to this. Close your eyes," Jaycee said, and then stepped forward delivering a massive shin kick to Rhonda's clenched stomach. The thud, mixed with Rhonda's scream, bounced around the room for a moment before dying in the soundproof panels near the ceiling.

Rhonda's insides felt like they had exploded, and she wasn't sure if she had blacked out. The pain was tremendous. Her vision pinched everything into a small tunnel, and her tongue became unbearably dry. Anything beyond that felt like a mystery. All that she knew was that when her wits came back, she was on the mat, Jaycee cradling her head and pouring small sips of cold water from a plastic cup into her mouth.

"Wh... wh... what happened?" she asked, weakly.

"You're a champ. But you're bleeding," Jaycee said, and Rhonda understood. "You just rest here for a few minutes, then we'll get you to the hospital."

Jaycee had the receptionist drive Rhonda to the ER.

"No, I don't mind giving you a lift. Pick up your car when you feel ready," she said, her impossibly perfect mouth forming each word with pinpoint accuracy. Rhonda mouthed *thank you* and hobbled towards the intake desk as the giant glass doors closed behind her.

"I'm bleeding," she told the receptionist, and signed her name to another set of X's while waiting for a nurse to call her name under the unflattering fluorescent lights of the hospital wing.

Eventually she was led to a private room while a few nurses scrambled to do X-Rays and blood tests to figure out what exactly had happened.

"Kickboxing," Rhonda told them, and the nurses looked at each other with hard eyes. They gave her some pills to take the edge off the agonizing pain in her pelvis.

When the doctor came in, he sat across from her and spoke in direct, unwelcoming tones.

"I'm afraid I have some bad news. The reason you're bleeding is because you were pregnant, but you've since miscarried. The trauma of the impact...I'm sorry."

"Oh," Rhonda said, and tried to will herself to cry. It was easier than she had planned and came too naturally. "I didn't know."

"We may need to keep you here under observation just to make sure you don't start to hemorrhage. If this injury occurred while kickboxing, you may have a lawsuit against them if you choose to pursue."

"Can't," Rhonda said. "Signed a waiver."

"Well they should really make women take pregnancy tests before signing up for anything high impact. Between you and me, you're not the first to end up like this."

"When you remove safe means, people don't just stop. They resort to unsafe means," Rhonda said, the pills working into her blood like snakes into the earth. "It's the Cobra Effect."

Lady Lampshade

D.J.W. Munro

I weep at night when I take off my tent and walk naked in my apartment behind my three locks. Sometimes, the guards conduct inspections, but they never just come in. I have time to put on my veil and robe and to hide the manuscript I'm writing under my floorboards.

It's funny.

The story of the denigration of our rights is so like the hundreds of fictions by women writers with dystopian fears from before everything got turned upside down–the fictions we used to teach as cautionary tales have now come true. Since they've become non-fiction, those books are banned from common use. Back when the wind was on my face and I lived where I wanted rather than this assigned apartment for fatherless, unmarried women, I'd read them all. Back then, I taught classes where we analyzed the critiques of the patriarchy in books where women wore red or were driven mad by wallpaper. Now, those books guide our leaders in tactics and stratagem. Our cautionary tales are made over into the bright lights the Ship of State set its course by.

"Let us in, Cass Smith," Joseph the guard says as he pounds on the door. We knew each other from before.

301

He used to be a custodian at the college. I remember him complaining about my Women's Studies students to the dean. About how rude and uppity the women were. I'd gotten him removed from my hallway. I'd told him to stop bothering my students in a voice full of indignant daggers. Now he had the power of life and death over me.

"Yes, sir." I unlock the door once everything is secure under the floor, and my body is covered.

He leads his band of goons on room checks almost every day. Most of the other spinster women in the building are only checked weekly. I bow my head and stand aside. He's hit me more than once when I moved too slowly, or I questioned the familiarity of them searching through my underthings.

I must be careful or...

"I'm going to catch you and then I'll let you have it," he mutters so I can hear. He curls his white-knuckled fist around his billy club and presses it hard against his leg as if he were holding it back from attacking. "I'll tear this fucking room apart if you make one mistake. Just one."

How did we let this happen?

It started with the reversal of Roe, then the Menanist movement took hold, and there were prosecutions for traveling to get birth control. Soon, executions for abortions dominated the newsfeed. The purge of women from all levels of leadership and strict rules about dress, occupation, and ownership of private property followed. We fought it. Complained. Wrote. Allies secreted women over state lines to get services and protections before the revolution erased those boundaries and created one big state. The loudest of us disappeared. Some, like me, were "reeducated."

"Pay attention to us, Cass Smith, or we'll make you sorry." Joseph brought me back to the moment with a spray of spittle on my cheek.

I nod once and drop to a knee in supplication, vigilantly watching them tear my room apart. So many of my cohorts are dead, hanging from trees or thrown into piles in front of the college. So many of my students, broken with me in the camps. Their faces swim up in my memory as I squeeze my eyes shut. Joseph uses the club to stroke my cheek, and I wonder how long I have.

How long do I want to have?

I still have nightmares about endless loops of government-mandated shows that fed me my role. I'm lucky they found a use for me: an example of what happens to women educated beyond their capacity and God-given calling.

I mop the floors of the museum.

At the museum, I'm allowed to wear a less restrictive uniform that swaths my body in fabric but allows me to move with my broom and mop. Though it's all browns and blacks, the shape reminds me of the Suffragettes' clothes right before the fashions of the 1920s took hold, back in the history we don't talk about anymore.

Puffy sleeves, fitted bodice with a high starched neck, hooped skirt that brushes the ankles of the knee-high boots that pinch my toes, and on my head I wear a flared cone that straps snugly beneath my chin. It looks just like a lampshade.

I am only supposed to wear it at the museum while cleaning, but it is so liberating. The freedom of movement it affords. Sweet breaths of fresh air and true sound that carries under the lip of my head gear makes me feel lucky to work in what those in charge thought would be a demeaning job, cleaning in their false history temple. Instead, it gives me access.

I've seen what they've done with the artifacts of Before. Mass burnings of mini-skirts and feminist tomes. More than one woman's degree was used as tinder at the museum's cullings. Nude oils and sculpture are draped for the after-hours visits of men for brandy and conversation, while their wives are safely tucked back at home under lock and key. Now what's left in the halls of the museum?

A history of invisible women.

I stole pages before the books were burned. Hidden inside the tent I wore home, I'd secreted vibrant fabrics and pieces of historical garb. Thread and needles were freely available in my apartment house, and no one questions a spinster woman sewing to pass her time. Even Joseph couldn't fault me for doing "women's work."

That's when I built Lady Lampshade.

~~~

The whispers in the grocery store grew over the next few weeks.

"Lady Lampshade gave me a book..."

"She snuck me an old radio that picks up Free Mexico and the Canadian provinces."

"...watercolors and paper..."

I heard their wishes and tried to find things in the old warehouse level of the museum. I brought out trinkets to cheer women, pencils and chalks, poem fragments, and old pictures of what women used to be.

"Lady Lampshade, Bringer of Light" was chalked on

the city wall with a powdery mural of flowers and books and a likeness of me that the guards sprayed off before the morning Women's Shopping Hour. The streaked rainbow of color ran through the lines in the grey bricks, bright as a rainbow, and the women knew what the guards had tried to wash away. Every woman who saw it knew that one of them had risked putting the message of freedom out in the world.

Women began passing encrypted notes at the shopping market, which continued even when public beatings were the result. Guards searched rooms and only found the quilts the women stitched with embedded directions.

Women started to disappear, and no amount of patrolling or threats revealed a path of escape that women might take. But I knew because I was one of those spreading the clues. I felt like I walked in the footsteps of women scrubbed from history–spies, escapees, soldiers.

At night, I used a bobbing light to draw them.

I'd found the plans to the storm sewers and turned them into a stitched pattern on handkerchiefs I shared with shopping partners and left in women's areas— nurseries, washrooms, and waiting areas designated for women only. Women taught each other to read the stitches and created a language to talk about what they'd lost, to talk to me about what they needed, and to tell me when they'd be following my bobbing light.

I collect them every other night or so, ushering them through the dark drains and concrete highways that run under hills and past the walls. When we get out of the city, I set them up in an abandoned Walmart we turned into a hub in the railroad. Those women mapped the world beyond.

Soon, Lady Lampshades popped up in every city doing the work of women. The stitched messages found me each week. Even though we had so many saved, so many little rebellions, the work cost so much. Lady Lampshades hung from trees and bell towers, exposed boots tapping together hollowly in the wind. Still, new Lady Lampshades spread across the expanse of what used to be the home of the free. I flushed every hanky, but the messages made me proud.

~~~

After a long shift at the museum, I report home for the night's check in. I stand at my door with Joseph as usual, keeping my eyes downcast as the others riffle through my closet, my drawers, and my bedsheets, though they seem less thorough than normal.

Usually, Joseph has some nasty curse or mumbled insult for me as the others do their work.

Nothing.

He stands silent and... relaxed.

Maybe he's accepted my facade of carved ivory acceptance and marble obedience. He doesn't say a word as they search and are surprisingly gentle with my things. Something is wrong, but I can't put my finger on it. His smirk or the sloppiness of the others? Maybe there's a new mandate?

"Have a good night, Cass," Joseph says as he pulls shut the door.

I lock all three locks and sit on the bed puzzling out what might be the source of his kindness. I spend a precious hour there waiting for the other shoe to drop. I can't wait longer than that.

I pull the boots and underskirts out of the panel at

the back of my closet. The dress itself I'd hidden in the lining of my mattress using Velcro I'd taken from computer cord wraps. The lampshade is... gone. I'd shoved it into the ductwork and screwed the cover over it tight, but it is not where I'd tucked it. Whoever'd found it had only halfway screwed the grate back on to the wall.

Fuuuuuuu–

He knocks on the door. Subdued. Gentle.

"Minister Gerry's here, traitor bitch. Open this damned door," he says calmly.

There are women waiting for Lady Lampshade to take them to safety. They'd crawled through their own ducts and down the rusted-out fire escapes. They'd snuck away with children leaving their husbands sleeping peacefully. They wait by the drain, covered in browns and blacks and tears, for a heroine.

Lampshade or no...

The banging on the door turns into a splintering. A cracking.

I'd given the map to others who'd memorized it and passed it along. Lady Lampshades would never give up to the beasts outside her door. Someone would find the women waiting. Another Lady Lampshade would step up.

"Let us in. You're only making it worse," Joseph yells now, though he sounded giddy. "We've got your fucking lampshade. You're done, dead to rights."

I think about putting on the dress, but I decide not to. Instead, I peel off my shift and stand as naked as I'd been born, skin kissed by moon and the breath of night. I open the window as much as I can, just four inches. Not enough to fit. I grab my chair and swing it through the window, creating a shimmering shower of glass that tumbles to the concrete below in a twinkling waterfall.

How would they see me? Would they know or would I be washed away like the chalk murals, no vivid rainbow river to announce I'd ever been. Maybe a velvety red ribbon tied around some lamppost to mark my passing.

I crouch in the windowsill as the door crashes open.

I scream the way women used to, full throated and unafraid. I howl as they push through, reaching for me. They'll hang me or beat me and then hang me.

I won't let them.

As naked as though being born again, pushing through the snaggled glass vulva of a window, I leap out into the void, hair flying, eyes wide and teeth bared.

I laugh, knowing the other women would hear even if they can't see what I'd done. I fling myself out and I am free. You can't hang an idea. You can't arrest us all.

Lampshade or not, we will find freedom.

Wading in the Rowe

E.P. Kennedy

he's had too much
but she serves the glass up
a maid in a Gilead bar

unlocking the car later
she smells the beer on his breath
as he grabs her and holds her down

now the lawyers argue
statute and precedent
of the medieval law
that guides her medical care

she wades
and rows
her swollen boat body to a butcher
in a back side street
on a bitter table
misery sends rage to play in the water
as her fluids drain out
fearing the final flow

where in her body does she feel the Good News?

The Audacity of Hopeful Women

D. Tewogbade

I waited with bated breath, hoping with every fibre in me that this nightmare (yes, I consider it a nightmare) would be over and the United States with the whole world at large would wake up from it.

But Alas! Almost fifty years of federal abortion rights vanished in a twinkle of an eye!

I could not believe it.

I still do not believe it.

For someone born, bred and residing in a third world country, I have always seen the United States as the land of the free, I have been idealistic and starry-eyed I guess. When my shock dissipated at the announcement of Roe v. Wade getting overturned, the fear started creeping in because I knew I did not have to reside in the United States for the decision to affect me. I am a woman after all; and patriarchy/misogyny is universal and does not care that I am so far away from the United States, the tentacles of the religious conservatism in the United States will eventually reach me in my own country.

Nigeria has always had one of the strictest laws on abortion rights in the world, making no provisions for abortions—EVEN in cases of rape and incest. I understand this, both as a poor woman (emphasis on POOR because at this point, the rich are not affected) and as an abortion rights activist.

I know that it's only a matter of time before the

311

already non-existing body-autonomy rights for women in Nigeria get even more smeared into the ground, so much so that we might lose the very concept that body-autonomy rights ever existed in the first place.

This overturn of Roe v. Wade is a universally recognizable attack on rights that unite women all over the world with no regard to their race and colour, sexuality and gender identity.

The question now is *what next?*

What do we do?

Do we cower and hide in a corner and talk in codes on the social media over *our own* bodies?

Or do we fiercely fight back?

I say we fight back!

"Gilead" is creeping up on us all and if we don't fight back, things will only get worse!

Next, they will come for LGBTQIA+ rights, the body-autonomy right to wear what we want, the right to use contraception, and even the right to choose when to have sex.

I do not exaggerate. *The Handmaid's Tale,* Margaret Atwood's predictions are scientific and those predictions have started coming to pass!

It will only get worse if we do not fight back! This is not the time to hide, to wait, to be meek. It is YOUR body. Talk OPENLY about abortion. About the rights of women.

Be angry! Be assertive. Read Mona Eltahawy's *The Seven Necessary Sins for Women and Girls.* Find your anger and express it.

In Nigeria abortion is considered a felony. We've never truly had body-autonomy rights to begin with, let alone have them overturned, so it has been really tough for women in Nigeria. But I did not hide. Not only did I have abortions, I wrote about them as a book. I released the book and dared the Nigerian Government to arrest me. Obviously, I am still free.

I believe that it is time for women all over the world

to take their rights back from some people somewhere who would use laws to oppress. It is time to make the law over our bodies very useless. Don't get me wrong, laws are useful in maintaining social structures, but when it comes to women's personal bodies, the law can go fuck itself. Nobody has any right whatsoever to decide what is "legal" or "illegal" over my own body.

It is absolutely NOT safe to wait on the "law" to give us body-autonomy rights as these rights can be taken away anytime just as with Roe v. Wade getting overturned. That is too much power these lawmakers, mostly men, have over our bodies, and it's time to take it back!

Without reverence to the law, the law is basically useless. I repeat, without *our* respect to the law, the law is basically useless! The law needs our consent to be useful in caging us, I tell you.

And if all women all over the world rally and make the law useless, how many women would they arrest? All of us? Is that possible?

I will finish this piece with a quote from Rosa Luxemburg:

"In all of our endeavours, we must exhibit the same determination, courage and ruthlessness mustered by the bourgeois revolutionaries which Georges Danton summed up in three words when he said that in certain situations, one needs only *three* words as a rallying cry: *audacity! more audacity! always audacity!*"

Now the question is where is *your* audacity?

.

About the Authors

A. Alexander—Alma Alexander is an Internationally published novelist and short story writer. She lives in the Pacific Northwest with an increasingly dyspeptic elderly cat. Although a writer of (occasionally lengthy) prose, she has always resorted to poetry for the deepest and most honest communication of truth and power.

K.G. Anderson—K.G. Anderson is a late-blooming speculative fiction writer, having spent most of her career as a journalist. She writes fiction as if it were fact and believes that, somewhere, on another timeline, it is. You'll find a list of her published short stories at writerway.com/fiction.

D.B. Baldwin—D. Brent Baldwin is originally from the tree-swept hills of the Missouri Ozarks. Brent lives in London with his wife, two daughters, and pet menagerie. His work has previously been published by *Nature Magazine*, *Fireside Fiction*, and *Analog*, among others. You can find him online at www.dbbaldwin.com and on Twitter at @dbrentbaldwin.

M.S. Barr—Dr. Marleen S. Barr is known for her pioneering work in feminist science fiction. She has won the Science Fiction Research Association Pilgrim Award for lifetime achievement in science fiction criticism. Barr is the author of *Alien to Femininity: Speculative Fiction and Feminist Theory*, *Lost in Space: Probing Feminist*

Science Fiction and Beyond, Feminist Fabulation: Space/Postmodern Fiction, and *Genre Fission: A New Discourse Practice for Cultural Studies.* Barr has edited many critical anthologies and co-edited the science fiction issue of *PMLA.* She is the author of the novels *Oy Pioneer!* and *Oy Feminist Planets: A Fake Memoir.* Her *When Trump Changed: The Feminist Science Fiction Justice League Quashes the Orange Outrage Pussy Grabber* is the first single-authored Trump short story collection. It is followed by *This Former President: Science Fiction as Retrospective Retrorocket Jettisons Trumpism.*

M. Belanger— M. Belanger is the author of over thirty books of fiction and non-fiction, including the *Dictionary of Demons,* recently released in a tenth anniversary edition. A two-time winner of the Joseph Cotter Memorial Poetry Award, Belanger has worked with Osbourne Media, Marvel AR, Wizards of the Coast, and Nox Arcana.

H. Brown—H. Brown is a long-time clinic escort organizer who dedicates much time and effort in making visits safer and more comfortable for all patients.

S. Bryant—Samantha Bryant is best known for her *Menopausal Superhero* series of novels through Falstaff Books—well, that and her banana bread.

Her stories mostly feature complicated women defying expectations. Check out her full catalog at http://bit.ly/SamanthaBryant or find her wasting time on Twitter and Instagram @samanthabwriter. If all else fails, check the woods. She likes to get lost there.

J.P. Burnham—Jason P. Burnham gratefully spends his time with his wife, children, and dog. Find him on Twitter at @AndGalen.

M. Candelaria—M. Candelaria's work has previously been published in *Daily Science Fiction, Everyday Fiction, Nothing Without Us Too*, and other venues. They find reality's tendency to steal their horror story ideas annoying.

C. Carmichael—Connie Carmichael is a poet living in Columbus, Ohio. She has been published in *Writers and Readers Magazine, Dyst Literary Journal, From The Waist Down: the body in healthcare, The Open Arms*, and *Better Than Starbucks*.

A-T Castro—Adam-Troy Castro is a science fiction, fantasy, and horror writer living Florida.

He has more than one hundred stories to his credit and has been nominated for numerous awards, including the Hugo, Nebula, and Stoker. These stories include four Spider-Man novels, including the Sinister Six trilogy, and stories involving characters of Andrea Cort, Ernst Vossoff, and Karl Nimmitz. Castro is also known for his Gustav Gloom series of middle-school novels and has also authored a reference book on *The Amazing Race*.

R. Dawson—Robert Dawson teaches mathematics at a Nova Scotian university. His work has appeared in *Nature Futures, Tesseracts 20,* and *Year's Best Military and Adventure SF*. He believes that the world needs more bicycles.

J. Dorr—Indiana writer James Dorr's *The Tears of Isis* was a 2013 Bram Stoker Award finalist for Fiction Collection, with his latest book, *Tombs: A Chronicle of the Latter-Day Times of Earth*, a novel-in-stories from Elder Signs Press. A short fiction writer and sometime poet, he currently harbors a Goth cat named Triana, and counts among his major influences Ray Bradbury, Edgar Allan Poe, Allen Ginsberg, and Bertolt Brecht.

T. Easton—Tom Easton has been publishing science fiction and fantasy since the 1970s and spent 30 years as Analog's book columnist. Latest novel: *The Last Masters* (Wildside, 2022)

Latest nonfiction book: *Destinies: Issues to Shape Our Future* (B Cubed Press, 2020)

J. Ganshaw—John Ganshaw, At the age of 53, retired to follow his dream of owning a hotel in Southeast Asia. This led to many new experiences enabling John to see the world through a different lens, leading him to write his story through essays, poetry, and a yet-unpublished memoir. John's essays and poetry have been published by *Native Skin, Run Amok Books/Growlery, OpenDoor Magazine, Open Minds Quarterly*, and more. There is hope, truth, and adventure in life, all leading to stories that need to be written and told.

D.L. Godfrey—Debora Godfrey was published in several *Alternative* anthologies, and co-edited the best-selling *Alternative Apocalypse* and *Alternative War*. She recently exchanged life in a cohousing community for an existence with a husband, a dog, several grumpy hummingbirds, and a usually even-tempered lawyer, not to mention a multitude of tiny frogs and a googly-eyed vacuum cleaner named Vinny.

P. Hammond—Paula Hammond is a professional writer and digital artist. Her fiction has been nominated for the Pushcart Prize and a British Science Fiction Association award. If you should spot her in the pub, she'll be the one in the corner mumbling *Ghostbusters* quotes and waiting for the transporter to lock on to her signal. She'd be delighted if you shared pictures of puppies with her on Twitter: @writer_paula

L.K. Hardie—Linda Kay Hardie writes short stories, poetry, and fiction for adults and children, and her writing has won awards dating back to the fifth grade. She also writes recipes and is the reigning Spam champion for Nevada (yes, the tasty treat canned mystery meat). Linda has a master's degree in English from University of Nevada, Reno, where she teaches required courses to unwilling students.

K. Herrmann—Kathleen Herrmann is called by life's unexpected happenings, expressing personal discovery in poetry and song. She has published her work in numerous anthologies and is currently writing a poetry book entitled *I Was There, Now I'm Here: Refugees In America.*

L. Hodges—Larry Hodges has over 130 short story sales and four SF novels. He's a member of

Codexwriters, a graduate of the Odyssey and Taos Toolbox writers' workshops, and a ping-pong aficionado. As a professional writer, he has 17 books and over 2100 published articles in 170+ different publications. Visit him at www.larryhodges.com.

L.J. Hogan—Liam Hogan is an award-winning short story writer, with stories in Best of British Science Fiction 2016 & 2019, and Best of British Fantasy 2018 (NewCon Press). He's been published by Analog, Daily Science Fiction, and Flame Tree Press, among others. He helps host Liars' League London, volunteers at the creative writing charity Ministry of Stories, and lives and avoids work in London. More details at http://happyendingnotguaranteed.blogspot.co.uk

Jane—"Jane" is a retired Family Nurse Practitioner and educator who has spent her career teaching, researching and practicing women's health. She currently volunteers and advocates for everyone's right to safe health care.

A. MayClair—Amanda MayClair is fascinated by Earth's past as well as deeply concerned about its, and our, future. In that spirit, she earned a Master's degree in Biology with a minor in Anthropology, and currently works in medical technology support. Her first foray into writing was in kindergarten, where she reworked the tale of the 'Three Billy Goats Gruff' as a poem, and has been exploring the realities of science and weaving those into the possibilities inherent in fiction ever since.

E.P. Kennedy— Eileen P. Kennedy is a binational author of two collections of poetry: *Banshees* (Flutter Press, 2015), which was nominated for a Pushcart Prize and won Second Prize in Poetry from the Wordwrite Book Awards, and *Touch My Head Softly* (Finishing Line Press, 2021) which was a finalist in the International Book Awards in General Poetry. She lives, reads and writes in Amherst, MA with the ghost of Emily Dickinson. More at EileenPKennedy.com.

E.M. Killian—Elé Killian is a Metís woman of French-Canadian descent, raised in Eastern Washington and currently residing in Portland, Oregon. She is a lifelong student of communications with a deep appreciation and respect for the power that resides in the art of storytelling. Her contribution to this anthology is the first time she has ever been published.

L.A. Kurth—Lita Kurth has an MFA from the Rainier Writers Workshop, has been published in three genres, and her works have been nominated for Pushcart Prizes and Best of the Net Awards. She co-founded a literary reading series in San Jose, The Flash Fiction Forum. https://LitaKurth.com.

R.M. Kyle—Rebecca lives between the Smoky and Cumberland mountains with her husband of 40-plus years and three cats. She's a retired researcher whose fields of research include everything from medicine to chicken-waste recycling.

A.J. Lucas—Andrew J Lucas has been writing poetry, short stories and tabletop RPG adventures since the late 80s. He is mortified to have just realized that his first published poem is almost 40 years old, but gratified that he has since had a few dozen published credits. He is especially fond of the handful of politically themed stories published since 2016 (a galvanizing year). Of these, *High Steel* in B Cubed's Space Force anthology takes the lead. He has also self-published *Fractal Visions*, a two-volume collection of short fiction.

S.M. Macdonald—Susan Murrle Macdonald is a stroke survivor. She has had two strokes and is engaged in an experiment to prove minor brain damage is not a hindrance to a speculative fiction author. Prior to her first stroke she was a substitute teacher. She lives in western Tennessee with her husband and two children. She is lady-in-waiting to a black cat. She has published about two dozen short stories, mostly fantasy, but also some science fiction and Westerns. This is her fourth time to appear in a B Cubed Press book.

J.A. McColley—John A. McColley writes from his cave in the woods of New England. He's a member of the SFWA, serializes Scifi and Fantasy novels: https://www.patreon.com/JohnAMcColley on Patreon and spends too much time on Twitter: @JohnAMcColley and TikTok: @johnmccolley631.

J. Mierisch—Jen Mierisch's dream job is to write *Twilight Zone* episodes, but until then, she's a website administrator by day and a writer of odd stories by night. Jen's work can be found in the *Arcanist, NoSleep Podcast, Scare Street*, and numerous anthologies. Jen can be found haunting her local library near Chicago. Read more at www.jenmierisch.com and connect on Twitter @JenMierisch.

L. Milton—Louise Milton is a writer, social worker, retired health care administrator, mother of four grown daughters, and a wife with a wife. She lives contentedly in a barn-like country home in northern British Columbia with her wife and two cats, including the fierce and semi-feral Samuel Levi who guards the household against the visiting bears. Many times she has thought that this home has been waiting for her all her life and now that she has arrived she can be at peace.

D.J.W. Munro—Donna J. W. Munro teaches high schoolers the slippery truths of government and history at her day job. Her students are her greatest inspiration. She lives with five cats, a fur-covered husband, and an encyclopedia son. Her daughter is off saving the world. Writing is Donna's painful passion. Her pieces are published in *Corvid Queen, Enter the Apocalypse* (2017), *Beautiful Lies, Painful Truths II* (2018), *It Calls from the Forest* (2020), *Borderlands Vol 7* (2020), *Pseudopod 752* (2021), and many more. Check out her novel, *Revelation: Poppet Cycle Book 1*, and her website for a complete list of works at https://www.donnajwmunro.com/.

W.T. Paterson—W.T. Paterson is a four-time Pushcart Prize nominee, holds an MFA in Fiction Writing from the University of New Hampshire, and is a graduate of Second City Chicago. His work has appeared in over 90 publications worldwide including *The Saturday Evening Post, The Forge Literary Magazine, The Dalhousie Review, Brilliant Flash Fiction,* and *Fresh Ink*. A semi-finalist in the Aura Estra short story contest, his work has also received notable accolades from Lycan Valley, North 2 South Press, and Lumberloft. He spends most nights yelling for his cat to "Get down from there!" Visit his website at www.wtpaterson.com.

M. Rainbird—Mir Rainbird is composed primarily of words. Mir's other hobbies include arguing with cats and being bad at art. Read more of Mir's stories in *Cosmic Horror Monthly* and *Alternative Holidays*, or follow mir_rainy on Instagram.

N.M. Rechtman—Nancy Machlis Rechtman has had poetry and short stories published in *Your Daily Poem, The Whisky Blot, Grande Dame, Impspired, Trouvaille Review, Fresh Words, The Writing Disorder, Discretionary Love*, and more. She wrote freelance lifestyle stories for a local newspaper, and she was the copy editor for another paper. She writes a blog called Inanities at https://nancywriteon.wordpress.com.

E.A. Scarborough—Elizabeth Ann. Scarborough distinctly recalls fighting the battle over this issue before and is irritated that the fight does not seem to have stayed won. Scarborough decided long ago to have cats and books instead of boys and girls, and lives with same. She is also a longtime and devoted fan of folk music, in which songs tell one side of a story. (Preferred pronouns she/her) decided to address a different side of a well-known song about a well-known situation for this anthology.

M. Shepherd—Mara Shepherd is an exhausted woman who likes tea, hiking, and bodily anatomy. She mainly writes speculative and science fiction. You can find out more at her website: marashepherd16.wixsite.com/mara. If you are in need of resources at any stage of pregnancy, you can find them at her friend's website: www.icantaffordababy.org.

L. Short—Lisa Short is a Texas-born, Kansas-bred writer of fantasy, science fiction, and horror. She has an honorable discharge from the United States Army, a degree in chemical engineering, and twenty years' experience as a professional engineer. Lisa currently lives in Maryland with her husband, youngest child, father-in-law and cats. A full listing of her work can be found at lisashortauthor.com

A. Sweet—Andrew Sweet writes dystopian science fiction novels. He is currently working on the *Virtual Wars* series, where the lines between reality and virtual reality thin to almost breaking. Adamant about rights and civic engagement, Andrew also dedicates much of his time to his weekly *Right and Freedom* podcast hosted at https://www.rightandfreedom.com.

P.B. Tacy— **Peter B. Tacy** is a retired educator. He lives in Mystic, CT. Peter and his wife Jane Yolen were pals (and fellow poets) when they were in college in the 1950's. Later both were widowed after long marriages. They re-united in 2019.

D. Tewogbade—**Dasola Tewogbade**, popularly known as Sisi Afrika, is from Nigeria. She is an intersectional feminist activist, a professional writer, a socialist and a Narrative Therapist.

J. Thompson—Jenny Thompson is an IT analyst based in Pittsburgh. You can find more of her work in *Strange Horizons*, *Star*Line*, and *Scifaikuest*.

P.E. Thompson—Purmelia E. Thompson lives across the street from a feed lot in Hill City, Kansas where she swat's flies and writes, both with great enthusiasm.

S.L. Weippert—Stephanie Weippert writes because of a slug. Ages ago, a sci-fi convention sent out an anthology call and since their mascot was a slug, they wanted slug stories. The idea tickled Stephanie's funny bone, so she wrote her very first story and submitted it. Of course it got rejected, but the writing bug bit and with her hubby's enthusiastic support she's been writing ever since.

J. Wright—Jim Wright is a retired US Navy Chief Warrant Officer and freelance writer. He lives in Florida where he watches American politics in a perpetual state of amused disgust. He's been called the Tool of Satan, but he prefers the title Satan's Designated Driver. He is the mind behind Stonekettle Station (www.stonekettle.com). You can email him at jim@stonekettle.com. You can follow him on Twitter @stonekettle or you can join the boisterous bunch he hosts on Facebook at Facebook/Stonekettle. Remember to bring brownies and mind the white cat, he bites. Hard.

J. Yolen—Jane Yolen has published over 400 books (413 I believe is the current number) and has her eyes on the big 5-0-0. Along the way she's won 2 Nebulas, 3 World Fantasy Awards, The Skylark Award, and a Caldecott Medal for her book OWL MOON. At age 80, she was in a band. She was the first woman to give the Andrew Lang Lecture at the University of St Andrews, Scotland, a lecture series that began in the 1920's and included talks by both John Buchan and J.R.R. Tolkien among others. She is a SFWA Grand Master, SFPA Grand Master, and a Grand Master of World Fantasy. At 82, and a widow, she married Peter B. Tacy, one of her college boyfriends.

About the Editors

This book exists in this form because of the uniqueness of the editorial team.

Every editor made their own unique contributions that shaped this book. It would have been a different book with any other combination of editors.

Debora Godfrey: This is the third book Debora Godfrey has worked on with B Cubed Press, and she continues to be impressed by the quality of the publisher, other editors and the writers. This project has allowed her to push back against a travesty in a way that feels important. Thanks, Bob, for making this work, and thanks to everyone who has been involved.

Phyllis Irene Radford: a.k.a. Irene Radford, has been writing stories ever since she figured out what a pencil was for. Editing grew out of her love of the craft of writing. B Cubed Press has helped liberate her as a writer, editor, and person swimming through the morass of modern life.

Lou Berger: Lou J Berger lives in Denver, Colorado with his high-school crush, three kids, two Sheltie dogs and a brilliant rescue mutt with a nefarious agenda. He has been published in a variety of anthologies and magazines. A member of SFWA, he is now working on his first novel. His author website is www.LouJBerger.com.

Follow him on the following social media platforms: Twitter: @LouJBerger. He is also found on Facebook: https://www.facebook.com/AuthorLouJBerger/

K.G. Anderson: My aim as an editor is to ensure that the reader can engage with the story. The stories for this anthology were passionate and imaginative; the editing was minimal.

Tom Easton: Tom Easton started editing when he worked at Scott, Foresman in the 1970s, always striving to cut the unnecessary. He once cut a contracted textbook down to the size of a journal article. Stories are much easier.

Marleen S. Barr: Marleen S. Barr edits with an eye for at once achieving the most clarity possible and adhering to the author's intention. She relishes creative titles and absurd fictive premises which have a feminist perspective.

Ellen Barnes: One hundred days from the proposal to the finished product, and I now have a deeper, more comprehensive understanding of what the resonance in the phrase "dropping the bass" means in the bimaris of resistance and resilience. That's a rocks glass full of some of the finest whiskey in the house.

Rebecca McFarland Kyle: What I learned from this anthology, Three words: Nevertheless she persisted.

Manny Frishberg: If a camel is a horse designed by a committee, this collection, edited by a committee of no less than ten, is a unicorn. Working as a team, it was useful to see the variety of perspectives through which we viewed the author's submissions. Then finally, like a herd of cats, the final selection was corralled by Fearless Leaders, Bob Brown and Phyllis Irene Radford.

To everyone involved, thank you for letting me play a part in creating this. And, if the opportunity ever comes again, just shoot me.

Bob Brown: Bob Brown is the Owner of B Cubed Press. He likes dogs, tolerates cats, feeds fish, and pets chickens. He owns three operable tractors and an old pickup truck. He likes his tea iced and his coffee hot, just as was intended by the creator. He believes in redemption. Remember that if you are trying to sell him a story.

This was not his first time working with this team of editors, just his first time working with them all at once.

It has been said that nine women cannot make a baby in a month. It felt that way at times working on this book, but because of the multiple perspectives found their voices. in the end, a healthy 348 page book emerged.

Thanks to the team. Always the team.

About B Cubed Press

B Cubed Press is a micro press that publishes big books about things that matter.

A percentage of EVERY book we publish is donated to the ACLU.

We can be reached at Kionadad@aol.com.

Our writers gather routinely on the "B Cubed Project Page" on Facebook and we can also be found at B Cubed Press.com.

Thanks to you all.
It has been an incredibly
humbling experience to work
with this utterly awesome
team of editors and writers in
putting out such an
important work.

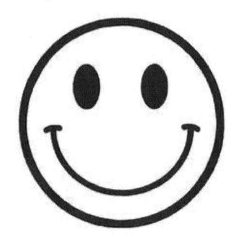

I can only hope this book
helps.

Made in the USA
Middletown, DE
15 October 2022